Max Pemberton

Kronstadt

Being the Story of Marian Best and of Paul Zassulic, her Lover...

Max Pemberton

Kronstadt
Being the Story of Marian Best and of Paul Zassulic, her Lover...

ISBN/EAN: 9783337168773

Printed in Europe, USA, Canada, Australia, Japan

Cover: Foto ©Andreas Hilbeck / pixelio.de

More available books at **www.hansebooks.com**

KRONSTADT

BEING THE STORY OF MARIAN BEST
AND OF PAUL ZASSULIC, HER LOVER,
TOGETHER WITH SOME ACCOUNT OF
THE RUSSIAN FORTRESS OF KRON-
STADT, AND OF THOSE WHO WOULD
HAVE BETRAYED IT

BY

MAX PEMBERTON

*Author of "A Puritan's Wife," "The Sea Wolves,"
"The Iron Pirate," "The Impregnable City," etc.*

WITH A MAP, AND 8 FULL-PAGE ILLUSTRATIONS BY A. FORESTIER

.

TENTH THOUSAND

CASSELL AND COMPANY, LIMITED
LONDON, PARIS, NEW YORK & MELBOURNE
1898

First Edition *April* 1898.
Reprinted *April* 1898, May 1898.

To My Wife.

To My Wife.

CONTENTS.

LIST OF ILLUSTRATIONS.

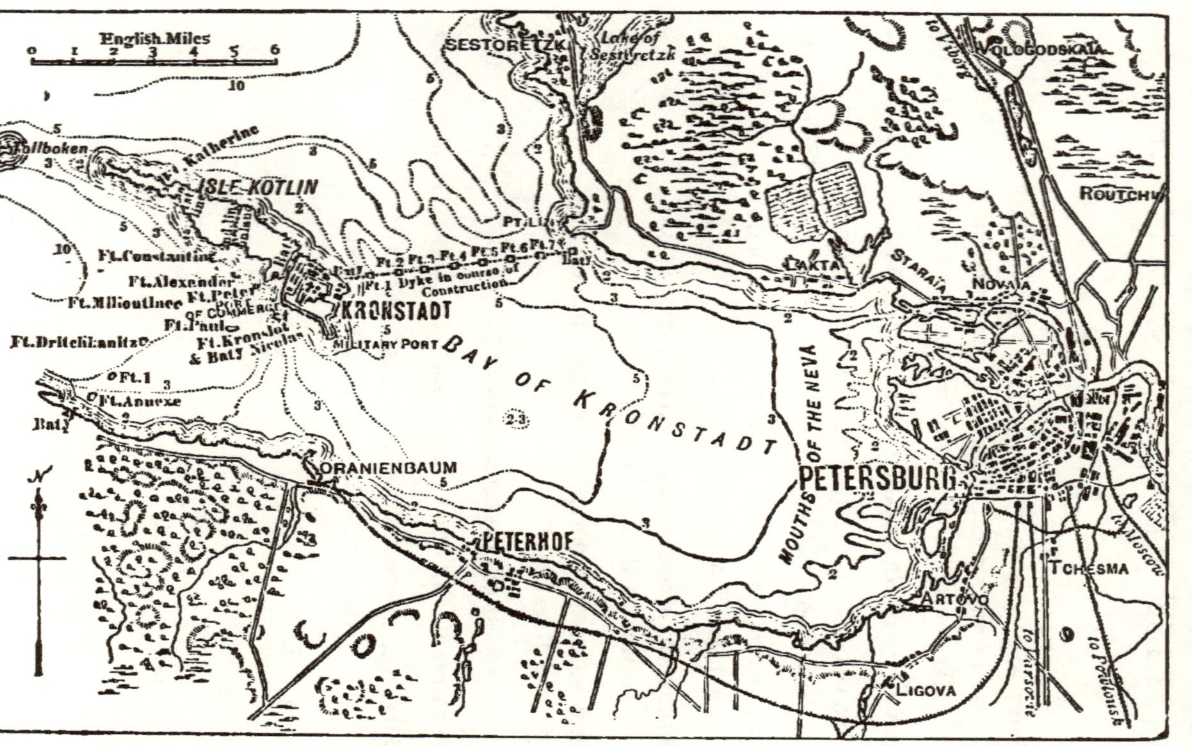

SKETCH MAP OF KRONSTADT AND ITS SURROUNDINGS.

KRONSTADT.

PROLOGUE.

SOMEONE cried out that the flashing light we saw upon the far horizon was Tollboken itself, and at this we left the quarter-deck and hurried to the bows of the ship. Even the invalid clergyman, who had not been more than an hour at the tea table, came panting up the companion and stood with us while the beacon magnified and gained majesty, and other lights shone over the vista of the waters, and the black line of the island fortress took shape as some terrible mausoleum of the sea. We had made Kronstadt at last—the Kronstadt of my dreams. While others turned the pages of their guide-books, while some were ready with history and some with anecdote, I gazed entranced as the mighty citadel shaped itself against the lurid canopy of cloud which hung in the eastern sky, and all the outward power and sullen magnificence were revealed to me. I stood at the gate of Russia indeed, at the impregnable gate, which the summons of war will never open. The

B

exclamations of wonder uttered by my companions seemed the lispings of credulous children. The chatter of the tourist was like a horrid discord in the temple of majestic silence. I had the wish to be apart from my fellows, to stand in some place of solitude and offer the worship of the imagination at the altar where I had worshipped in spirit so many months.

A Russian stood at my side, a young officer of artillery, who spoke English with some fluency. He had found our pleasure yacht at Copenhagen, and had taken passage with us to the island of Kronstadt, where his duty lay. We had found him a pleasant companion—a man who gave his laughter no holiday. But when the shores of the gulf began to draw in toward one another, and the lights of the great citadel flashed upon the horizon, I observed that the Russian was silent. Awe of his own home possessed him. He leaned heavily upon the bulwarks of the yacht, and had no eyes but for the ramparts and bastions before him. When I spoke to him he came down from some high place of the imagination to answer me; moments of time passed before he realised that he stood upon the deck of a ship, and that gaping tourists were his companions.

"Forgive me," he said, while he watched the group contemptuously. "You asked me—— ?"

"If those two lights to the right of Tollboken are the lights of Menzikoff?"

The question interested him, and after a word of surprise that I knew the name of the harbour fort, he began to explain many things to me.

"Yes," he said, "that is Menzikoff, though the lights are not the lights of the fort but of the harbour gates. The seven-fathom channel is there, and that flashing light, still more to the right, is the lantern upon the fort of Kronslott. Away a little to the south is Fort Paul, and that battery which crosses its fire is Battery 3. You see how well we protect the channel, which is no more than three hundred yards wide, though covered by a hundred guns."

I asked him how long the island was, questioning at the same time the accuracy of the statement that the southern channel was so narrow.

"I should have given it a breadth of at least a mile, but of course there are shallows."

"Exactly; the Oranienbaum spit runs out as far as Kronslott itself. It is a spur of sand creating shallows—another barrier which nature has put between Russia and her enemies. Though I am a Russian, and my word may be the word of prejudice, I say that there is not in all the world another citadel such as this; there is not one stamped out of the earth so clearly, a work of God unmistakable, for the defence of an empire. Observe the great bay into which we are sailing. It is in the shape of a V; the mouth turned toward the Baltic, the apex toward our capital. Kronstadt itself is also V-shaped, but the mouth of the letter is now turned toward Petersburg, the apex toward the open sea. Observe this clearly and you will see how the island, fitting into the neck of the gulf, becomes a vast and natural wedge which foreign ships may never pass. If they come by the north channel, there is the great boom of granite which a hundred navies could not destroy. If they attack us by the south channel, there are the guns of all the forts, a tremendous armament, which would crumble cities to the dust. No, my friend, you may search all seas and you will never find another citadel like this. She is invincible, the terrible gate of my country. We call her the tomb of spies, for no spy has betrayed her or ever will betray her. She stands for all that is dear to us—our liberty and our freedom. Her secrets are entombed in a heart of granite. He who seeks for them walks with Death for his guide."

He turned upon his heel and left me to wonder as much at his eloquence as at his earnestness. I had supposed him to be a mere lieutenant of artillery doing his duty soberly and with no concern for the romance of war. But it has been my good fortune since that day to meet many of those who serve the fortress of Kronstadt, and I have found the same love of the citadel, the same pride in its power influencing them all. To them it is more than the mistress of the Gulf of Finland, it is the temple of their country's freedom, the arsenal of God's weapons, a barrier given of the Eternal for the safety of their kingdom. When it shall fall the empire must fall with it. But that day will be the great, the dreadful day.

It was almost dark when our yacht came abreast the eastern end of the island, where the lieutenant took leave of us. We seemed at this time to be hemmed in by forts and batteries and by the tremendous walls which protect the town and harbours; lights flashed from every side, the lights of war-ships, the lights of barracks, the red and white and green lanterns of the bastions. I thought as I watched the lieutenant rowing away to the service he loved so well, that he had spoken truly when he named Death as the comrade of him who would snatch the secrets of this mighty fortress. Death indeed; or if not death, then the terror worse than death, the sunless labour of the mines, the eternal solitude, the groans and sufferings of the desolate land.

To write a story of this fortress, and of certain people named in its recent history, I had come to

Russia. No books or plans could help me to measure the achievements or the courage of those I was to speak about. I must see with my own eyes the things which they had seen, must stand where they had stood. As far as it lay in my power, I must realise the grandeur and the greatness of that sanctuary of war which they had invaded so resolutely; must hear the tramp of armed men and the bugle's blast where they had heard them. In that spirit I left my yacht and entered the city which the Russian had called the tomb of spies. And I thought as I went of Marian Best, the Woman of Kronstadt, of her love and of her sorrows.*

* The author would wish it to be clearly understood that the characters in this book are entirely fictional.

CHAPTER I.

THOUGH the great bell of Kronstadt had struck the hour of nine and the bugles had called "lights out" in the barracks of the town, there was no perceptible curb upon the merriment of those who kept the carnival of the sea. For Kronstadt was ice-bound, and the New Year, bringing an end to the stress and storm of the earlier winter, had sealed the waves with the seal of the welcome frost. Where ships sailed a month ago, the merry skaters now ventured. Far out from the great citadel the gulf was still and frozen. No longer was the call of the pilot heard or the voice of the seaman crying to his men. The whirr of skate and sledge, the music of artillery bands, the prattle of pretty women, had taken their place. But here and there vast fires blazing upon the ice drew the busy throngs to the door of tent or wooden theatre. The light of many torches made golden rings upon the fields of glistening snow. Old and young, generals and ensigns, rothmisters and feldwebels, hurried to the joy of the whirling life. As prisoners from the cells of solitude and silence they rushed from their island home to the sea, which frost had stilled and the ice made war upon.

Conspicuous upon the field of the frozen sea, for it was built in the ring of light shed by the beacons of Menzikoff, stood the palace of ice, which the officers of the garrison had set up as the monument of a winter so generous. Ready hands had hewn blocks from the shallower waters of the military harbour; stout arms had dragged the glistening boulders and piled them up for the foundations of the temple of the frost. Soon a vast building arose, a tabernacle of shimmering and transparent whiteness, into which cunning engineers carried wires for the electric light, while zealous corporals brought the flaming eagles of their regiments, and laughing girls bedecked the temple with draperies of silk and satin. The enduring frost looked upon the work and found it to be good. A keener breath of winter breathed strength upon the palace and made it a perfect whole. Its builders spoke of masquerade and carnival. Generals shook their heads but did not refuse. The 29th of January in the year 1895 brought the proposal to maturity, and all social Kronstadt came out that night to offer the incense of laughter at the shrine. Old and young, poor and rich hastened to enjoy an opportunity so rare.

CONSPICUOUS UPON THE FIELD OF THE FROZEN SEA STOOD THE PALACE OF ICE (p. 8).

While the palace within shone with countless lights, which gave a glittering radiance to the uniforms of gold and white and green, the dark field of the ice without was vantage ground for the townspeople and sailors weary of waiting for an open sea. Frenchmen, Dutchmen, Swedes, but English outnumbering all, they stood shivering in the icy blast, or warming themselves at the great fires, or roaring with laughter at the jests and the antics of the masqueraders. For them the sup of vodki must suffice; no frothing champagne, no warmth of fur or dance, no occupation of looking love gave them armour against the cold. But they were critics always, and being critics, they spoke their minds and were not afraid. Half an hour had not passed before they had a name for every prominent person in the palace. The fat general perspiring in an effort of agility, the gorgeous cuirassiers of the Guard in their dazzling uniforms of white and blue—"flour mills," the English sailors called them, and qualified the noun; the mincing cornets of cavalry; the three-starred colonels of artillery groping for the honours of the clown—as each made the tour of the frozen ballroom and came to clearer view of the uninvited, his new name was roared lustily by the volleyed voices of the seamen.

"Higher up, spangled shanks—lift 'em up!"

bawled the bullet-headed skipper of a trading steamer as an exceedingly stout lady came shuffling into view. "There ain't no bally 'oop in Roosher as you're a-going to jump through, marm."

"Leave the lady be, Bill," retorted his mate. "'Tain't often as you see a fine growed thing like that—at her age too! You ain't got no manners. If she weighs more than twenty stun, I'm a nigger!"

"She shall pose for Venus!" said a merry little Frenchman; but a German protested—

"Blitzen! it is her harvest time. In ze summer der zun will melt her down!"

"Why, here's little 'Sixpence-a-box,'" chimed in a burly engineer as a mannikin in the green uniform of an artillery officer came prancing by. "'Sixpence-a-box' along with the 'Tower of Babel'!"

"He'll want a ladder to hail her, I guess!" cried an able seaman who surveyed the tall lady in question with the expression of one who could not take in the whole of her height and magnificence at a glance. "You'd have to take three reefs in that lot, Bill, before you could lay your course for 'Ampstead 'Eath on a Sunday!"

"Two to one St. Frusquin!" roared the purser of a small passenger steamer when a lank and lean *stabcapitaine* came galloping round with feet lifted high as though he must crush the earth beneath him. "I'm damned if he don't fancy he's running for a cup."

"I'll be thinking he's took with the spasms," exclaimed the red and shaggy-haired mate of a Scotch trading vessel.

"Which shows your ignorance, Jack," cried the engineer. "Don't you know a valtz when you sees one? Look at him cuddling Miss 'Fore-and-aft'! It don't want a book to tell you that she likes it neither."

"I hear as cuddling's come in again with the quick valtz," said the purser. "They've give up walking round one another like hands round a capstan now. Maybe the weather's too cold."

A few ejaculations of approval greeted the surmise, one of the most melancholy among the company hazarding the opinion that the infernal regions were already "froze up"; but thereafter the conversation began to dribble away and was almost run out when a shout from the Frenchman awoke all to attention, and a new buzz of talk was born of the passing of a dancer whose steps were followed with pleasure and approval by every eye in the group of the uninvited.

"La voici! la belle Anglaise! la voici! Comme elle sait danser la polka!"

"That's her right enough," exclaimed the bullet-headed skipper; "and ain't she a beauty afore the wind. By gosh! I'd pay off with her myself, I'm damned if I wouldn't! See how she goes about—and sudden too! It wants a head for that, mates, if so be as you've not been brought up to it."

"She's a daisy!" exclaimed the purser. "I told you so yesterday when she was out at Fort Paul with 'Sixpence-a-box.' Look at the way she carries her canvas! There's style about that, mates, as anyone can see."

"And look at the way her hair is wove! Oh, I tell you she's a beauty!"

"If you lofe her, you lofe little," said the German, nettled at the unanimity of the admiration.

"Little it is for me, by thunder!" cried the skipper. "I don't want a wife, as I've got to walk round every morning to see if any of her is missing. Give me the English miss, and the devil take all fat Rooshians!"

The argument waxed hot, but *la belle Anglaise* skated on unconscious of it. She was a brown-haired girl whose bright eyes and white skin had cheated Time so that he forgot the day of her birth, which was twenty-five years ago, and had come to believe her still in the teens. A slightly-built, fragile creature, whose face was ever changing and rarely carried the same expression; a creature of quick impulses and unresting gaiety, whose words cost her nothing, whose gesture was the gesture of a Frenchwoman. They called her "La Petite" in the fortress, where she had won much love and many friends—none more zealous than the deputy-governor, General Stefanovitch, who painted his eye-brows and wore stays. He had followed her like a dog this night of carnival, and she repaid him generously with many a word of compliment whispered into his willing ear and many a press upon a hand which, younger men said, should have been already paralysed. For they begrudged him *la belle Anglaise.* There was no man in all that company of glittering masqueraders who was not the happier for her word or the message of her eyes. And one, at least, there had given her the best offering an honest man can give—the offering of his love.

He skated with her now, and had earned already from an approving audience the name of the "Green-baize-tree." A tall flaxen-haired man, for whose fine figure the neat uniform of the artillery betrayed close friendship, he had something of the manner of the more civilised West; and had learnt in Paris and London, as many of his brothers had not, the elements of those polite arts which win upon a woman's favour. For the moment he applied such arts to the purpose of pleasing his partner, *la belle Anglaise;* and it was plain to be seen that he had eyes only for her. In and out of the glittering throng they skated, a harmony of gold and green, and soft furs and azure stuffs lifting to the breeze like wings of gauze. But while the man looked ever into the girl's face, she, in turn, was spellbound by the trance of sensuous music; and being carried from the world about her to a kingdom of her imagination, she forgot all else and abandoned herself to the exalting rhythm of the dance. Not until the last chord was a lingering harmony upon the air did she so much as remember that a man's arm was close about her waist, or that his head was bent down toward her until his lips almost kissed her ear.

"You suffocate me," she said, drawing back from his embrace and fanning herself vigorously. "Am I so very like a rifle, Captain Paul? Really, I thought you were going to present arms with me."

The great artilleryman began to pull his moustache and to look foolish.

"I thought you might fall," he stammered. "It is very slippery, Mademoiselle Marian. Besides, when I come to think of it, you are very like a rifle—your bullets wound and your eyes are bayonets!"

She took his arm and they walked with the

others ; the whole company being drawn by a subtle law of gravitation to the refreshment-room, where the corks popped, and silk petticoats rustled, and laughter struck many chords, and champagne frothed in silver goblets. The touch of her little gloved hand was like the caress of a rose ; she seemed so slight and fair and fragile that he had the impulse to crush her in his strong arms and make her a part of his being.

"You repent ?" he asked her in a low voice, while he handed her a cup of boiling tea.

"I ?—of what ?"

"Of many things—of all the dances you have not given me !"

She laughed lightly, and turned to hear the complaints of an ensign who wished to tell her that she had promised him the next dance ; but had not the courage to do anything but devour her with his eyes. When she had sent the boy away, and had drunk her tea, she answered her companion.

"Repentance is a virtue," she said, " but to repent you must sin. The moral is obvious. I am going to dance with the ensign, and remember the time when I was fifteen, and wrote my own romances. Have you ever made heroes of your boy friends, Captain Paul ? Oh, the bitterness of it, when the divinity of your youth goes through the bankruptcy court, or a judge reads his 'Ode to the Chorus Girl,' with emphasis. But of course you don't understand—how should you? It is only in England that a man—a certain sort of man—writes poetry because he is in love. You will come to that state of civilisation by-and-bye. Meanwhile you are barbarians, and would be impossible if you could not dance so beautifully upon skates. When I leave you I shall write a book dividing you into two heads——"

Captain Paul, who understood little beyond the fact that she was to dance with the ensign, interrupted her with a laugh which rang out like the note of a bell.

"Into two heads? Moi! ça, c'est bien! I shall have four eyes to watch you while you dance. After that there are no more numbers. It is one long waltz and I am your partner, hein?"

He twirled his moustache fiercely, seeming to watch every movement of her eyes or hand; but when she was about to answer him, a voice at her elbow jarred upon their privacy and stilled her laughter. It was the voice of Mademoiselle Varia, the General's daughter—the eldest of the two children whom *la belle Anglaise* had come to Russia to teach—and at her side stood her yellow-haired sister Rina.

"Ma'mselle, it is time to walk abroad."

" Ma'mselle, eleven does beat upon the clock."

Sixteen years and fifteen were the ages of the children, but their English was not yet six months old and was unweaned from the jargon of polyglot phrase inseparable from civilised Russian speech. They stood now like two waxen figures beside their governess, whose art was incapable of disguising the coldness of her welcome or her little love for their company. She answered shortly and almost with irritation, suffering Captain Paul to lead her back to the great ballroom; but thither the intruders followed, and were not to be put off.

" Ma'mselle, veux-tu partir ? "

" Ma'mselle, nous sommes parfaitement prêtes."

Mademoiselle looked over her shoulder and said, " In a moment, children." Then she made a doleful grimace.

" I had forgotten ' the Dolls,' " she said. " Does not it speak well for your dance that I should forget them ? "

" But you are not going ? "

" Indeed and I am. Eleven o'clock is my curfew to-night. I am like the little criminal who turned from his dark deed when he remembered that the clock used to strike eleven in his mother's house. You haven't read Dickens, equally of course."

Captain Paul made a gesture of impatience. "Why do you torture me? why do you not ask me to walk with you?" he asked eagerly; "you know that I am ready."

"Who am I to say to you, 'Walk,' and you will walk. Besides, you have partners."

"Partners—I—partners when you are in the room! To the devil——!"

He stopped abruptly, biting his moustache and rocking upon his heels. But she turned from him with a gesture of one inexpressibly shocked, and ran to the room where thicker furs awaited her, and old Ivan with the lantern, and "the Dolls," who still held each other's hand and seemed to say, "We are the good children from the fairy book." She was not at all surprised when, presently, she found him waiting for her at the door of the palace; nor did she protest as he expected.

"I am forgiven?" he asked.

"I will tell you to-morrow?" she said.

"You are glad it is not the General who walks with you?"

"Gladness is a large emotion. Say that I am content."

"Only content?"

"Why 'only'? Is content so common an experience?"

The man sighed, but pressed the arm which

he held, and drew her closer to him. They had crossed the ice which lay between the harbour and the temple of the carnival, and had entered the town of barrack and rampart and bastion. Though Kronstadt slept, her robe of war was still upon her; the shadows upon her pavements were the shadows of her mighty guns; the tramp of sentries, the sign and countersign, were her music. Marian Best never entered that citadel of steel and granite without a little shudder of indefinable fear. Captain Paul felt the tremor upon her arm now, and it helped to an anxious sympathy.

"You are cold," he said; "then wait a moment and I will wrap you in my cloak."

"And leave yourself a target for the east wind? No, I am not cold, but I fear the shadows!"

"They fall upon us both," said the man; "we share them as we shared the bright lights just now. Would that we might share them always, Mademoiselle Marian, the light and the dark, the sorrow and the joy!"

The girl tossed her pretty curls from her forehead and laughed up at him.

"Is it not too cold to talk nonsense?" she asked. "I thought poets waited for the spring."

He took advantage of her words, for the lantern-bearer appeared now like a star upon the

c 2

road before them, and "the Dolls" were hand in hand at old Ivan's heels.

"But I cannot wait," he said earnestly, while he felt for her fingers and tried to lock his own in them. "It is always spring when you are at my side; it is always winter when the night takes you away from me. Why do I read your English books all day? Is it not that I may find words to speak to you? But I have no words— I have nothing but myself, myself and my poverty, and my love for you. Some day, perhaps, it will be different. Some day I shall be able to come to you and to say, 'I am no longer Paul Zassulic, of the Artillery, but Paul of Tolma, the master of many and the servant of none but the Czar.' I dare not think that such a day is near—the gifts of life come too often in the autumn of our years. But I shall be rich always while I possess my love for you, Marian; you cannot rob me of that; you cannot make me love you less; there is no one in the world who can take my riches from me!"

They had come up in their walk to the curtain of the bastion which defended General Stefanovitch's house, and therefrom could look down upon the town, now darkened, yet showing in the moon's rays a forest of spires and turrets and the gloomy shapes of fort and barracks.

Away upon the ice a great blaze of light, focussed by the translucent walls of the palace, marked the scene of carnival. Faint strains of music, the note of horns, and the rolling of drums, came up to them for a memory of their dance and of their pleasure. Some instinct held them to the place, and they stood together with quickening hearts and muted lips, the man trembling with a strange excitement, the girl dumb because the word she had long awaited was now spoken. It was no secret to her that Paul Zassulic loved her; it was no reproach to her, she thought, that she had no answer for him. While she had been content in his friendship and devotion, her busy life had forbidden that she should reckon with herself or examine her own heart to see if any treasure of an answering love were locked therein. She was dumb because no certainty of self came to assist her; she would not wound, yet knew not if she could heal. A great seriousness possessed her, a realisation that such moments were supreme in every life. She had few friends in all the world. The thought that this friend might be taken from her was bitter.

"Paul," she said, when a sudden movement of his snapped the seal upon her lips, "Paul, what shall I say to you—you who have been my friend, who will be my friend always? Shall I tell you that I have done wrong to listen to you? No, indeed, for I owe you that—I owe you more than I can ever repay, a thousand times. Perhaps I am not like other women. When I ask myself if I love, I cannot answer—I do not know what love is. I am happy because you are my friend. I welcome the days which bring you to me. But a wife should be able to say more than that. Some day, perhaps, I shall know all. When that day comes I will not fear to speak. I will answer as you wish. I will tell you that I have learned to love you."

It was not the answer that he wished; but the word that he might ever count himself her friend, and that she was happy when he was with her, made his pulse leap, and he drew her towards him again, kissing her upon the forehead many times and refusing to release her from his strong embrace.

"God bless you, little Marian! God bless you for the promise!" he said.

"It was only a promise, Paul," she answered. "I cannot give you more—I cannot lie to you, or how should I be worthy of your friendship?"

"There is no woman more worthy in all the world!"

A voice from the ramparts brought them to a recollection of the hour and the place. It was the voice of old Ivan, who wished to close the gate of the enceinte, and at his call Marian broke swiftly from her lover's embrace and entered the fortress. But Captain Paul stood long watching the lights in the Governor's house. When he turned to go down to the barracks he saw that carnival was done and the great palace in darkness.

"It is night now," he said to himself, "but to-morrow the sun will shine and I shall see her! She is to go with me to the batteries. I shall show her everything, and that will take a long time. God bless the little woman I love!"

But Marian herself knelt by her bed, and heavy tears gathered in her eyes.

"If he knew!" she cried bitterly, "if he knew!"

CHAPTER II.

"A SPY WITHIN THE GATE."

GENERAL STEFANOVITCH, the deputy-governor of Kronstadt, entered his library every morning at half-past eight precisely that he might kiss his daughters upon the cheek and wish their governess "good-day." The years brought no variation of the ceremony; the same words were spoken, the same compliments passed. When the General had unusual leisure, he devoted some moments of it to a measured flirtation with the young lady who taught his children. When he had no leisure, he gave her a haunting leer or kissed the tips of his fingers to her if his daughters were not looking.

"Bon jour, Varia."

"Bon jour, cher papa."

"Et tu, Rina?"

"Bien, cher papa."

Marian Best, the General's governess in the year 1895, always said that when the old soldier laughed the top of his head threatened to come off like the half of an egg. But this alarming effect was rather the result of his weakness for painted eyebrows than of any deficiency of head or skull. Sixty years of life had not satisfied his vanity. A glance from a woman's eyes could still release the flow of compliment and childish affectation. Marian said that he seemed at such moments to be treading upon hot plates. His shrivelled body swelled until his close-laced stays were strained to bursting point; he bowed continually, and laid upon his breast a hand blue and long and almost fleshless. She dreaded those mornings when he was not busy; it was a relief to her when she heard his sword clanging in the stone passage of the house or saw old Ivan running for his great boots.

"Ah, you must learn our language," he would say often; "you must learn the verb 'to lofe.' Some day we will have the lesson by ourselves, mademoiselle. You shall repeat the little word after me until you are perfect. Ho, ho, ho! Will you not have me for your master, Meess Best? Shall I not teach well, hein?"

"Cher papa, qu'est-ce que tu dis à mademoiselle?"

"Rien, ma chère, rien du tout."

Sometimes, when "the Dolls" sat staring with inquiring eyes at his amatory contortions or strange pursuits of nimbleness, he would entertain for them anything but a father's love. He could not caper as he would with the children for his audience. The snatched whisper or stolen leer was not satisfying. He tasted the dry bones of flirtation when he was hungering for the baked meats. It was difficult to believe that this perfumed old dandy, whose head was like a shining ball of mahogany, and whose eyebrows were an uncertain quantity, was the master of Kronstadt and of her garrison, the sentinel of the mighty Russian Empire, the keeper of the gate and of the freedom of millions. Yet Russia knew no more faithful servant; there was no more devoted soldier of the Czar in all the kingdom; no man whose pride in the citadel of the gate was so enduring and ever-present. General Stefanovitch lived for his work; the gaunt and bare Governor's house upon the north shore of the island was a palace for him; he desired no other gardens but the garden of fort and bastion, of shallowing sea and impassable rampart. His world lay in that calcareous, barren island which God had set in the Gulf of Finland for the protection of Russia. His vanities, his personal "scenery and effects," as Marian Best described them, were trifles of his leisure. He forgot them in an instant when Kronstadt was named. She was all to him—the mighty tablet upon which his life's work was recorded.

Thus it befell that the moments when he could employ himself with amatory recreations were few. The half of an hour with his children in the morning, a few words to them at night, sufficed for the proper performance of the domestic *rôle*. At other times he was the martinet, the hundred-eyed guardian of the gate, the precise soldier who ruled with an ungloved hand of iron. Men feared his look; the dungeons of the fortress echoed with the groans of those upon whom the lash of his displeasure had fallen; the lightest breath of his suspicion, blowing upon any who served him, withered up the blossoms of that man's fortune. They saw he was a just man, but one who knew not forgiveness.

Nine o'clock in the morning was the hour which found the General at his writing-desk in the private cabinet of the Governor's house. Neither fast nor feast gave grace to those who awaited him. He would enter the room as the clock struck; the echoes of the bell would not have died away before the grim Colonel Bonzo, the second in command, would have saluted and laid the report before him. Upon the morning which followed carnival, the young officers, who had not been to bed, declared his punctuality immoral. No rose gathered at the hour of the dew was fresher than Nikolai Stefanovitch when he saluted the Colonel as the clock struck nine. Painted, powdered, prim—he bowed to those who awaited him with the inflexible courtesy of an automaton. The eyes which had just beamed upon Marian Best, as they had beamed upon eight governesses during the past five years, were now cold and steely and devouring. A great silence fell upon those in the ante-room when he passed through. Even the iron-framed Bonzo stiffened at his approach.

"Good morning, Colonel. You have the papers?"

"Here, my General."

General Stefanovitch fixed his eyeglass and began to peruse the bulky document. He had read but a few lines when a subdued exclamation and a shuffling of feet again drew his attention to his subordinate. Such a breach of the discipline of silence was not to be endured; a sudden flight of the General's eyebrows, which seemed to run up to the top of his head, marked his displeasure and impatience.

"You spoke, Colonel?" he asked.

"I wished to speak, my General."

"Now, when I read the despatches?"

"If you please, my General."

General Stefanovitch let his glass fall and deliberately rolled up the report. Such an interruption had not been known during the twenty years he had spent at Kronstadt.   It remained for Bonzo to justify himself.

“ Well, Colonel ?.”

“ It is this, my General : the plan of Battery No. 3 was put into the hands of the English Government a week ago.”

Colonel Bonzo stood like a statue when the words were spoken.   The terrible news had been the burden of his night; he had heard it, and yet twelve hours had passed before he had dared to speak.   Now the deed was done and the blow would fall—the blow of anger, of recrimination, it might be of punishment.

Five minutes, it may be, passed before General Stefanovitch found his tongue.   During that time he seemed outwardly to be unconscious of the place or the word, but in reality his mind was seeking to and fro for the first link of the chain which reason must forge for him.   To Bonzo’s surprise no martinet answered him. The voice was low and in command; he did not speak in anger.

“ Where does this news come from ? ”

“ By telegram last night—from the Prince.”

“ How is it that I did not hear of this before ? ”

Bonzo half raised his hands as though in a gesture of excuse.

"There was carnival upon the ice, my General."

" Yes—— ? "

"And when I returned at midnight, and you were still down there, I did not think you would wish it."

He stood stammering and stuttering, but the other, awakened by all the impulses of duty, smote the table with his fist until the very glass in the windows of the room was shaken.

"Not wish it?—I—whose honour is at stake By heaven, Colonel Bonzo, what do you mean?"

The Colonel's heart quaked, but he was glad that the moment had come. He had waited for this, and now he took courage.

"I mean, my General, that we have first to ascertain if the plan of Battery 3, which the English Government is said to possess, is the correct plan or no. These English would give much for the secret of Kronstadt. Is it not possible that a part of the ten thousand pounds they offer to him who shall help them has gone into the pocket of an impostor? I say that it is possible. I say that it is the only explication. The Prince is deceived; the plan is a forgery. We shall laugh in our sleeves by-and-bye, and sell the people in London more secrets. It will keep their tongues still and help us to hang the spies. Oh! be assured, my General, if there is any man in the city who has betrayed us, many hours shall not pass before we lay our hands upon him."

The Colonel spoke with great earnestness; there was a light of anger and of determination in his eyes; his great hands trembled with his desire to be acting. Like his master, the island fortress was to him a sacred citadel; his life, his work lay there; his honour was offered upon that altar of granite and of steel. The two men had laboured side by side for twenty years; they were more than friends, they were brothers in a great and insurpassable trust. And now a common peril was before them both. They could not wholly realise it; they dare not tell themselves that a spy was within the gate; they were ready to be deceived if it were only for a day.

"I was a fool not to think of it at the first," said Stefanovitch, taking heart as the other spoke. "If they have a plan of Battery 3 in London, it is not our plan. I will tell the Prince so to-day. He should not have been deceived like that. He should not charge the fidelity of those who have grown old in this service. We will see to it that he is answered, Bonzo. You shall make it your business to draw up our case, if that be necessary. Why does he not suggest at the same time that these English have a plan of my house——"

"Or of heaven?" said the Colonel bluntly. "They are as likely to get it as the drawings of Battery 3. And why of Battery 3, my General? Why not of Fort Peter, of Alexander, of Menzikoff? They have sought these things long enough. Why should one be taken and the other left? Are they children at Petersburg that they believe any tale which is told them in London? Do they think that we sleep while spies are busy on our ramparts? Oh, it is a jest, Nikolai, a jest, and we should be the first to laugh at it."

Colonel Bonzo's laugh had grown rusted from long disuse, so that when he asked help of it the answer was loud and grating like the bark of a dog. His earnestness had led him to address Stefanovitch in the familiar style which the men assumed when no janissaries of office overheard them, and this familiarity was not resented.

"You say well," replied the General, fixing his glass for the first time since he had heard the tidings; "the Prince jests with us and we shall anwer him with another jest; it will be a list of all the people who have entered Battery 3 since it was built. He shall then tell us who is the spy, and we shall know what to do. Eh, Colonel, we shall know what to do? Then let Captain Paul come to me."

Paul Zassulic had gone to bed at four o'clock in the morning. During two short hours he had dreamed of Marian Best—of a garden of eternal summer of which she was mistress. But when six o'clock struck and twenty trumpets sounded the reveille from the ramparts, he had dragged himself wearily from his couch and turned gloomily to his monotonous work in the fortress. A roseate flush of the lagging sun which fell upon the field of the ice as a die of crimson and of gold, awakened him at last from his depression. A crisp wind of morning gave colour to his face; the keen air was as a tonic to his veins. When he stood up to salute his chief there was the seal of health upon his cheeks, the light of untroubled youth in his eyes.

"You sent for me, my General?"

Stefanovitch, who loved Paul as a son, surveyed him critically through the searching eye-glass before he answered.

"Certainly, Captain, I sent for you. "You have heard the news?"

"The news, General?"

"As I say, the news—that they have the

D

plan of Battery 3 in London, sold to them by someone who knows it as you know it or as I know it."

Stefanovitch spoke with assumed unconcern, as though the matter were the most trifling he could mention. It was his habit to avòid any outward display of anger; his glance was ever more feared than his word. Paul knew this habit well; he dreaded it as a criminal may dread the jests of his judge.

"They have the plan of Battery 3 in London, General! Oh, but that is a lie!" he cried, looking from one to the other with dazed eyes and questioning glance; "it is a lie, I say, and I will tell them so! They cannot have the plan; it is impossible. Who should have given it to them? Who is there in Kronstadt who would sell his country's secrets? Who is there that could sell them? You know that it is not true, my General. Lord God! that they should bring such a charge against me!"

Moment by moment he began to realise the gravity of the unspoken accusation. Sweat stood upon his forehead, tears welled up in his eyes. He had worked so unselfishly to make himself a good servant of Kronstadt that this overwhelming blow seemed to strike at the heart of his honour and his life. They had implied that he was unworthy of the trust—he, Paul Zassulic, who would have died willingly if the citadel had asked his life of him.   They could put no greater affront upon him.

“It is a lie!” he continued to repeat, while Nikolai Stefanovitch watched him approvingly, and old Bonzo’s grey eyes twinkled cunningly; “it is a monstrous lie, General!   No one has entered the fort but those who have work there; I will swear to it upon the Holy Gospel.   If you doubt me, send for Seroff Ossinksy—he can tell you; he will laugh at the story as I would laugh at it were my honour not at stake.   Oh, they cannot have the plan in London—you know that they cannot.”

He appealed to them pitifully, looking from one to the other questioningly, but he read nothing in their faces, neither of sympathy nor of reassurance.   Bonzo wore, as ever, the changeless mask of iron severity; Stefanovitch lolled back in his chair and stared at the speaker as he would have stared at some defaulter hurried to the judgment.

“I know nothing,” he said in answer to the earnest protestations, “nothing at all beyond that which I am told by those in Petersburg.   They say that the plan of the fort has been sold to the English; you, who were in command of the battery until a month ago, answer that it is impossible, because no stranger has ever been permitted within the enceinte. Is that so, Captain ? "

" I will swear it, General, and my successor will swear it too."

" You shall both swear it before the court which will investigate this report. If your word be accepted, there is an end of the matter. For my part I will tell you that I regard the story as ridiculous. The plan which the English have bought is a forgery; there can be no doubt of it. It rests upon us to convince the Prince of that, and to be unresting in our vigilance. I need say no more, Captain; I am not here to teach you your duty; the city is well served when she has servants like Paul Zassulic."

Captain Paul opened his eyes. He had believed that they brought a charge against him; he knew now that they did not. The burden of suspicion was more than he could bear, and when it fell from his shoulders, an impulse of gratitude and devotion came upon him.

" Thank you, General," he said simply. " I could ask nothing more than your approval."

Stefanovitch dismissed him with a wave of the hand. He went from the room gladly, and with the purpose to seek out his sergeant at once

and to question him. But before he had crossed
the great courtyard of the house, someone touched
him upon the shoulder; and when he turned about
quickly he found that Bonzo had followed him
from the room.

“Ha! Colonel, you are going my way,” he cried.

“I am going to the prison,” said the old soldier
grimly. “It will be full enough by-and-bye if
there is anything in this news.”

“But there cannot be anything, Colonel—I
am ready to swear it upon the Gospels. No one
has entered the fort——”

Bonzo shrugged his shoulders, his little eyes
were screwed up until they shone like the eyes
of a ferret.

“You say no one?” he asked.

“Certainly. I would swear it to the Emperor.”

“Do you forget that you had a visitor at the
fort yesterday?”

“Yesterday?”

“I say so—the little Englishwoman, La Petite.
What of her?”

Captain Paul could not have stopped in his
walk more abruptly if a chasm had opened at
his feet.

“You mean Mademoiselle Marian, my Colonel?”

“Certainly. Is she no one? Did you think
so last night when you danced with her for two

hours, eh, my friend? Shall I tell her how soon you forget the little lessons in gunnery? Shall I say that you are prepared to swear to the Emperor that she is nobody, hein?"

Captain Paul roared with laughter.

"Sapristi!" he cried, "that I should forget Mademoiselle Marian, and that you should remind me of her! Of course there is our spy. Why did I not think of it before? Oh, this will amuse the General when I tell him to-night. La Petite—who does not know which end you load a gun? She has made the plans, there cannot be a doubt of it. We will tell the people of Petersburg so. Jest for jest, n'est-ce pas, mon Colonel, and ours a little more foolish than theirs. *La belle Anglaise*—that I should forget her. Oh, quelle bêtise!"

The humour of the idea seized upon him uncontrollably, and upon the old soldier, so that they went down to their work laughing as lads at play. When they separated at last before the doors of the church of St. Vladimir, Captain Paul stood a moment to watch the other walking toward the prison. Then, being quite alone, his face paled suddenly, and he seemed about to reel against one of the pillars of the cathedral.

"My God!" he thought, "if the jest should be no jest!"

*   *   *   *   *

Old Bonzo, lumbering along the narrow streets of Kronstadt, was saying to himself, “She is too innocent; she shall be watched—night and day— the little Englishwoman.”

CHAPTER III.

AT THE COMING OF THE LIGHT.

MARIAN BEST opened her eyes dreamily, expecting
to hear the boom of the morning gun ringing in
her ears. She saw that it must be six o'clock of
the day—time for her to think of " the Dolls " again,
and of all the uncoloured drudgery of her life. She
had travelled far, in her sleep, from the ice-bound
fortress and the melancholy, prison-like abode of
Nikolai Stefanovitch ; had sojourned awhile in the
lanes and orchards of her own Devonshire, there to
gather flowers of her affection and to kiss the lips of
the child she loved. But when she awoke, with a red
glare of light playing in her eyes and the grip of
the frost to benumb her limbs, she came quickly
from the garden of her dreams and steeled herself
to face the solitude and the gloom of her island
home. And she knew that the child, whose lips
she had touched in her sleep, was himself sleeping
more than a thousand miles away, and that between
them lay the barrier of city and of sea—and of a
woman's poverty.

She was surprised at the first that her room
was not in darkness, and that she did not hear the

voice of old Ivan asking if " Missa " would " take a tea"; but anon the rustle of her silk skirt and the shape of the great stove looming up in the ruddy light brought her to a remembrance of the time and place, and she knew that she had dozed before her fire at the hour of the General's dinner.

That was her moment of respite ; the moment when she could shut herself in her room and be mistress of her thoughts and enjoy that dominion of self which no eye may share. When first she came to Kronstadt to teach the General's daughters those scraps of· English which pass for culture in Russia, she had welcomed this hour as the ultimate possibility of her day; an hour when she could write to little Dick, her brother, and remember the home she had left—the unforgotten voices and the harvest time of love. As the months passed and the terrible winter fell upon the land, and even the friendly sea below her windows was bound in the chains of the frost, she began almost to be afraid of herself and of the solitude. It may be that the work to which she had set her hand could not fail to react upon her mind, and so to war against her nerves that the creak of a door or the fall of a foot upon the stair would bring her to piteous trembling and dread. The secret she guarded so well was a heavy burden. Grim spectres followed it, haunt- ing her, or whispering words that seemed to still her heart and to bring cries of fear to her lips. There were moments when a realisation of all she had done, and would do, drove her to such depths of terror that her reason seemed to be leaving her. At other moments she could call herself a spy and laugh at the word. The living death of the mines, the horrid sights and sounds of Russian prisons, were no more than fairy tales to such a mind. She was only a woman, she said, and who would harm her? She would tell them it was a jest, and they must believe her. That pretty assumption of a child-like innocence, which had befriended her often when she had cajoled Captain Paul and obtained from him those secrets of the citadel for which her friends in London were willing to pay so great a price, that innocence should befriend her to the end. And the end was near now. She carried bound about her own body, a very part of herself, as it were, the precious sketches and maps and diaries for which she had laboured so earnestly. She foresaw the day when the shadow of the living death would lie upon her path no more; when an English home would harbour her and English hands would shield her from peril, and the child she loved would be ever near her. For his sake she would go on, for his sake self should be forgotten with that new and sweetening impulse which the winter months had brought to her. She dare not tell herself that such an impulse was love for the man whose country she had betrayed and whose honour she had played with.

Many of these thoughts came to her in the moment of waking, when she sat in her great chair and watched the fantastic shapes of light and shadow; or listened to the moan and crash of the ice now mastered by the warmth of later February and losing dominion over the sea. Her room lay in the north wing of the Governor's house, and was built out upon the ramparts, so that when she pulled aside her curtain she beheld a mighty moving field of shining floes, here decked with hummocks which had the glitter of jewels, there broken into tiny bergs and floating islands of snow; or again washed by the foaming waves which cast the waters up in fountains of spray and displayed a hundred changing lights as the moonbeams fell upon them. Grim and forbidding, above this holocaust of the driven ice, stood the forts and batteries of the northern channel. Marian remembered the long summer days she had spent with Captain Paul in those steel-walled chambers of the secrets; how she had paced the ramparts for a measurement of them; how greedily she had learnt the lessons in gunnery; how in the silence of this very room she had written down the answers to the questions her English friends asked her, that thereby she might purchase liberty for herself and for the child. To-night these memories were full of an unexplained sadness. She recalled carnival— three weeks had passed since that folly—and the words of love spoken to her then. A yearning for sympathy, a sense of weakness, a consciousness that one man at least in Kronstadt could bring blood to her cheeks and light to her eyes, contributed to her sense of solitude. She found herself standing in the darkness and telling herself that she was utterly alone. Then fear—fear she knew not of what—swept upon her like a freshet; there came to her the horrid thought that she was watched; that unseen eyes followed her even in the privacy of her room; that a man stood close to her and had but to stretch out his hand to touch her own. The terror of such imaginings served to freeze her very blood in her veins. She staggered to the wall and switched on the light. But the lamp showed her an empty room—she was alone with her fears, to laugh at them, to forget them as she had forgotten them a hundred times since she had come to Kronstadt.

The friendly light helped her quickly to this task of forgetfulness. The hand which pressed upon her beating heart dropped to her side. She ran to the door and looked out into the great corridor of the north wing. The silence of night lay upon it. Gladly she turned back to her own cosy room, to the warmth of the stove and the welcome privacy. A moment at the glass, a moment before a photograph of little Dick set boldly upon an easel, a touch of the dress here, a touch of the hair there, a pose of the dainty head, a silent question, " Will he be there to-night?" satisfied the personal instinct. She knew that they awaited her in the drawing-room ; " the Dolls" would sit, one on either side of her, just now and hold her hand. The General himself would leer at her from the depths of an arm-chair and ask her to sing " Bid me to lofe." It might be that Captain Paul would join them if his duties were done; and that he would linger on when Nikolai Stefanovitch had gone to his library, and would remind her, not by word, but by look and unspoken appeal and the silent tributes of homage, of the night of her promise, of the night when he had touched her forehead with his lips and she had not refused him.

The thought brought a deeper colour to her cheeks. She moved about her room with the quick, nervous gesture of suppressed excitement. A man, observing her, would have said that a well-trained mind governed every act; he would have wondered, at the same time, that so fair a face should have led its possessor so rarely to the mirror.

Marian Best knew little of the weapons with which nature had armed her. The thick brown hair straggled in picturesque disorder upon her forehead and her neck; rebelling curls showed themselves at every movement; her dress was "thrown on," but it fitted her to perfection; she had no rings upon her fingers, but the white hands were the prettier for the need.

Eight o'clock was being struck by the church bells of the town when at last Marian left her room to join "the Dolls" in the salon of the house. She had quite forgotten her strange fears of an hour ago, and laughed at them when she trod the soft carpets of the corridor and peeped into the chambers which opened off it. No one moved then in the north wing. The rooms about her were tenantless and in darkness. When she passed the library where old Nikolai Stefanovitch had set up his holy of holies, she wondered to see the door of it open and a flicker of red light upon the low-pitched ceiling. Once only since she had been in the fortress had she dared to enter that room and to pry into its secrets. She knew well that the book-shelves, upon which she beheld the glare of the dancing light, were garners of maps and documents which, could she possess them, would be a fortune to her; she knew that here were locked away treasures for which spies had laid down their lives unavailingly.

Never did she pass that study without some little tremor of heart and mind. Now it would be the devil of rashness saying, "Enter and see"; or, again, the spirit of prudence telling her that therein lay the living death. To-night she heard the first of the voices, and prudence was no more her friend. The desire to have done with it all, to flee Russia and the land of bondage, possessed her to the exclusion of all else. She longed for the sound of little Dick's voice in the English lanes she loved. There came to her out of the darkness a message which said, "Search, and all that you want shall be found there." She refused to listen to it, and answered in her heart that she would betray no more the country of the man who loved her. And this drove her from the door, but not many paces, for presently she stood quite still to listen for any sounds, and, hearing none, she gave herself up to the less subtle arguments. She told herself that when the summer came she would be in England, that the price of her work would have been paid by the British Government, that she would build a home to be the haven of her love.

So was she held, chained by hesitation to the precincts of the corridor. The silence tempted her the more; she was sure that no man in the house then thought of the north wing—that all were busy in the kitchens below. A strong and conquering impulse sent her, at last, with muted feet, back to her own room. She picked up a volume of stories and deftly inserted a sheet of notepaper and a pencil between the leaves. Quick and daring, and armed with all her courage, she ran back to the General's cabinet and entered it. She stood within the holy of holies, and the shadow of the living death was all about her.

It was a spacious room, ill furnished and bare, save for the many volumes which gave ornament to the walls. A ponderous writing-table had the place of honour, and this was littered with bulky documents and official books decorative in their disorder. Marian could see, even by the feeble light cast from the open door of the stove, that the General had been occupied very recently with public affairs, for a big blue paper was open upon his blotting-pad and his pen had rolled from the inkstand and smirched the paper. A heavy volume, bound in red, lay cheek by jowl with the letter he had been writing; and a wine-glass, half emptied, spoke of an occupation interrupted only by the gong for dinner. That occupation would be resumed when the clock struck nine. Marian remembered that it had just gone eight, and with the remembrance there came upon her another moment of apprehension — such a moment as she had known when she awoke from her sleep in the armchair. A panic, overwhelming and irresistible, seized upon her. She thought again that unseen eyes watched her in the darkness. She ran from the room and stood panting in the corridor.

But the panic surrendered swiftly—as these fits were wont to do. She laughed at herself when a minute had passed, and took heart of her new resolution. She said that if anyone found her in the room she must be ready with many an excuse—the excuse that the door of the stove was open, that a cinder had fallen. When she entered the cabinet for the second time, a great hope nerved her to resolution. It was the hope that among the General's maps there would be one of Fort Peter. She lacked this alone for the completion of her work. She said that she must have light; and growing bolder at the impulse, she found the switch, and a blaze of soft rays illumined the apartment.

The brightness of the light awed her. She shielded her eyes with both her hands, and

E

stood irresolute for the third time. Not until many minutes had passed was she able to read the gilt lettering of the books upon the shelves. When resolution came at last generously, she took a map down and unfolded it. It was the map of the southern channel wherein Fort Peter stands. She saw the name joyfully, and opened her book that she might have pencil and paper. But before she could use them a hand was laid upon her shoulder; and when she sprang up with a cry unsuppressed upon her lips, she found herself face to face with Paul Zassulic.

All the little comedy of excuse she had planned so well failed in that supreme moment to defend her. When she had faced her lover for a moment, she knew that she had no word with which to answer him; and all her courage deserting her, she stood white and trembling to hear his accusation.

CHAPTER IV.

LOVER AND JUDGE.

THE red book with the plan of the southern channel had tumbled to the floor when Marian started up from the table. Paul replaced it upon the bookshelf before he spoke to her. She thought the act deliberate to the point of cruelty, but she saw that the hand which held the volume trembled, and she knew then that the man feared for her greatly with a fear such as her own.

"Paul," she cried, finding her tongue after many minutes, "what are you doing? Why do you not speak to me?"

He turned swiftly to show her a face stern and angry.

"I am putting away the map which interested you, mademoiselle; it is ten years old and could be of no use to you. There are others, but we do not leave them about for the amusement of everyone. They are locked up in the safe, and I have no false keys, mademoiselle."

The mocking tone was as a blow to her. Chagrin at her own folly, the certainty that the secret of her life was a secret no more, brought tears to her eyes. This, she said, was the end of it all, of her dream and of her liberty. To-morrow—she dare not think of to-morrow. When she feigned to laugh, the laugh was hard and forced and must struggle for mastery with a sob.

"Oh," she said, and every word cost her an effort, "you think that I care whether your map is new or old. What an idea, Captain Paul! Why do you not say that I came in here to read the General's letters?"

Paul, who had put away the book and possessed himself of the pencil with which she had begun to draw, faced her for a moment and gave her a look which withered her smile and silenced her excuse.

"Do not lie to me," he said; "God knows, there is enough without that. You will not laugh to-morrow when the whip cuts your shoulders and the prison blinds you. Fool! fool! Who but a woman would commit a folly like this?"

She did not speak when he charged her, but leaned back against the wall as though in defiance of his anger. Her clever mind had begun to be busy again, and she reproached herself that she should cut so sorry a figure; but he did not permit her to speak. A door shutting in the hall brought an exclamation to his lips.

"Hark!" he said, "there is Ivan Grigarovitch If he should find you here—my God!"

He switched off the electric light and dragged her from the room, back to her own apartment. She did not resist him, but went with a mind unconscious of her surroundings. Yesterday seemed far off; the thread of her life had snapped, as it were, at the moment of the discovery; she hoped nothing, could realise nothing; she thought that she passed through some valley of her dreams, but would never pass out of it again. When he had shut the door of her own room she dropped into an arm-chair and sat staring vaguely at the red embers in the stove. She tried to think that she had awakened from her sleep; the voice of the man was as a distant sound coming to her across the sea.

"Mademoiselle," he said, crossing over to her and standing at her side, "before I tell them what I have seen to-night, as my duty and my honour compel me to do, I would ask you if you have anything to say to me?"

She continued to look into the fire, a smile hovering upon her face.

"What should I say to you?" she asked, with a shrug of her shoulders. "Is it so great an offence in Russia to look at a book which does not belong to you?"

"It is an offence," he answered quietly, "for which men and women are now dying in the dungeons of the fortresses or at the labour in the mines; it is an offence for which we have lashed many a man to death in the courtyard before this house; it is the one crime which Russia neither forgets nor forgives. Great God, that it should be you—you who sent the plan to London, you who brought this trouble upon us all! I cannot believe it, Marian, I cannot believe the things I have seen with my own eyes."

Again she had no answer for him, but the laugh left her face and she clasped her hands together across her knee.

"You do not understand," she said after a while; "you will never understand."

She was telling herself, secretly, that this trance of the mind which held her tongue-tied and impotent was not to be explained. She knew that if anyone but her lover had found her in the cabinet of Nikolai Stefanovitch, she could have played her part to perfection; aping the ingenuousness and the surprise which had been able hitherto to shield her from suspicion. But she was dumb before Paul. A great shame of her employment came upon her. She did not fear its consequences yet, for she did not wholly realise them; but the thought that her lover knew of it paralysed her understanding. He, meanwhile, paced the room in an agony of uncertainty and of distress.

"You say that I do not understand," he exclaimed in anger at her silence; "not understand, when I find you with the map in your hands and your pencil busy! Not understand! Am I a child, then? Shall I tell myself after this that it was someone else, and not you, who sent the plan to London? Shall I look for another spy in Kronstadt? Pshaw! that I should waste words when every minute is precious."

"You need look for no one, Paul," she said, rising and facing him as the resolve took her; "I alone did what you say. No one helped me. I drew the map and sent it to London. I am the spy, if that is the word. I do not ask you to pity me nor to think of me; I am not worthy of your help, God knows. I can stand alone in the future as I have done in the past. You say that your duty compels you to tell them of what you have seen. Very well, tell them now, and I will wait until they come for me. I am not afraid; why should you be afraid for me?"

She had gathered up her courage and stood before him with blazing eyes and flushed cheeks. He said that he had never seen so beautiful a creature, and her spirit won him to a sudden remembrance of his love.

"Why am I afraid for you, Marian? Can you ask that? Would not I give my life for you? Is not your hurt my hurt? Oh, you know that it is. If they take you from me, they take all that I have in the world. Why could you not trust me? You have done this thing for money; why could you not have told me of you trouble?"

"To beg of you?" she cried, with scorn in her voice.

"Certainly, if by begging you might have saved yourself this dishonour."

"It is no dishonour to buy bread that a child may eat. That is my crime; I am ready to suffer for it."

He stared at her in astonishment.

"It is my turn to say that I do not understand," he cried, "and I must understand, I must know all, Marian I may yet be your friend if you will be frank with me. But to do that you must hold nothing from me, you must speak to me as you would speak to your own brother."

"I will hold nothing from you, Paul—there is nothing to hold. I sent the letters to London because they offered me money for them, and I am very poor, and there is a child in England who is dependent upon me. God help him!"

She sank upon her sofa sobbing, for a memory of little Dick brought her back to reality. But Paul's arms were about her in a moment, and he held her to him and forgot that he was her judge.

"They shall not hurt you, little one," he said; "if you will only trust me, I may yet see a way. Have I not loved you too well to wish to see you harmed? Be frank with me, then, that I may know how to serve you. You say that there is a child in England?"

She looked at him gratefully through her tears. A photograph stood upon the easel near her. She took it up and put it into his hand.

"It is my brother Dick," she said; "that is his picture. He and I were left to face the world together three years ago. He will be six next year. It was for his sake I came here. I have no other relative in the world but my cousin Walter, who is at the Admiralty in London."

"Then he it was who asked you to commit this crime?"

"He told me that the English Government would pay ten thousand pounds to anyone who could secure the plans of the unknown forts here. Then he sent the book which was written about Vladivostok, and the way the English got the maps of that. I asked myself why a woman could not do what a man had done. It was nothing to you that your plans should be known. You say always that Kronstadt is strong enough to defy the world. If that is so, what have you to fear from anyone? And it meant so much to me—a home for myself and the child, and exile no more. Cannot you understand now, Paul?"

He kissed her upon the forehead.

"I understand," he said. "God help us both!"

Her courage appealed to him, for she was quite calm now, saying to herself that for the child's sake she would do again what she had done. And her mind was already occupied with a multitude of ideas, but chiefly with the idea that her lover would save her.

"Paul," she said suddenly, "if you understand, are you not my friend again?"

He began to pace the room again, his spurs clanking over the bare floor and his long cloak hanging loose from his shoulders. A voice of conscience whispered to him that he was one of the children of Kronstadt and must not betray her. The kiss of the girl was still warm upon his lips as a kiss of mercy. But even in the crisis a memory of smaller things intruded, and he spoke of them.

"Mon Dieu!" he said, "what an actress you are, Marian! I remember the day I took you to the battery and showed you the breech of a gun. You asked me if a shell was a torpedo, and how we measured the ten-inch Armstrong, which seemed to you three yards long. You remember that, do you not? How you ran about from rampart to rampart like a schoolgirl. If I had known!"

She laughed, forgetting all that had gone before.

"But you did not know," she said; "and I measured the mole by pacing it while you were making tea. I can see you now, scalding your fingers with the kettle and saying that it was an honour. I wrote down the number of the guns when old Seroff the sergeant went to look for bread. He told me how deep the channel was, and repeated it over and over again because I was so stupid. You were all so kind to me!"

The love of jest was not conquered even by this, the tragedy of her life. She laughed with the laugh of a child at the remembrance of the comedy she had played upon the ramparts; and Paul laughed with her, content that she and no other had acted for him.

"Oh!" said he. "You have the cunning of

the devil! If it had begun and ended in this; but now — now when we have to-morrow to face, I cannot laugh long when I think of that, Marian. How shall I help you? How shall I do my duty? How shall I forget that I love you? Why, to-morrow, holy God! they may send you to the fortress, and I may never look upon your face again!"

He stopped abruptly in his walk, but she, standing by the chimney, looked into the ashes of the stove as though still seeking dream pictures there.

"They will do that if you tell them," she said.

"And I must tell them; I have no other course. My honour compels me. I would give half the years of my life to get you out of Kronstadt to-night, Marian; to-morrow it will be too late. I must tell them then. I cannot delay—you know that I cannot."

The words cost him an effort, and when he had spoken them he came and took both her hands in his and looked into her eyes.

"My love! my love!" he said, "how shall I help you? How shall I save you from this folly? Swear to me that you will do nothing more—that you will never write another line to England while you are in this house."

"I must write to little Dick," she said petulantly.

He stamped on the floor impatiently.

"Promise—give me the promise!" he cried.

"I promise," she answered, clinging to him with a pitiful appeal; "oh, I promise all. I will do anything if I may see the child again! You will not tell them, Paul? Oh, for God's sake pity me—listen to me!"

"I must tell them," he answered doggedly—"I must, I must!"

He pushed her from him, for there was a sound of voices in the corridor, and he reeled rather than walked from the room. But she stood trembling and still, and she counted his footsteps as he crossed the snow-clad courtyard.

CHAPTER V.

FOREBODING.

THE echo of the footsteps grew fainter and fainter, and was lost at last in a murmur of other sounds — the sound of a sentry tramping and the clang of arms. Marian listened keenly for some while in the hope that she would hear the steps again, and that Paul would come back to her, repentant of his determination. But the deeper silence of the night fell again anon; the wind moaned dismally across the frozen sea; the crash of the rending ice prevailed, and she knew that she was left alone.

There had been a buzz of voices in the corridor when Paul left her, and she opened the door of the room to hear who it was that had come up to the place. She thought that she could distinguish the deep baying tones of old Bonzo and the cat-like purr of the servant Ivan; but these were silenced in a little time; and she said to herself that she could delay no longer, but must go down to "the Dolls" and to the farce played every night in the gloomy and depressing salon. Though her hands still trembled, and there was a stain of tears upon her cheek, she would not think of that which had happened in the last hour. She cheated herself with the assurance that her lover would not tell; she believed that his love for her would prove stronger than his resolution to guard his honour. At the same time, her prudence did not desert her. Remotely and vaguely she realised the possibility that the work of the night might bring some swift and terrible punishment. Just as she had told her lover everything, so did she determine to tell other accusers nothing. She would play the part of the *ingénue* again; she would answer their accusations with laughter and little gestures of assumed fear and the weapons of the coquette. The utmost that Paul could do, she said, would be to speak of a suspicion. It would be her business to laugh that suspicion away, to make it ridiculous.

While this was in her mind her fingers were busy in the execution of the plan. Although she was dressed for the comedy of the drawing-room, she began to undress swiftly, loosing the laces of her bodice and casting off her clothes until she was able to unwind from her body a scroll of paper, upon which were many little sketches and names innumerable, and the depths of soundings and the armament of forts. She laughed to herself when at last she thrust into the fire this treasure which had cost her so many months of secret labour and daring schemes. She knew that its contents were written also upon her memory, and that she could make a copy of it from memory alone whenever she might choose.

"They will search me and will find nothing," she said to herself when the ashes of the paper were scattered. "I shall write to England to-morrow a letter for them to open. They cannot prove that I sent the map to London, and Paul will not tell them. I shall go away from here when the sea will let me, and that will be the end of all. Paul will forget, and I——"

She turned from the fire with a sigh and began to lace up her dress again. A tremulous excitement possessed her, so that she went from place to place in the room, now pulling aside the curtain that she might look upon the moonlit sea; now standing before her glass to discover that her face was drawn and pale and almost haggard; or going to the door to listen for the voices of "the Dolls." It was nine o'clock when she entered the salon, to find the children sitting like mutes before a picture-book, and old Stefanovitch himself dozing peacefully in a chair. The scene was one with which she was familiar. She took courage of it, and whispered that nothing had happened. She tried to think that Paul had not spoken to her, that she had imagined the scene in the cabinet and that other scene with her lover. It lay upon her to play courageously the part she had played always. When the General awoke with a start, and sat staring at her stupidly through the after haze of sleep, she had a winning smile for him and a ready word.

"How stupid of me!" she cried, with a gesture of feigned amazement. "I did not see that you were resting."

She paused as though she would draw back, but the General silenced her gallantly.

"Tais toi, tais toi," said he, sitting upright and searching for his glass; "how shall I keep awake when you are not here? Tell me that, mademoiselle?"

"But I have no business to let you know that I am here—at such a time, General."

He twisted in his chair, seeking to follow her with his eyes as she crossed the room.

"Du tout, du tout," he said pleasantly; "you shall sing to me and I shall forget everything. One of the English songs, ma petite—a little song of the lofe—hein, mademoiselle, of the lofe?"

She looked at him prettily over her shoulder,

F

and "the Dolls" rising mechanically to stand one upon either side of the piano, she began to sing the ballad of the King of Thule. She had a voice surpassingly sweet and tender, and music was for her more than an accomplishment, it was an art. The excitement and the passion of the past hour seemed to mingle with the harmonies of the exquisitely tender ballad. Even Stefanovitch, who thought that the angels must play upon trombones, was held in a trance of admiration.

"Magnifique! magnifique!" he cried again and again; "it is the genius which sings like that. You shall be heard in all Russia by-and-by, and the Emperor shall applaud you. Eh, mes enfants, would you not sing like mademoiselle? Is she not superb? is she not beautiful?"

He cackled and applauded again and again, while the children repeated the words after him, though their wooden faces had no change of expression, and the music was meaningless to them.

"Quelle une chanson delicieuse!"

"Oh, mademoiselle, si j'etais vous!"

"It is the song of Marguerite."

"Sans doute—the song of Marguerite."

"Si je l'avais connu, Marguerite!"

"Stupide! she is dead; n'est-ce pas, mademoiselle, Marguerite est morte?"

Old Nikolai listened to their chatter and hugged himself at the trend of it.

"Eh, what is that—you wish mademoiselle to tell you about Marguerite? Ho, ho! Another time, children, another time. Mees Marian will first tell that story to me—hein, mademoiselle, you will tell me the story of Marguerite when we are alone?"

Marian rose from the piano, telling herself that it would be a pleasure to box the ears of Nikolai Stefanovitch. But she continued to wear a contented face, for the thought that the friendship of the master of Kronstadt might yet serve her was strong in her mind, and she acted upon it.

"I could not tell you anything, General," she said; "I should not have the courage."

"The courage—not have the courage—with me? Oh, but I will give you the courage; you shall lean upon me, mademoiselle. Ho, ho! you shall lean upon me and be strong, and I will put the flowers in the garden—the English flowers, hein? You shall find them and sing the song again."

She answered with a coquette's glance. The Dolls stared at their father open-mouthed. They could not understand how it was that he slept when they were with him, or answered them in reluctant grunts, while no sooner was their

F 2

governess in the room, than these spasms of gesture and ridiculous antics seized upon him, and he became another man. Nor did they recall an occasion when Mademoiselle Marian had responded so willingly to his foolishness. The *rôle* of the demure and shy little governess was cast off; she had become the coquette to the "tips of her fingers." Possibly, Mademoiselle Rina and Mademoiselle Varia were very glad when old Colonel Bonzo entered the room and put an end to such strange goings-on.

"You are engaged, my General?" he said, standing motionless at the door.

Stefanovitch was on his feet in a moment. If he had shame to be surprised in such employment, he did not show it.

"You wait for me, Colonel?"

"If you please, my General."

"There is news, then?"

"There is grave news, Nikolai."

Marian, who had been turning over the leaves of a book, looked up quickly. The tone in which the Man of Iron spoke, his neglect to pass a word with her, were warnings of instinct. She felt the colour rushing to her cheeks; her hands trembled upon the pages; a voice whispered to her—a voice of her imagination—"Paul has told them that is the news." Excitement of the hour alone had enabled her to bear up before the General and the children. She had almost cheated herself into the idea that her alarms were foolish shadows created by her fancy; but now, when she looked Bonzo full in the face, it was as though the hand of the accuser already touched her shoulder. Grim, and stern, and unbending, the Man of Iron watched her with a searching gaze which stifled the words upon her lips and held her chained by fear to the lounge. "He knows," she thought; "he knows, and has come here to tell the other. Paul has spoken, and this is the end."

"Mademoiselle, voulez-vous monter en haut?"

"Mademoiselle, I have the wish to sleep."

The children spoke, and Marian rose with an effort. She turned to bow to the men, but they had already left the room. She did not know that minutes had elapsed while this agony of uncertainty troubled her. She had not seen the stately salute with which the master of Kronstadt had taken leave of her; the dreaded searching eyes of old Bonzo still seemed to look her through and through, although the Colonel was no longer in the room. They followed her, she thought, from the salon to the bedrooms of the children; they watched her again in the corridor; the same sensation of dread, and the desire to hide herself, was with her when she entered her own apartment and locked the door, and sank, weak, and trembling, and afraid, upon the couch.

It was near to the hour of ten o'clock by this time, and the bugles were blowing in the barracks of the town. Marian had heard them often when she sat alone in the room, and had welcomed them as a message coming from the haunts of men. She asked herself if she would hear them to-morrow. She looked across the jagged sea, billowed with pinnacles of ice and swirling floes, and found in it the frozen barrier lying between her and freedom. She began to ask herself if she could seek any place of shelter upon the island. Had it been summer, some English ship might have given her harbourage; but now, when the Gulf was wrestling with the fetters of the ice, and no ships could venture from the harbours, what hope was there of that? She could distinguish in the courtyard below her window the shining barrel of the rifle which the sentry carried. The vast mass of the ramparts beyond showed other sentries swiftly pacing the outworks of the fort. The tomb could not have caged its victim more surely than Kronstadt had caged the woman who had betrayed her.

Midnight was struck in the town before she began to undress. Her unwilling fingers went clumsily to the work; and when she had laid her pretty gown upon the bed she asked herself if she had worn it for the last time. Fear had wrought upon her nerves so pitilessly that she could neither sit nor lie; but must be listening ever for the fall of a foot in the corridor or the sound of voices in the courtyard without.

"They will come in five minutes—in ten," she would say. And she began to plan the defence she would make, repeating the excuses she must plead and the arts she must practise.

Or again, she would trust in the man's love, telling herself that Paul would not harm her, that he would find some way. She could not believe that Fate would cut her off in a moment from the light of life and the love of life, and that little world of self-content she had created. All the comforts about her—the cheery fire in the stove, the pretty chairs, the pictures, the bed wherein she had dreamed of little Dick so often—she thought of these, and asked herself what magician's wand could spirit them away and set up in their place the reeking walls of a prison. She had dared much, but the penalty of her daring remained for her a phantom of her fears.

Her long brown hair was tumbling upon her shoulders now, and she passed from her sitting-room to the little white alcove wherein her bed stood. All was very still and quiet here; she could distinguish no longer the wash of the waters over the ice nor the tramp of the sentries upon the ramparts. She shivered with the cold, and lay for hours wondering why the great house slept and no one came to accuse her. When, at last, the lagging dawn was winged, white and misty across the sea, sleep took pity upon her, and a befriending dream put her arms about the neck of the child she loved, and she held him close to her; and anon she walked with him through the lanes and gardens of her beloved England. Nor did she know that when next she slept it would be in the lightless dungeon of Fort Alexander at Kronstadt.

CHAPTER VI.

THE HONOUR OF PAUL ZASSULIC.

CAPTAIN PAUL crossed the courtyard of the Governor's house and began to walk rapidly toward the town of Kronstadt. Marian had listened to his footsteps as he went, but her thought that he would return again was not in his mind. Indeed, he scarce knew whither he went or upon what errand; so that the sentry crossed himself as he passed and said that his officer was drunk with vodki, a condition which every right-minded artilleryman considered to be the ultimate possibility of bliss. But Paul never saw the man. The snow, white and crisp upon the ramparts, was so much slush and mud beneath his feet. The keen north wind nipped his ears and cast flakes of the driven hail into his eyes; but he had no thought to draw his fur hood closer or to button up his cloak. An impulse to flee the house, the city, to escape at any cost from the terrible position he had been placed in, was paramount. Once he thought that death was the way, and at that he stood very still in the roadway and asked himself what would be the consequences of his death.

"It would not save her," he thought; "she would be alone then. Even if I hold my tongue they will know sooner or later. There is nothing hidden long in Russia. It may be a week, it may be a month, but they will know, and then——"

He walked on with tremendous strides, ignoring the salutes of the troopers who passed him by the way; deaf to the music in the cafés; blind to the lights flashing over the frozen sea. His life had been so barren of difficulties until this time; his duty had claimed absolute and ready obedience. If anyone had told him a week ago that the day would come when he would hesitate to do that duty, he would have struck the speaker upon the mouth and have shot him afterwards. But he loved Marian with a tenderness and a whole-hearted devotion of which none but an honest man is capable. Proud of his own strength, her helplessness and gentleness appealed to him with pathetic insistence. If it had been permitted to him to suffer in her stead, he would have laid down his own liberty gladly. He pictured her cast out from civilisation, alone, and friendless, and weeping in the pitiless prisons of Siberia. The sweet touch of her hands, when she had put them about his neck and craved

mercy of him, was an ecstasy of memory. That
she should ask mercy of him who had worshipped
her so long in silence, that was a bitter day indeed !

"It cannot be—it cannot be," he said to himself again and again. " She did not send the plans
to London; she did not mean to copy the map
it is all a mistake ; it will be proved so by-and-by.
I will wait and see. My God ! if I should tell and
she should be innocent ! But she must be innocent
—she is !—I will swear it."

All the chivalry in his nature waged war with
the more subtle pleadings of conscience. He told
himself that it would be a crime to speak of
what he had seen, or to take Marian's words
seriously, until he was sure that she had sinned.
"She did not know what she was doing. They
tempted her in London, but we cannot blame her
for that. It is impossible that she can have sent a
correct map. We are strong enough to laugh at
a little enemy like that ; and I shall make her
our friend. She will learn to love Russia as she
has learned to love me."

He went on with a lighter step, happy in this
contenting reflection. But he was still oblivious
of all about him—of the narrow streets of the
town which he entered, of the great looming
buildings, of the cathedral square, and of the
soldiers' cafés. When a man touched him upon

the shoulder and spoke to him, he awoke from his meditations as one may wake from a broken sleep.

"It is you, my Colonel! You wish to speak to me?"

Old Bonzo, for he it was who had stopped him, laughed good humouredly.

"You have long legs, Paul, my friend," he said. "Do not let them walk away with you into the sea. Upon my life, you look as though you had seen a devil!"

"I was in a hurry to get to barracks, Colonel; they will not begin until I come, and it has struck nine."

Bonzo's eyes twinkled curiously.

"Old Nikolai will be gone to his room and La Petite to her children—hein, my friend? You can come away from the big house while the Englishwoman is still at the piano? I do not believe it. Ho, ho! She is not well to-night, and that is why you walk fast."

Paul shrugged his shoulders impatiently. He was thinking that Marian's very life might depend upon his words.

"Mademoiselle Best is now in the salon," he said unconcernedly; "you will find her there if you are going up. For myself, I prefer the conversation of my friends."

Bonzo gave a great guffaw and slapped the younger man upon the shoulder.

"You shall tell that to the little Englishwoman to-morrow. I will remind you of the words. When I go up to the house just now it will be something to talk about. My friend Paul running away from the petticoats! Bon Dieu! what a spectacle! Come and drink a glass of wine with me, my son, for I have news for you."

They turned into a café, and the Colonel called for the wine of Burgundy. The place was full and busy, the gold and green of many uniforms shining under the tremulous rays of many brilliant lamps. But they got a table to themselves, and Paul hastened to gulp down a glass of wine that he might hide his curiosity from one who could read and interpret the slightest gesture of friend or enemy.

"Your news is from London, Colonel?"

Bonzo nodded his head and pretended to light a cigar that he might watch the face of his companion.

"Yes," he said, "from London."

"And, of course, the story we were talking about the other day proves to be ridiculous."

Bonzo leaned over the table and whispered his answer.

"It is not ridiculous at all; it is true. The

map which was sent is a correct map. Every
gun is marked; the depths of the channels are
given. The names of the garrison are accurate.
We could not have made a better map ourselves."

Paul sat very white and still. He was asking
himself whether he should feign surprise or doubt.
A little reflection led him to believe that doubt
would serve him better than surprise.

"Quelle sottise!" he said, leaning back in his
chair and smoking quickly. "You do not believe
that story, my Colonel?"

Bonzo took up his glass.

"I believe every word of it," he said; "more
than that, I know it is true."

"You know?"

"Certainly I know."

"Then there is a spy in the city! My God,
what a thing to hear!"

Bonzo drank off his wine at a draught.

"Tut!" he said indifferently, "we shall know
how to deal with it. And mark you, my son,
it would be another thing altogether if the man
who made the map were out of the city. It is
just because we have him trapped by the ice
here that I can drink a glass of wine with you
instead of hurrying to the General with the
news. To-morrow, perhaps, we shall go and look

for this man. There is no need to disturb ourselves. No letters can leave us, no more maps can be sent to London — at present. Why should we hurry? There is plenty of time, and we do not see a man shot every day."

Paul started in spite of himself.

"But you don't shoot spies when there is no war," he exclaimed hurriedly.

"It is a fashion of speaking, my son. For my part, I would shoot no one when there is the whip—when you have only to raise your finger so, and your enemy is an enemy no more."

"And you are sure that the man is still in the city?"

"I know it!" cried Bonzo, bringing his fist down on the table with a great crash. "You will know it too, directly. You shall see the fellow for yourself. Who can say? perhaps we shall send him to you at Alexander. To-morrow you must have the cell swept, and the irons ready, and the whip waiting. Certainly, we shall know how to deal with it; but with those at the capital it is another thing. Voyez-vous, mon ami, we can say no longer it is a jest, there is no spy in Kronstadt. If we report this arrest, there must be inquiry, blame, recrimination. But if we do not report it"— here Bonzo lowered his voice until it was but a whisper—"if we do not report it, and the man who made the map should die in the cell at Fort Alexander—hein, how would they accuse us then? You understand, my friend?"

Paul's heart beat quicker, for he understood perfectly. They would flog the spy to death in the dungeons of Fort Alexander, that blame might not rest upon their own shoulders. At the same time he did not fail to remark that his companion spoke always of "the man." Marian's secret was safe then!

"It is a clever thought, my Colonel," he said quickly. "Why should we be bullied by people at Petersburg who do not know of our difficulties? If I were the General, I would report nothing. But he must be sure of the man; and is he sure? You say that he is, and I believe you. But I should be glad to see him for myself."

"You shall see him to-morrow," said Bonzo rising and buttoning his greatcoat about him, "meanwhile, Captain, do not let us forget our responsibilities. There is no officer here who should not be ashamed that this work was ever finished; there is none who should not say to himself, 'My duty must be done.' You have said so, I know. You will do your duty and nothing will stand between you and the Czar you serve."

He laid his hand on the young man's shoulder almost affectionately. Paul shuddered at the touch and the words, for he seemed to read a deeper meaning in them. He told himself that he was already a traitor in his heart, for he had kept the great secret, had kept it with an effort which was an agony.

When he left the Colonel at the door of the café, the lights of Kronstadt were dancing before his eyes; a fever of self-reproach and doubt heated his blood and quickened his step as he went onwards to the barracks.

"They will know to-morrow," he said again and again; "they will know to-morrow, and she must suffer."

And he was impotent to serve her, impotent to do anything but remember his love for her and bewail the doom she had brought upon herself.

Those who met Paul Zassulic in the streets that night declared that he walked with the step of a drunken man. He passed them without recognition, or jostled them rudely from the pavements. Here and there he was upon the brink of a brawl. A cornet meeting him before the Observatory, and being thrust aside with little ceremony, ran after him to call him "hobbledehoy." When Paul turned swiftly the

G

youth slunk off.　There was no better pistol shot, no quicker swordsman in Kronstadt than the young captain of artillery.　Men spoke of his cleverness as a thing of which the city was proud.　Bullies gave him the wall and proclaimed their desire to meet him only before other bullies.　He had proved his courage in many a difficult moment; his word was a bond to them.　Could they have read his mind as he stalked past them on his way to the barracks, they would have known that courage was now wrestling with the agony of self-reproach; that he was saying to himself, "I will tell at midnight, at dawn, before the sun sets to-morrow."

A hearty welcome always awaited him in barracks, but to-night the men who rose to make way for him could not suppress an exclamation upon his appearance.

"You are ill, mon vieux!"

"Fichtre! you have plastered your face with the snow, Paul."

"He has quarrelled with La Petite, and comes here to be cured."

Paul turned upon the speaker, a grinning ensign, savagely.

"Hold your tongue, or I will cut it out," he said, and the boy slunk from the room.

"There is nothing the matter with me," he

continued, throwing off his cloak and helping himself liberally to the absinthe ready upon the table, "or, if there is," he added, "it is the wine of old Bonzo. I have been drinking with him up there. You understand?"

The men exchanged glances swiftly. Some shrugged their shoulders, others fidgeted with packs of cards in their hands. Paul turned to the cards as to a refuge from perplexity.

"What are you waiting for?" he said brusquely. "Is it to make more complaints about my appearance? You, Sergius, Karl, are you going to sleep there all night? or is it Lent which troubles you?"

The lieutenants addressed rose from their chairs and seated themselves in silence at the card table. They were asking themselves what was the matter with their friend. They had a vague idea that the Englishwoman was at the bottom of it; but were too careful of their skins to hazard the opinion openly.

"I shall win your money, Sergius, and cure my headache," cried Paul boisterously, as his friend began to deal; "there is always a headache if you meet Bonzo after dinner."

"There is sometimes a headache if you meet him in the morning," said Karl, throwing a card upon the table. "That is the worst of these

G 2

silent men; you are always asking yourself what they are thinking about, and so you get a headache. What is more, you never find out the thing that perplexes you. I would wager old Bonzo against the devil at any kind of cheat or cunning you like to name. He can read the papers which lie in your pocket-book; I have known him to do it."

"Did he drink Burgundy to-night?" asked Sergius, passing some roubles across the table with the air of a man not yet warmed to the game. "I keep out of his way when he drinks Burgundy—it is a danger signal. Champagne, now, that means peace, and possibly a pair of twinkling eyes. He has even patted me on the shoulder with the paw of a domesticated bear—after champagne."

"There will be no twinkling eyes to-morrow," exclaimed an onlooker who watched the game. "You have heard that he has news from the Prince —at least, that is the story. It should mean that we are to learn all about the map which went to London."

Sergius laughed; Paul continued to watch his cards.

"For my part," continued the speaker, while he lighted a cigarette indolently, " I do not believe any such story—pas si bête. Someone has played a joke upon the English, and we are paying for it with all this fuss and trouble. As if a woman——"

"A woman!" cried Paul, looking up suddenly.

"Yes; have you not heard? They say that the map was drawn by a woman. There is no doubt of it. Our own people in London have been at work, and they are sure that a woman's hand is to be traced. It is an extraordinary story—to be told to a fool."

The man strolled away to the stove, while the others played intently for a little while, until, indeed, Paul of a sudden threw down his cards and rose from the table.

"I cannot play," he stammered; "you must excuse me, mes amis; my head is going round. It is the cursed wine which old Bonzo drinks. I shall walk in the cool air and then go to bed."

He threw his cloak about his shoulders and quitted the room with no further exchange of words. The cry of one of his companions, that he had left his money upon the table, did not arrest him. He was saying to himself over and over again, "A woman's hand—they know that the map was drawn by a woman!" He had the desire to run up to the great house to warn Marian that the hour had come. He dared not to think that he had touched her lips for the last time; nevertheless a voice told him that it must be so. The blow was about to fall, the gate of the prison to shut upon the woman for whom he would have laid down his life.

"Sacre bleu!" cried Sergius the lieutenant, staring after the retreating figure. "So Paul is like that to-night. And he has left his roubles."

"Not at all," said Karl. "He has gone up to see La Petite; he goes there every night. They have quarrelled, I say, and he is off to tell her that it was his fault. He will not be in such a hurry by-and-by. He should have waited. It is much prettier to forgive a woman than to be forgiven by her, and it does not cost you forty roubles."

"Or make you ridiculous," said one of the ensigns. "For my part, I would not lose my temper for any woman in Russia."

Sergius cut the cards idly.

"Vive la jeunesse!" he exclaimed gaily, "you will know better by-and-by, mon vieux. I used to talk like that when I was twenty; but I would not look twice now at any woman who could not provoke me. Fichtre! it is not love at all until you have made her angry. And he is very much in love, for he forgot to finish his absinthe. Let us go to the square and hear more of the news from London. There will be plenty to talk about by-and-by if the Sasha does not laugh at us."

"Of course he laughs at us," replied Karl; "how should it be otherwise? Where is the woman who could make a map of Battery 3 ? Who took her there, and where did she learn her gunnery ? It is a child's tale and the General is wise enough to laugh at it."

"Child's tale or not," chimed in the grinning ensign who had spoken of La Petite when Paul first entered the room, "there has been one woman in the battery. I saw her there myself. She took tea with Captain Paul a week ago."

"You mean the Englishwoman ?" asked Sergius, turning swiftly upon him.

"Certainly. Ask Seroff if you do not believe me."

A great silence fell upon the room, the silence of embarrassment and of sudden revelation. There was only one man there who did not love Paul Zassulic, and he had spoken. The others heard his words, but knew not how to answer.

"You shall tell Paul that in the morning," said Sergius, breaking a troublesome silence; "it will amuse him and amuse us afterwards." But to the others he said, "This is no place for the friends of my friend. Who is going with me to the square ? "

They went out together, leaving the ensign alone in the room. They did not speak to each other of the meaning of the things they had heard; the honour of a friend was in their keeping.

Paul, meanwhile, had retraced his steps to the Governor's house, and now paced the courtyard regardless of the hour or of the night. Streams of light were cast out upon the hazy air from many rooms in the forbidding and barrack-like building; but one room alone was for his eyes. He could distinguish, through the interstice of the curtains, the depending lamp and the gilt mirror upon which Marian displayed her photographs. Once he saw her pass the window swiftly, her hair falling upon her shoulders. He was tempted to scout prudence and to speak to her again before she slept. Although he had quarters in Nikolai Stefanovitch's house—for he was attached to the staff—it was long before he could find the courage to enter or to learn what Bonzo had done. The little star of light shining from the window of the English girl's room was for him as the lamp of a sanctuary. He tortured himself with thoughts of Marian sleeping in the shadow of the doom; he remembered her prettiness, her gentleness, her winning pride. He said that they would crush that pride in the dust of suffering and humiliation. The cruel severity with which the keepers of the gate of Russia could punish even their own children was remembered by him with loathing and regret. They would put unnameable indignities upon her, he said. He foresaw the day when the childish face must become the haggard face of the woman branded with the furrows of pain, and torture, and mental agony. He swore that he would save her, though her fate should become his own; and, swearing, he cursed his own impotence and the very uniform he wore.

Snow fell in lagging flakes at this time; the wind had fallen somewhat, so that all sounds, other than the sound of men's footsteps, were plainly to be heard. Paul observed the passing lights in the great house, but could detect no omen of warning. The lamp in Marian's room was a message to . him telling of her safety. He could peer in through the window of the General's cabinet and make out old Bonzo standing by the side of the writing-table; but the Colonel's attitude was one of patient waiting, and it reassured him. "It is not for to-night," he told himself; "it may never be at all. Even if they know that the map was drawn by a woman's hand, how can they trace it to her? If they had any news she would not be sleeping in her room, she would be in——"

He ground his heel into the snow when he dared thus to think of the possibilities. His mind was made up that he would stand sentinel no more. He feared the observation, the chatter of the sentries. Old Bonzo might find him in the courtyard when he returned to barracks; he could imagine no greater calamity than to raise suspicion in the mind of the Man of Iron. And this fear drove him into the house at last, but with reluctant and halting steps. His own room, the bare room of a soldier, was in the north wing, remote from Marian's, but not so remote that he could not hear the creak of her door when it opened or shut. Nor did he enter before he had walked with a woman's step to the end of the corridor and had listened a little while to assure himself that she slept. Then, delaying but a moment before the cabinet of the General, he turned wearily to his bed and lay long listening for the voice of Bonzo and for sleep to come upon the great house.

There was no light in his room, nor had he kindled one. The moonbeams, striking upward from the glittering fields of snow, made glorious lamps of the night to shed a softening radiance upon all things. He welcomed them, for they spoke of rest, and sleep, and the balm of the mind. He thought that they were playing upon the face of her he loved; putting a crown of gold about her white forehead and kissing her eyes with the kiss of dreams. When sleep took pity upon him at last, he was carried in thought to the night of carnival and the love message it bore him. He walked with her again through the silent streets of Kronstadt, but anon, as he walked, she fell at his feet and a scream of terror awakened the sleeping city. No word, no prayer of his could hush that cry of dolour which he heard in his dream. It rang in his ears, terrifying him; he bore her in his arms, but awakened troopers pursued him; men came from the looming buildings to exclaim upon her; he looked back upon the grim forts and mighty ramparts, and the angel of death hovered over them; he clasped his burden the closer in his arms and ran on; but the cry was unchecked, and phantoms of pursuit multiplied until they became an army.

And so he awoke and sprang from his bed. There was a glimmer of sunshine in his room, but the woman's cry he had heard in his dream still rang out in the silence of the great house. He listened for one instant of agony and then reeled to the door. The corridor without was full of the figures of gunners; he saw Bonzo, silent and grim; he saw Marian, white and trembling.

"My God!" he cried, "the hour has come!"

CHAPTER VII.

PAUL BEARS WITNESS.

PAUL returned to his room and began to dress, maladroitly, but with some deliberation. The irons upon Marian's wrists seemed to hurt his own hands; her cry still echoed in his ears. He heard the heavy tramp of feet in the passage; he thought he could distinguish the voice of General Stefanovitch; but anon these sounds died away and silence fell upon the house again. He said that it was typical of the silence which henceforth must wait upon his life. He thought that he had looked upon the woman he loved for the last time. She had gone from him with that terrible appeal upon her lips; to what fate he knew not, save that the impassable gates had shut upon her, that the herald of the living death had struck her down.

He was glad that she had not seen him when he stood for a moment at his door and watched the gunners drag her from her room. The pitiful figure, the babyish face, the beseeching eyes, would be for him the everlasting remembrance of her. He knew well that the measure of her guilt or innocence was not to be weighed by those who were to judge her. She, the mere girl, alone and unaided, had set herself against the might and the power and the terrible justice of Kronstadt, and had been vanquished in the contest. She had looked upon the world of light for the last time. No cry of hers would ever be heard by the world again. She would go from the city and none would dare to ask whither.

Now that the blow had fallen, Paul was surprised that his mind was so ready to serve him and that he could think so clearly. The arrest of Marian lifted one burden at least from his shoulders. There was no longer a confession to make, he argued. That which he knew was known also to the governors of the citadel. And he must defend himself from the possibilities of suspicion; must be ready with words of surprise and wonder. He alone in Russia remained the friend of the stricken woman; for her sake he would dare anything in the hope that he might yet be of service to her. And this hope began to give him courage, he knew not why. His clumsy fingers became supple; he dressed swiftly and walked boldly from the house. Old Bonzo was in the courtyard waiting for his chief to come out. Smart and trim, with well-squared shoulders and firm tread, the Man of Iron greeted the young officer with no more concern than if this had been a *festa* and they had been going together for a picnic on the sea.

"Bon jour, Captain Paul; I see you well this morning?"

"Thank you, Colonel; and you?"

Bonzo's eyes twinkled cunningly.

"All my nights are good," he said; "it is the old bird who knows how to roost. And I am just going to breakfast with a lady. You hear, my son; then you will not tell madame—hein?"

His jocund efforts were like the labour of a shire horse. They angered Paul, whose feverish impatience scarcely brooked control.

"Colonel," he exclaimed, unable to hold his tongue any longer; "it is said that they have just arrested Mademoiselle Best. Is the news true?"

Bonzo stopped suddenly in his walk.

"You know that it is true, Captain Paul."

"I, my Colonel? how should I know?"

"Because you stood at your door while they were taking her down yonder."

Paul bit his lip.

"Certainly I saw that, but I did not know

the meaning of it. You suspect her, then, my Colonel?"

"We suspect her so far that we know it was her hand which drew the map of Battery 3."

"Her hand, my Colonel—a woman's hand! But she is as ignorant as a child."

Paul wished to assume an air of great surprise, but his gesture was false, his voice had a hollow ring in it. Bonzo watched him with little twinkling eyes and read him as he would have read a book.

"You shall learn how ignorant she is when the accusation is made just now, my son. Did I not tell you that I would show you the spy this morning? Well, if you will go up to the ramparts, you will see her in the launch which carries her to Alexander. We will follow her there when the General is ready, Captain Paul. It is not every day that we can breakfast with a lady in Kronstadt."

"I cannot believe it!" cried Paul; "I cannot believe that she could have——"

"Cannot believe it! Bon Dieu! you tell that to me when you know that it is true, when you know—but I will leave you to tell us what you know, my son. I will leave you to remember that you are a servant of the Czar. You do not forget that, Captain Paul."

Bonzo's voice rang out in varying notes, loud and accusing, or gentle and cooing. All the colour left Paul's face when the words were spoken. He had a great awe of the man whose eyes could read his very thoughts; he began to ask himself, "What has he learned? What has he seen?" But Bonzo, who served a purpose with every word, now laid his. hand upon the shoulder of the younger man and the gesture was a kind one.

"Come," he said, " I do not forget that you are a man as well as a soldier, Paul. Go and get your café and then meet me upon the quay. We will cross together, and you shall hear the story for yourself."

Paul thanked him incoherently and hurried away. The Colonel watched him as he went, and with no unfriendly eyes.

" There goes a lover bewitched by a pretty face," he said at last. " He will come to reason by-and-by, or, if he does not, we shall know how to deal with him. We will send him to the fort often. If there is anything more between them, that will be the opportunity to find it out."

Content with this design, Bonzo resumed his measured walk; but Paul went swiftly through the town, avoiding the haunts of his fellows. He saw nothing, heard nothing of the awakening life about him. "Marian is arrested," were the words ever whispered into his ear. Men saluted him, he forgot to observe or to return their greeting; the sun shone brightly, but for him the city was in darkness. "They will send her to the mines, they will torture her," he thought. The moment when he must see her again was one to be dreaded. He feared his own courage, for he knew that his courage alone could save her —if she was to be saved—from the terrible days to come.

It was eight o'clock when he arrived at the quay, and Bonzo had not yet come down. Paul entered a little café just by the merchants' harbour, and called for tea and for prune brandy. There were many soldiers and sailors in the place, but their talk convinced him that they had no news of that which had happened. He began to see that the authorities would keep their acts as secret as possible; but whether this would help or hinder him, he could not say. He remembered Bonzo's words—if the prisoner should die in Fort Alexander, what inquiry would then be held? He knew that they would not put a woman to death; but Russian prisons have other weapons whereby the ends of

H

death are attained. Paul's hand shook when he lifted the glass to his lips ; he left the café, driven on by all the impulses of fear and dread. "She shall not die!" he said, and then laughed nervously at his own helplessness.

Fort Alexander, with its one hundred and sixteen guns, 8 and 10 inch, in casemates, is perhaps the most imposing of the seven detached forts which stand up, islets of steel and stone, in the southern channel of Kronstadt. Built entirely of granite, in the shape of an ellipse, there are four tiers of embrasures in its front; while its rear wall bristles with great guns *en barbette*. A foundation of piles driven down in a channel, here eighteen feet deep, carries the tremendous blocks of which the battery is constructed, and its guns are so placed that they cross fires with the guns of Fort Peter and of Battery 3, thus rendering impassable the one narrow channel by which an enemy's ships must seek passage to Petersburg. The interior of the fort has all the aspect of a gloomy and forbidding prison. Dark cell-like rooms accommodate the garrison in charge of it. There are other cells below into which the light of day never comes, tomb-like cavities hidden in the very womb of the citadel. Upon this morning of Marian's trial, late in the month of February, the breaking ice scarred and groaned beneath the bastions of the fort, but the sappers had blasted a passage for the small steam launch with which the garrison reached the merchants' harbour, and through this passage General Stefanovitch and two of his staff were carried to see the prisoner who had been arrested so surprisingly in the earlier hours of the morning.

Paul was already in the vaulted stone chamber where the inquiry was to be held when Stefanovitch and Bonzo entered together. The General answered his salute but did not speak. Bonzo exchanged a quick glance with him and then busied himself with the bundle of papers which seemed inseparable from his equipment. So dark was the place that the figure of the sergeant at the door was like some phantom shape. The feeble candles, flickering upon the table, cast a weirdly yellow light on the faces of those who sat within their aureola. Paul saw that Nikolai Stefanovitch looked wretchedly ill. The very neatness of dress and affectation of manner aggravated the pallor and unrest of his face. His hands wandered aimlessly, now touching a pen, now a paper, now seeking to straighten the hair which should have been upon his shining forehead. When he ordered

H 2

the prisoner to be brought in, his voice was hollow and unnatural. He cast his eyes upon the table and did not look at the woman before him. Paul, in his turn, shrank back into the shadows. He saw Marian enter that gloomy chamber, and the impulse to speak to her, to stand at her side, was almost irresistible. But prudence kept him still. He had decided upon the part he would play; the keen air from the sea had stimulated him mentally and bodily. He had said to himself, " I alone am her friend, and I will save her."

They had arrested the girl shortly after sunrise, that none in the town might whisper abroad the business upon which she had been carried to Fort Alexander. So great was their haste that she had scarce time to bind up her untidy tresses of silky brown hair or to get furs against the cold of dawn. But she had used the intervening hours in winning from the Sergeant permission to practise those arts which help a woman's victory. Paul said that she never looked so pretty. She entered the gloomy room with a laugh upon her lips. The dainty head was thrown back disdainfully; the fur about her neck and wrists contrasted with the exquisite whiteness of her skin; her gesture was one of amusement and of surprise.

"Oh!" she cried mockingly, "comme je suis effrayée, comme je me sens criminelle."

Stefanovitch looked up from his papers.

"Silence," he exclaimed sharply, and there was that in his voice which compelled obedience. Paul trembled for her then.

"She will act a part, and they will condemn her out of her own mouth," he thought.

"Mademoiselle," said Stefanovitch, beginning to address her in a low voice, "there is no need for me to tell you why you are brought here; you are as well aware of the reasons as I am."

"Indeed, General, I know nothing of your reasons."

The lines upon Stefanovitch's face hardened perceptibly, but he did not display any anger.

"We will not argue the point," he said quickly. "If I speak to you this morning, here in this room, it is in the hope that you will help us to lighten the punishment which your actions have deserved. For some months now you have been sending to the British Government in London such information concerning Kronstadt as our hospitality put you in possession of. Within the course of the last month you have sold for money a plan of Battery 3, and have prepared other plans which, but for our prudence and foresight, would now have left the city. It is not for me to tell you, mademoiselle, that these things are an outrage upon the hospitality you have received. You came here to us as a stranger, and we made you as one of our own people. We trusted you as we should have trusted a daughter. It is possible that you are unaware of the heinous nature of your crime and are willing to atone so far as it is in your power. Should that be so, you have now the opportunity to tell us how you came to do this thing, and whose was the help and the promise you relied upon. The truth alone can help you here, mademoiselle. I rely upon your good sense and your cleverness to withhold nothing from us."

He paused and looked the girl full in the face. She had ceased to laugh, for his accusation, that she had outraged the hospitality of those who had befriended her, was one that she could not jest with.

"I did not wish to be ungrateful," she cried despairingly; "I did not wish to injure or hurt any of those who have been kind to me. I drew the map to send to a friend in London; he asked me for it, and I did not think you would mind. It was such a little thing, and you are so strong. Oh, General, you will not judge me for that; you will not believe me guilty."

"Mademoiselle," interrupted Stefanovitch sternly, "of your guilt there is no doubt. Believe me that it is idle for you to stand there and seek to mislead us. We do not imagine what you have done, we know."

"You know, monsieur!"

"We know," repeated Stefanovitch; "our chain of evidence is complete. Six months ago this friend of yours in London, your cousin, mademoiselle, told you that the British Government was willing to pay a heavy price for such facts concerning the new forts here as it had been unable to find out for itself. He sent you, at the same time, the book which described how that other spy, your fellow-countryman, obtained the secrets of Vladivostok. That work was your guide. As the man had learned to measure a fort by pacing it, so you measured our batteries. You sought to make us believe in your ignorance and your childishness that you might win our confidence and profit by the sale of it. You spied upon us while you were receiving our hospitality. You feigned friendship for us that we might betray our secrets to you. You entered even my own cabinet to copy the maps which lie there. Was that also to amuse your friend in London, mademoiselle ? "

Marian shivered. She turned toward Paul eyes which beseeched his help, but he stood silent. For a moment she sought still to wear the mask of indifference and of ignorance, but the laugh froze upon her lips.

" It is not true ! " she exclaimed wildly; " you cannot know that. I did not steal the maps in your cabinet. How could I have done so ? It is a foolish tale."

" Mademoiselle," said Stefanovitch, raising his hand warningly, " there is no need to add to your guilt by falsehood. I am waiting to hear that you are willing to tell us the names of your friends both in Russia and in England."

" I will tell you nothing ! " she answered doggedly. " You know nothing. The falsehood is yours, monsieur. You have no right to bring me here. I am an Englishwoman ; you dare not harm me ! I will write to England. You are cowards to torture me with these questions."

She clasped her hands together and stamped her foot angrily, for excitement had mastered her, and, having robbed her of her arts, had left the woman, weak and resourceless, but with courage undaunted. As for her lover, the accusation with which she was charged stunned him.

They were the very words she herself had spoken in the privacy of her own room when he had discovered her secret fifteen hours ago. There was no longer a loophole for him. "I must tell all, for they know all," he argued. And yet his pity for her was an agony. Her childishness, her helplessness, the days of suffering awaiting her, prompted him to dare everything, to take her in his arms and ask that he might suffer with her. When anon he heard his own name called, and must come out into the light to answer the questions of the General, his tongue, his limbs, seemed paralysed. He spoke in a thick voice and swayed often against the slight table.

"Captain Zassulic," said Stefanovitch, "you have heard this woman's story. Have you anything to say to it?"

Paul squared his shoulders. He dare not look at Marian; the figures around seemed unreal and shadowy.

"I have heard the story, my General," he stammered.

"Is it true or false, Captain?"

"It is false, my General."

"You are sure of that? Then please to give us your reasons."

Paul leaned against the table and put his

hand to his throat as though to compel himself to speak.

"Last night you sent me to your room, General, to leave there the despatches from the Prince. It was at eight o'clock—after you had dined—at eight o'clock, my General."

He wiped his brow with his hand and stared about the room in a dazed way. For a moment his eyes rested on the face of the girl. She was looking at him as she would have looked at one risen from the dead to accuse her.

"Well," said Stefanovitch, " we are waiting for you, Captain."

Paul squared his shoulders again. He began to remember that the words which now condemned the woman might save her in the end.

" When I entered the corridor," he said, speaking quickly, "there was a light in the room, General ; the Englishwoman was there. She was copying one of the maps which she had taken from the shelf."

"To amuse her brother in London," grunted Bonzo, who had stood hitherto, motionless and voiceless, at the side of his master.

But Marian did not hear him. She had fallen in a swoon, and, senseless still, they carried her back to her cell.

" Pshaw!" said old Bonzo, folding up his

papers quickly, "we waste time, my General. If I were in your shoes I would flog the truth out of her. She is not alone here, be sure. There are others."

"It shall be your work to learn their names, Colonel," cried Stefanovitch, rising from the table. "Stand at nothing which your duty dictates. And to you, Captain, I would say that the Emperor is happy in such servants. Let the woman be watched night and day. I count upon you, my friends, in this hour of danger, upon your zeal and your silence. Our honour is at stake, and we shall know how to guard it."

He saluted and returned to his launch; but old Bonzo lingered a moment to whisper a word in Paul's ear.

"There were two prisoners this morning, my son," he said, with a kindly pat of his great hand, "two prisoners, but one is acquitted."

"You mean, my Colonel——"

"That the woman was watched last night, and that the words you have just spoken saved your life."

He lurched from the room to join his chief, but Paul remained long standing by the table where the damning words were spoken.

"She will never believe," he thought. "I have lost her love. God help me!"

CHAPTER VIII.

AFTER FORTY DAYS.

THE iron hand of winter relaxed its grip upon Kronstadt when the last bitter winds of March had exhausted themselves. Gentle breezes followed upon the devastating gales; trees blossomed generously as the snow sank through the face of the land, and the grass lifted its head again. No longer was the sea imprisoned nor the ships that had wintered in the merchants' harbour. Marian, awake through long nights in her cell at Fort Alexander, could hear the waves gambolling in their new-found freedom or surging heavily against the granite walls with which the vast fort opposed them. There were even days when a kindly ray of sunlight came down through the barred windows and shone upon the icon set up in the corner of the dungeon. Marian welcomed these days, though her welcome was not without a certain pathos. She remembered that it was spring-time in Devonshire and that the child was alone. An intense longing for the freedom of the lanes and the perfume of the flowers possessed her. It was not that the intended discomforts of the cell galled her, for she was schooled now to privation and to suffering; she had made up her mind to pay the penalty which was the guerdon of her rashness. But the thought that she was never to hear little Dick's voice again, that he was dependent now upon charity for the very food he ate, drove her almost to madness. She had been forty days in prison; she asked herself how it would be when days had become years.

Few visited her cell in those first hours of silence. They had sent a woman from the Governor's house to wait upon her, and she had seen the Sergeant once or twice, though he had never spoken to her. But old Bonzo came nearly every day and brought always the same promise.

"Tell us the truth, mademoiselle," he would say, "and it will be well with you. There is a room in Fort Katherine where you can see the sun and watch the ships upon the sea. You shall go there when you are sensible. But first we must know the names of those who helped you—your friends in Kronstadt, your friends in London. You cannot save them by silence. We shall catch them sooner or later; we shall know how to reward you when you help us in the attempt."

"I have no friends," she would answer. "I have told you the truth. I was poor, and they tempted me. I can tell you nothing more."

Bonzo would lose his temper at this, and threaten her, but her courage remained unbroken.

"You shall have the whip, and we will see what you can tell us then," he would cry. "Do you think to defy us, mademoiselle? Sapristi! I could crush you with my fingers."

"They are large enough, monsieur," she said simply.

Bonzo would leave the cell and slam the door after such a scene. He had hesitated until this time to carry out any of the threats he uttered so glibly. He did not forget that Marian Best was an Englishwoman; that the day might come when her story would be made public. But he left nothing undone which could appeal to the natural weakness of the woman; and there was a morning when she was carried up to see a man flogged in the courtyard of the fort. The lash falling brutally upon the bare flesh seemed to cut her own shoulders; the screams and groans of the wretched victim were so many appeals for her merciful intercession; she swooned when she saw the blood flow, but her answer to Bonzo was unchanged.

"You are cowards here," she said, "and you are not clever in your cowardice! You do not know the truth when you hear it. And you have no manners, monsieur. Oh, you do not frighten me at all. I laugh when you look like that. If

you could only see yourself, you would laugh
too."

She bore herself bravely indeed; but when the
iron door groaned upon its hinges, and she was left
alone, and no sound but the surging of the sea
against the bastions was borne in to her from
without, she would sink down upon the bed, and
tears and wretchedness would conquer her. She
had no longer a friend in all the world, she said.
Her love for Paul struggled for a while bravely
against the damning testimony he had given in the
council-room. She was clever enough to think
that possibly some deep and hidden meaning was
behind his words; but when the days passed and
he did not come, when no message, no word from
him reached her, the well of her love began to be
dried up; she accounted him her friend no more;
she was, in spirit and in thought, a broken-hearted
woman.

The morning of the fortieth day dawned generously, for there was a gift of April sunshine in her
room and the gaunt stone walls were touched with
its warming glow. Marian awoke at daybreak,
and being permitted to walk for an hour upon the
ramparts—a concession made to her but thrice in
the weeks of her imprisonment—she beheld the
town again and wondered that the sun of spring
could so transform it. Even the grim shapes

of the barracks were softened by the splendour of the morning light. She could distinguish the gilded domes and minarets of the churches; the cramped yet picturesque houses huddled about the merchants' harbour; the masts of ships in the docks; the stately hulls of ironclads and cruisers; could hear the blasts of bugles, the shrill piping of whistles, the clank of the great hammers at the arsenal. But the sunshine touched every outstanding object with its transforming rays. The muzzles of the great guns, peeping from the tremendous mole of the island, were capped with gold; there were flashes of fire upon all the bright places of the ships; the sea sparkled and foamed and rolled merrily over the silver shallows of sand. She could perceive the Ingrian coast and the woods creeping down to the water's edge; it was for her an emblem of the life she had lost. The very beauty of the morning awoke in her that intense longing for liberty which is the swift punishment of the prisoner. Everywhere the new day spoke of life and work and the gladness of being; but for her it had no message.

The short hour passed all too swiftly. She returned to her cell at seven o'clock and to the meagre repast prepared for her. She asked herself, while she drank the welcome tea and ate the coarse bread, if Bonzo would come again upon that morning to threaten her or cajole her as he had threatened and cajoled so often. An inconquerable spirit of mischief prompted her to tell him some fool's tale with which he might occupy himself for a season. When someone knocked at her door presently, she made sure that this was her opportunity, and began to rack her brains for a plausible story. But the door was opened and the man who entered was not Bonzo.

"Paul!" she cried, and then stood silent and wondering.

Her lover, for a truth, stood before her. She saw that he was dressed in the full uniform of a captain of artillery—the green tunic with the scarlet epaulettes and the scarlet and black facings, the pipe-clayed belt, the high black boots, the fur cap with the golden eagle for its crest. But his face wore deep lines which had not been there at carnival, and the hand which rested upon the hilt of his sword was thin and white. For an instant he could not find his tongue. He stood rocking upon his heels as his habit was, while he sought vainly for some word which might give his tongue release.

Marian had risen from her seat as he entered, and when her first cry of wonder had escaped her she was quick to take pity upon him. Instinctively she had hidden the plate of coarse bread behind

I

her cup that he might not see of what kind her food was; instinctively, too, she touched her wind-blown curls with her fingers and looked down at the shabby dress she wore.

"It is you, then," she said, with a poor attempt at gaiety. "I might have known that no one else in Russia would knock at my door."

Paul did not answer her. He was staring at the wretched furniture of the cell. He shivered as though the cold of the granite walls had struck his own heart.

"My God!" he cried; "is this your new home, Marian?"

She expected that he would begin to excuse himself, and to tell her why he had been a witness against her in the council-room. His pity for her was an enemy of her resolution to hide the truths of her misfortune from him.

"Yes," she said, standing defiantly with her back to the wall; "I am always at home here—to my friends. You need not ask me if I have a day. I shall be glad—no, do not touch me—I am quite strong—Paul——"

How it was she knew not, but when next she opened her eyes Paul's arms were about her and she was held close in his strong embrace. The tears still glistened upon her cheek, but they were tears of gladness.

"Beloved," he said, "do not wound me; I suffer too—oh, God knows! Every hour has been an hour of pain since they took you away; there has been no sunshine for me, no day, no night; my life has stood still; I have lived in the darkness; my eyes have seen no image but the image of her I love. Marian—you will not turn from me now?"

He held her closer for the passionate words to be whispered into her ear; nor did she restrain him. The long hours of loneliness were remembered too well that this new love should not win her gratitude.

"You told them," she sobbed; "it was your word. They knew nothing until you spoke. If I suffer, it is by your hand; your love for me has brought me here. How can I believe——"

The reproach was choked suddenly upon her lips. The arms which held her trembled as with cold. She looked into the face of the man, and the pain written upon it turned her anger to pity.

"No, no, Paul—do not listen to me," she cried in turn, clinging to him. "It is not true. Oh, I am not changed; I am only weak, and ill, and lonely. Tell me you are my friend; tell me you will help me!"

His answer was to kiss her again and again upon the forehead and the lips.

I 2

"I am your friend always, little Marian. Would to God I could promise as you wish! How shall I help you here—in this place? It cannot be. You have made them your enemies, and they do not know how to forgive. I am the servant, and it is my duty to obey."

She looked up at him, and smiling now through her tears.

"And you have obeyed. Oh, I understand," she said quickly. "When you spoke against me I knew that you must speak. Paul, I do not love you less because of that—how could I?"

She kissed him prettily, but a flush of shame coloured his face, for he remembered how much fear for himself had prompted his confession in the council-room. It was upon his tongue to make a full confession to her, for his simple honesty rebelled at her generous confidence; but she began to speak of other things, and chiefly of the terrible forty days which had passed.

"You did not come," she said, "and I counted the hours. Then I said you would never come, or that you were ill. Paul, you have been ill— your eyes tell me that."

She held his face between her hands that the sunlight might fall upon it, but he shrugged his shoulders indifferently.

"It was nothing," he answered "nothing at

all. The work has been heavy, and I am tired —I do not sleep. It will be better when the summer comes."

He did not tell her that for ten days after they had arrested her he had been at the point of death, and was newly risen from a bed of sickness to visit the fort. Nevertheless, a woman's instinct guided her unerringly.

"Oh, my love, my love, if I had foreseen all —if I had told you of my folly and my trouble! And now it is too late; you suffer when you should forget. Oh, you must forget, Paul; forget that I ever came to Kronstadt; forget that you were my friend!"

He laughed brusquely.

"Shall I forget that I live, or that the sun shines?" he asked. Shall I forget that your freedom is to be won, that we are both upon the threshold of our lives? No, for a truth, such things are not to be forgotten. Let us ask ourselves, rather, how the folly is to be undone, how our enemies are to be made our friends. It is because I believe in the possibility of these things that I am here this morning. If I can help you, Marian, it will be by telling them the truth as you have told it to me?"

There was a question in his words, the

unspoken thought that she had hidden something from him.

"Paul," she said earnestly, "you know that I have told you all as I have told it to them. I have no friends in Kronstadt, none in London. What I did was for the sake of the child. You see how it has helped him, when they will not even let me write to him now."

"They will not let you write! You have asked them, then?"

"God knows, I have asked them on my knees. You do not know what humiliations they have put upon me here. I hope that you will never know."

Paul laughed again. She looked up at him with startled eyes, but he held both her wrists and pushed her from him that he might watch her while he spoke.

"You think that little Dick has had no message?" he asked.

"How could he?" she exclaimed, though a suggestion of the truth began to dawn upon her.

"You think that he will write to you no more?" continued Paul, with a child's pleasure in his words.

A smile lighted her face.

"Tell me!" she cried; "do not torture me!"

Laughing still, he released her hands and took a letter-case from his pocket. His thin fingers trembled while he fumbled with the many scraps the case contained, but at last he found a paper scrawled over with a child's writing.

"There," he said, laying the scrawl upon the table, "that is how little Dick forgets to write."

He turned away and walked to the door of the cell, a subtle delicacy forbidding him to watch the tears upon the blotted paper or to listen to the half-spoken words of love and gratitude. Almost his first thought on the morrow of the dreadful day, when he had seen the soldiers at the Governor's house, was one for the child for whom this sacrifice was made. And now he reaped his reward.

"Dick shall write every week," he said, "and I shall be your mouthpiece. Do not be afraid; I have planned it all, and he will learn to call me brother. Are you not glad, little girl?"

"I love you," she said simply. "I am lonely no more, for your love shall be with me always."

The footsteps of a sentry in the court without forced them apart, and Paul began to remember again the purpose with which he had been sent to Fort Alexander.

"I am come here to question you," he said; "we must not forget that. They think that you have friends, but I shall tell them all, and then we shall see. They must not keep you in this place. I will not rest until you are at Fort Katherine. I will see the General at once; he shall know how it is, and he will not refuse me. Oh, you are to be lonely no more, Marian—that day is past. We will begin the summer together, and it shall be our summer always. The sun will shine upon us and we will forget the shadows."

"You make me forget them already, Paul," she answered; "it is summer for me now. I am happy even here when I know that to-morrow will bring you to me again."

"To-morrow and all the to-morrows," he said cheerily. "I will find a way, be sure; there is no door which my love for you shall not open; no night so dark that I shall not see the brightness of your eyes; no day so silent that I shall not hear your voice. God guard you, little girl, and give you back to me!"

He stooped once more to kiss her and went from the room quickly that he might say nothing which should awake her from this new dream of content. There had been a ray of sunlight in the cell, but when he was out upon the sea again

it seemed to him that the sun shone no more
and that darkness lay upon the land.

"God help me! how could I tell her the
truth?" he thought. "They will send her to
the capital and I shall see her no more."

CHAPTER IX.

OUT OF THE DARKNESS.

THE launch crossed the narrow channel between Fort Alexander and the mainland swiftly. Paul did not linger in the town, but, full of his promise to Marian, he went straight to the Governor's house to seek the General. He found Stefanovitch in his private cabinet, and was welcomed with a questioning movement of the eyebrow which meant, "Well, why are you here?"

"I come to tell you that I have been to the fort, my General, and have seen the prisoner."

Stefanovitch put down his pen and turned in his chair. Though it had been a month of swift anxieties, the master of Kronstadt showed no trace of them either by carelessness of dress or weariness of face. He was as well groomed and dainty in his personal adornment as when last he had racked his brains for compliments which should win the favour of his governess.

"You have been to the fort!" he said, fixing his glass that he might study Paul's face. "By whose order was that?"

"By the Colonel's order, my General."

Stefanovitch nodded his head two or three times.

"He sent you there to question the woman?"

"He thought that she would tell me things which she would not tell to others," exclaimed Paul, speaking eagerly. "I have been—that is, I called myself her friend."

A smile crept over Stefanovitch's face. He nodded his head again, as though he understood perfectly.

"You called yourself her friend!" he repeated, as though weighing the words. "But that is a *rôle* you play no longer, Captain."

"I am the friend of none who is the enemy of my country," said Paul stolidly. "It is because I do not believe Mademoiselle Best is our enemy that I come here now."

"But the documents, the plan which she sent to London?" exclaimed Stefanovitch testily.

"She did not understand—she did not know what she was doing, General. She made the map because her relations in London offered her money. She did not think it was a crime. I have questioned her, and I know that she has told you all. There is nothing to find out now. The man to be punished is he who asked a woman to do such work. If *he* were in Russia——"

Stefanovitch laughed a little hardly. The

instinctive gesture which had carried the young soldier's hand to the hilt of his sword was not lost upon his chief.

"But he is not in Russia, and he will be too wise to come here. When you want to cut his throat, you must go to London and be hanged by a judge in a black cap afterwards. That is how they reward one who defends his honour—là-bas! And they call us barbarians! But I am waiting to hear more of your visit to Alexander. The woman has spoken to you? She has made a confession, possibly?"

"She has told nothing but that which she told to you in the council-room, General. A child could see that she spoke the truth. I would stake my life upon it."

Stefanovitch regarded him with some amusement. He knew perfectly well whence came this earnestness surpassing the earnestness of the advocate. As a principle Nikolai Stefanovitch loved all women, but he could not understand the worship of the unit. Marian had amused him when she was at his house. Another governess would take her place in a day or two, and she would amuse him too. But that he should disturb himself at the change was a possibility to be laughed at.

"You value your life at a low price when you stake it on a woman's word," he said.

"Upon the word of some, true, my General; but not upon the word of Mademoiselle Best. He is a foolish man who cannot tell when a woman is lying to him. This one has never lied; the truth is written in her eyes."

"And you have been reading it there. Ho, ho! I must send this book to the Censor. He will tell me if it is good for my officers to read a work like that."

He leered pleasantly, delighting in the embarrassment of the younger man. There was no purpose either in his questions or his assumption of curiosity. Those at Kronstadt knew now the whole of Marian Best's story. Their perplexity was the difficulty of keeping that knowledge from Petersburg, and of saving themselves from the charge of negligence which might be brought against them. This perplexity was helped by the presence of the prisoner at Fort Alexander. They hesitated to send her to the capital. They feared that her story would be made public by some prying Englishman, and that unpleasant revelations would follow. And this thought was in Stefanovitch's mind when he asked—

"Have you told Bonzo that which you are telling me?"

"I have told him nothing, my General."

"And why not?"

"Because I wished first to speak to you; I wished you to know that the prisoner is ill. They have put her in the south cell, and they give her black bread to eat. God knows, I did not like to see that when I spoke to her. She hid the bread behind her plate, General. She did not complain, but I could see many things. They are starving her, and she will not live long. Oh, she is so little and helpless; she has not meant to harm us. I said that I would speak to you, for you could know nothing of what has been done. I said that you would hear me, and remember that she is an Englishwoman and have her taken to Fort Katherine. The Colonel would not understand. I could not speak to him; but with you it is different. You will listen to me; you will not forget that she has been the friend of your children. Kronstadt will gain nothing by this woman's death. She would suffer eternal shame if her story were known in England. And it will be known—I am sure of that. The English spies are everywhere. Someone will tell them that we have a prisoner at Alexander and that she is dying. They will say that it is your act—you, who are the father of the city and have won the love of your children. My General, you will send her to Fort Katherine ; you will not refuse me this."

His earnestness surprised even Stefanovitch, who had always regarded him with an affection which lost nothing from the indispensable formality of their rank and duty. In all the years he had known him the General had never seen Paul so moved or so eloquent of purpose. For his own part, he disliked eloquence and all that disturbed the easy ripple of his life; but his affection for the younger man came to his aid now, and there was added to the force of it that warning word which Bonzo had forgotten to speak. Stefanovitch said to himself that Paul was right. They were dealing with an Englishwoman. The political friends of an Englishwoman could be troublesome.

"Come," he said, "you speak like the woman's brother—or lover, my friend Paul."

Paul's face flushed until it was crimson.

"I ask nothing for myself, General," he said; "that day is gone. But I speak as any honest man would speak when he sees a woman suffer."

"And you think that this woman will cease to suffer when she is at Fort Katherine."

"She will not cease to suffer, but she will live no longer in the darkness; she will not eat black bread; she will see the ships; she will hear men's voices. Will Kronstadt be hurt because of these things, General ? Oh, you know that she will not."

Stefanovitch's glass dropped from his eye. For a moment his quick brain ran over the gamut of the possibilities.

"It would be for a few days at the most," he said, while Paul began to tremble with the excitement of success. "They will hear of her sooner or later at Petersburg ; it may be that the police will wish to talk to her, and then our duty will be done. After that, my son—the deluge."

He took a pen in his hand and wrote an order quickly. Paul watched him as a hungry man may watch one who sets food upon his table.

"Take that to Sergius," said Stefanovitch, when the order was written. "Your English friend will be in Fort Katherine at sunset."

CHAPTER X.

TEMPTATION.

PAUL left the Governor's house with a light step. The sun shone for him again; the surge of the sea was sweet music for his ears; the green heights of the distant shores were a joy to his eyes. "To-night," he said to himself, "to-night she will leave Alexander, to-night she will eat white bread and see the sky again." But more often the thought was, "To-night she will be near me, she will think of me, she will know that I have spoken to the General."

He walked swiftly, holding the paper as he would have held a jewel, in the hollow of his hand. It was his purpose to seek out old Sergius and to make sure that the hardly-gained order was enacted without delay. This purpose carried him through the heart of the town toward the arsenal. He had a cheery word and a nod for such of his friends as he passed; but he would stand to speak to none, and when he met Bonzo face to face in the great square he begrudged the minutes of delay.

"Sacré bleu! you walk like the devil!" said

J

Bonzo, taking from his mouth a cigar as long as a pistol. "Are you going back to Alexander, my son?"

Paul laughed, and displayed the paper triumphantly.

"There is no more Alexander," he said with fervour; "she is to be at Fort Katherine to-night. I have the General's order. He remembers that she is an Englishwoman, and he is wise."

Bonzo opened his cunning eyes.

"Oh," he said, "it is that, then. I thought there was something. So Nikolai is touched. Ho, ho! She has been on her knees to him. Now he will go on his knees to her. Quelle farce!"

Paul wondered if this man had ever known a moment's love, or sympathy for a fellow-creature; but he was careful to conceal his thoughts and to overlook the jest.

"The General is afraid of the English tongues," he said simply. "I think that he is right to be afraid. She is no criminal, my Colonel, and we are not a savage people. She will be just as safe at Fort Katherine, and we shall not suffer because she eats white bread."

Bonzo laughed.

"You should all wear petticoats!" he exclaimed boorishly; "you should go to a nunnery and mope and mew together. How shall such fellows be soldiers?"

He turned on his heel, for he remembered he was speaking of his chief; but as he resumed his walk he cried with a careful assumption of indifference:

"Mind you don't run away with her yourself, Captain Paul; she is not in Fort Katherine yet!"

Paul stood still and choked the word which rose to his lips. He was about to resent with heat the suggestion that he could be guilty of this dishonour; but Bonzo had already turned the corner of the square, and the younger man stood still to repeat the words of temptation again and again.

"She is not in Fort Katherine yet!"

Paul laughed and walked on. At a distance of ten paces he stopped again, and began to read the paper he had treasured so earnestly.

"The Englishwoman to be removed at sunset, and to be delivered into the custody of Rothmister Siebenski at Fort Katherine. "STEFANOVITCH.

"At Kronstadt, April 19, 1895."

Paul read the paper three times. He turned it over and over, as though seeking for some name which should be written upon it.

J 2

"So," he said to himself, "he has forgotten to write the name of Sergius upon it. He who delivers this paper may carry the Englishwoman from Fort Alexander. The Captain will not be there at sunset; he will be in the café or at the barracks. The Sergeant would not question my authority, since I come straight from the great house, and here is the General's order. Holy God! what an idea!"

He continued his walk, but at a more rapid pace. The suggestion which Bonzo had thrown out jestingly began to haunt him. He heard a voice whispering: "It is possible. She would suffer no more. She would lie in your arms. It would be your business to see that she did not betray Kronstadt. She would be your wife —the friend of Russia."

He laughed aloud as men will at the first swift advance of some triumphant temptation which they have the wish but not the strength to resist. His hurried walk carried him from the square to the café, where he had drunk with Bonzo on that night of Marian's arrest. He entered and called for a glass of absinthe. Destiny, now busy with him, contrived that he should take a seat wherefrom he could look over the harbour and spy out his own little launch lying a biscuit toss from the quay. She had been a present to him from his kinsman, Prince Tolma. They said that there was no faster yacht in all the Baltic; men pointed to her as the work of the great Yarrow, and wagered that she would outsteam the fleetest cruiser then lying in the roads. Paul spent most of his money upon this little ship. She was his toy, his plaything. He loved to steam in her to the islands of the Finnish shore, and there to camp for days at the zenith of the summer. He had a better knowledge of the Gulf than many a master mariner. His servant Reuben, the young Englishman sent out by the Yarrow people to tend the launch, was devoted to him heart and soul. "He would be the very man for this," Paul said to himself; "he would remember that she is an Englishwoman." And so he drank off his absinthe and went out into the sunshine again.

Kronstadt had begun to sweat with her day's work then. The great hammers clanged unceasingly in the arsenal; the bellow of steam whistles echoed across the water: the cries of seamen, their oaths, their songs, filled the nearer harbour. Squadrons passed weary from long drill; the courtyards of the barracks were full of troops hungering for dinner; launches steamed swiftly between the outlying forts and the mainland. Paul remembered that this tumult of the active life was very dear to him. He loved Kronstadt as a child loves its home. He looked across the sea to the granite walls and to the guns shining as silver in the blaze of sunlight, and he asked himself how it would be if he were cut off from this iron home for ever, branded as a traitor, spoken of with curses, the mock of those who had honoured him.

"Bah!" he said, "that day will never come. I shall deliver the paper to Sergius; he will take a file of men and conduct the prisoner to Fort Katherine. I must do my duty. I am a servant of the Czar. I will forget that she has loved me."

But as he walked the voice of the tempter spake again.

"Reuben is down there upon the quay. He would have steam up in your yacht by sunset. You could find a few drunken artillery men to act as your file. It would be a long time before they would discover your flight. She would be a wife to you—the woman you love."

He cursed the tempter, but called to his man Reuben, and was answered.

CHAPTER XI.

THE BEGINNING OF THE FLIGHT.

MARIAN in her cell could hear the bells of the ships striking the hours; and she would count them and wait to see if the harbour clock answered to their signal. There was little else to do through the long days of darkness, save it were to listen to the cries of the seamen as they warped their ships to the buoys or exchanged a word with one of the sentries at the fort. Until this time her jailers permitted her no other occupations. Designedly, that she might become acquainted with the whole meaning of imprisonment in a fortress, they kept her hands idle and shut the daylight from her eyes. She thought sometimes that she would lose her reason for very dread of the silence and the darkness. Or she would succumb to the frenzy of the prisoner and be tempted to beat upon the door with her fist, or to dash herself against the granite walls, seeking thus an escape from the living death. But upon the day of Paul's visit a new sense of resignation possessed her. The man's great love, surpassing all she had imagined, spoke to her still when he had quitted her cell; she heard his voice again bidding her to be of good courage; she had kept the letter which little Dick had written, and tears of affection sealed the childish words. She asked herself what craven spirit had mastered her, that she should be the victim of this weakness and despair. They had accounted her a woman of unfailing nerve; no shackles of cowardice had hampered her will during those months of excitement when she had filched the secrets of Kronstadt one by one; had measured the forts, and counted the guns, and cried with delight at the successes she numbered. She determined to remember those days and to live them again.

"I will not show him that I suffer," she said; "he shall find me laughing when he comes here to-morrow. And he shall write to Dick for me—a long letter about our home that is to be. After that he will speak to them. They will not keep me here always. It was such a little thing."

This spirit of courage breathed upon all her actions of the day. She showed a smiling face to the Sergeant when he brought her dinner. Surrendering herself to childish anticipations, she began to think of a hundred things which Paul would do—how he would write to England, or see the Governor, or even go to the Czar for her. The hours hurried now, each bell telling her that her lover was up and working for her. To-morrow she would see him again. Perchance he would bring good news. At least she would touch his hand and hear his voice.

They were wont to bring her a little supper at sunset—the boiling tea and the black bread which was as earth in her mouth. But she ate it to-night with relish; and when her supper was done she let her head sink upon her arms and so was carried away to a dreamland of wood and meadow, to gardens warmed with everlasting sunshine, and woods alive with music of song-birds. Therein she walked awhile, holding her lover's hand; she heard voices long forgotten, the voices of dead friends and the laughter of the child. The sleep was sweet, for it was a sleep of hope new born and of courage rekindled; but when it had endured a little while, the harsh skirl of the outer door turning upon its hinges awoke her rudely. She opened her eyes to see the Sergeant standing before her, and with him rough artillery men in their great grey cloaks, and others who were strangers to her. She thought for the moment that they had come to take her to Petersburg, or even to the nameless punishment beyond. She began to tremble, and stood back against the wall as though she would find protection there—the weak woman shrinking from the terrible hand which was about to touch her.

"What is it?" she cried, while she shielded her eyes, dewed with sleep, from the garish rays of the lanterns. "Why do you come here? what do you want with me?"

"To take you to Fort Katherine, mademoiselle, by order of the Governor."

Marian clenched her hands; she scarce dared to believe what she heard. Paul had spoken, then; the night had passed; she would see the sun again.

"You wish to take me now?" she asked, vainly seeking to cloak the excitement which possessed her.

"Now," said the Sergeant gruffly—"that is, if you have finished your supper."

She laughed joyously, as though the suggestion were a folly.

"Oh!" she cried; "as if one would wait for that!"

Her hands were busy with the cape of fur while she spoke, and when she had buttoned it about her shoulders and had drawn the little fur cap over her untrammelled hair, she was ready for them. The men watched her with admiring eyes. The youngest among them was saying to himself, "What lips to kiss!"

"I am ready, quite ready," she exclaimed, looking up with eyes awake and laughing. "You are sure it is to Fort Katherine, Sergeant?"

The Sergeant shrugged his shoulders.

"Sei tchas! are we here to play at being children, mademoiselle? Read that paper—it is the writing of the Governor."

"I can read nothing to-night," she said, pushing aside the lantern; "my eyes are blinded by the light. I cannot breathe in this place. It is good of you to come for me."

"It is not good at all, mademoiselle. I am the servant, and it is my business to obey."

He turned from the cell and the girl walked beside him still babbling like a child. No thought of prudence could have stilled her tongue in that hour. The burden of her punishment fell from her shoulders when she quitted the cell and ascended the short flight of steps leading to the quay above. The mighty granite walls terrified her no longer. She could see the heaven above her, gray-blue through the silver haze of night; the stars shone down upon her; they would be shining down upon England, she said; and she would watch them every night henceforth from her windows in Fort Katherine. The joy of liberty half possessed quickened her heart and released all her impulses and affection. She could have

kissed the hand of the Sergeant who conducted
her to the launch. She talked to him unceasingly while they traversed the corridor and the
courtyard of the fortress; she was talking still
when he threw open the iron-bound door and
stepped out on to the quay which lies upon
the north side of Alexander.

It was a glorious night, a night of soft
winds and rippling sea. Though the sun had
sunk, there was still a glow of crimson light
in the West, a vast arc pointed with jagged
spikes of orange and green and purple flame.
Kronstadt herself stood silhouetted as an island
of rock and pinnacles in an atmosphere of
quivering haze. Great ships, belching clouds of
smoke from mighty funnels, passed noiselessly
behind the curtain of the eastern mists; lanterns
flashed from all the forts, here white and far-
reaching, there scarlet and dim; strange rays
played upon the fretting waters; lakes of golden
waves glistened where the warships spread the
searching arcs of their lamps; the steam whistle
moaned distantly or bellowed warningly from the
nearer harbours. The West was a splendid
canopy of flame hung in the heavens, as it
were, above the throne of liberty and of freedom.

Marian stood upon the quay and the fresh wind
scattered her curls and cast refreshing spray

"KRONSTADT HERSELF STOOD SILHOUETTED AS AN ISLAND OF ROCK AND PINNACLES" (*p.* 140).

upon her weary eyes. The scene around her was bewildering and not to be realised. She beheld a steam launch lying at the quay; she heard its timbers groaning as the swell lifted it against the granite wall and the fenders were flattened and twisted at the rush of the seas. But her eyes were rather for the West. There lay her own England. She could have stretched out her arms to the befriending light and have prayed that some messenger of God might come down to carry her from this tomb to which folly had brought her.

"Oh," she said, "I am ready, quite ready, Sergeant. Is this the boat?"

The Sergeant ignored her question. He was bending down to speak to one who stood in the bows of the launch, a tall man wearing the rough overcoat of an officer of artillery. Notwithstanding the light in the West, it was very dark in the loom of the walls of Alexander. Marian could see little of the faces of those about her. The flickering rays of the lanterns danced upon the white deck of the yacht, but not upon the figure of the man who seemed to command it.

"I am to go on board?" she asked of one near her. "Why have you brought me here if you are not ready?"

The soldier laughed good-naturedly.

"We are quite ready, mademoiselle; it is the Captain for whom we wait."

"The Captain!"

"Yes, for Captain Zassulic, who is to take you to Fort Katherine."

She laughed in her turn, nervously and with the desire that surprise should not betray her. She did not dare, for some moments, to look again at the little ship or at the tall figure now standing by the engine-room. But when she was sure of herself, when she had driven from her mind the wild thoughts that occupied it, she saw that the figure was the figure of Paul, her lover; and at this the lights and the stars, the ships and the men, swam before her eyes, and she leaned heavily upon the arm of the trooper.

"Why do you keep me waiting? I am weak and cold," she cried petulantly. "I cannot stand here."

"Mademoiselle," said the Sergeant, turning to her, "there is no need to keep you waiting any longer."

Marian suffered herself almost to be lifted upon the launch. So soon as her feet had touched the deck a strong hand seized her own and drew her towards the companion. It was the hand of Paul, hot and burning as the hand of one in a fever.

"Let go!" he cried to the engineer, speaking in a voice which rang across the sea; and, almost with the words, the ropes were cast off and the launch stood away from the quay.

It was the work of a moment, so dexterously done, so unlooked for, that the Sergeant stood staring stupidly as one dazed with drink.

"Stoi, stoi!" he cried; "there are the others, my Captain."

"I have no need of them. Do you think the girl is going to jump into the sea?"

"But the General's order, my Captain."

Paul laughed and took his place at the woman's side.

"We shall know how to answer the General. Good-night to you, Sergeant."

He cried again to the engineer and the little ship leaped into the waves. Foam flew from her bows and sparkled upon her decks. The whirr of her screw was as the whirr of a cascade thundering. The surrounding forts seemed to recede back to a more distant horizon. The lights of Kronstadt, the black shapes of barrack and church, were hidden in the deepening mists. Into the West, outward to the greater seas of the Baltic, the launch was bearing them. But the man continued to keep his eyes upon the great citadel he was leaving, to look upon it as one may look upon a home which shall be a home no more.

"My God!" he said, "it is for ever!"

And so he turned to the girl as though to shield her with his arm. The lights around him began to vanish one by one; the salt of the sea was on his face; he waited to hear the boom of the guns which should signal his flight and tell the city that he was a traitor—he who had served Kronstadt with an abiding love.

CHAPTER XII.

THE CITADEL AWAKES.

Marian sat in the saloon of the *Esmeralda*, and
the saloon was in darkness. She still wore her
pretty cap of fur, and the cape was unbuttoned
upon her shoulders. Her impatient imagination
told her that she had been a full hour in the cabin
of the ship waiting for Paul to come to her. But
no more than twenty minutes had passed since she
had quitted her cell at Fort Alexander. The yacht
was still running down the southern shore of the
island; the great guns still threatened from the
mighty ramparts.

Until this time she understood nothing of her
lover's purpose or of the meaning of her journey.
She believed that Paul was compelled thus to steer
toward the open sea that he might come to Fort
Katherine, which lies upon the northern shore of
the island. Little as she knew of ships, the
tremendous vibration of everything around her,
the rattle of glass, the swirl of the seas against the
ports, spoke of high speed and freshening wind.
It was her argument that they were making Tollboken, the great lighthouse at the western point of

K

Kronstadt. The ship would put back presently and run down the northern shore to the new prison awaiting her. The sweet hour of liberty would be at an end; the door of a cell would close upon her again unpityingly. When the launch was not put about, but continued to hold its course for the Baltic, she could not understand why it was, and was puzzling her brains to think, when her lover entered the cabin brusquely, with spray shining in crystals of salt upon his oilskins and the dew of the sea upon his cheek. He answered her unspoken question, but not as she wished him to answer it.

"You have no fire and no light," he said cheerily; "and this is your welcome to the *Esmeralda*. Well, it will be better presently."

She took his wet hands and held them to her lips.

"Paul," she cried, "for the love of God tell me, what does it mean? Where am I? where are you taking me to?"

He kissed her upon the forehead very tenderly.

"I am taking you to London—to your friends," he said.

"Oh, you do not mean it," she answered impatiently, "you do not mean it, dearest. It is to Fort Katherine. I heard them say so."

"If you think that I do not mean it, Marian,

come up to the deck with me and you will see the light of Tollboken. You had better come, for we shall never look at Kronstadt again."

He did not wait for her answer, but led the way to the companion and to the deck above. When she stood there with him the wind blew so freshly and the spray so blinded her that she must cling to him for a while and cry that she could see nothing. But anon she got footing by the shrouds of the mainmast, and from that place she looked over the gathering seas and beheld a great white light hanging, as a globe of fire, above the northern point of the island. She remembered that she had seen the light for the first time when she came to Russia to be governess to the children of Nikolai Stefanovitch. But now she was leaving it; the yacht had not rounded the point as she thought it would; it held a course straight for the open sea. She dare not ask herself what this course meant.

"Well," said Paul, "do you believe me now? Yonder is Tollboken. You are looking at it for the last time."

She began to tremble at his words.

"For the last time—and you?"

A shadow rested upon his face.

"Moi c'est égal. I am weary of Kronstadt and of my friends there. I shall find new friends in

England.　Besides, I do my country a service since I take charge of one who has been her enemy. Tell me, little Marian, you will be the enemy of Russia no more."

He drew her beneath the shelter of his oilskins and kissed the lips upraised to his.　But the girl was silent.　She could not then measure the sacrifice he had made so willingly.　Of all the thoughts crowding upon her mind this thought predominated, that her lover had saved her from the living death.

"I do not understand," she said at length, "I do not know what you are saying to me.　Oh, it is not true, Paul, it cannot be."

"You shall tell me to-morrow whether it is true or not," he answered merrily.　"Meanwhile, there is supper to think of, and after supper, rest.　It is time that we lighted the saloon; you are tired, Marian."

She was about to tell him that her fatigue was only the fatigue of joy, when a flame of light leaped up from the shore of the distant islands, and the boom of a great gun rolled across the darkening seas like the rumble of approaching thunder.

"Hark!" she said, starting involuntarily; "they have fired a gun from Tollboken."

Paul turned impatiently.

"It is a captain's salute, little girl."

"I think of the shadows again," she exclaimed with a shudder. And then she asked—

"Paul, whose yacht is this?"

"It is mine, Marian."

"And you had the Governor's permission to take me from Alexander?"

"Certainly, or how could you be here now?"

"He gave me my liberty, then?"

Paul laughed.

"You ask too many questions, Marian, and supper should be waiting."

A second gun fired from the ramparts of Tollboken arrested the laugh upon his face. He could conceal from her no longer the terrible dread which had possessed him since the yacht left Alexander. She read his secret upon his face; she knew that he risked his life for the guerdon of her love.

"Paul," she said, clinging to him now with a passionate gesture of reproach and gratitude, "I understand all. Oh, God forgive me for bringing you to this!"

"No," he said, "where you live I must live, Marian; where your home is, there must be my home. It could not be otherwise. Without you there is nothing for me—the sun does not shine, there are no stars at night. We will stand together for good or ill until the end, as God wills."

"I am not worthy," she answered through her tears. "Oh, God knows, I am not worthy!"

"You will be my wife," he said simply; "you will repay a thousand times."

A grinning face, appearing above the coamings of the engine-room hatchway, put them apart. It was the face of Reuben the engineer.

"Well," said Paul, turning to him, "you wish to tell me——"

"That she is doing twenty knots, sir."

"She must do more. Spare nothing. We must burn the very ship if need be. Hark to that! It is the gun at Menzikoff, which means that the garrison is alarmed. We shall see the lights of their ships soon."

The grinning face disappeared, and anon thick smoke rolled from the funnel of the *Esmeralda*. She plunged with new speed into the choppy, spuming waves which the fresh wind drove in from the Baltic. The water washed her bows and ran ankle-deep over her flush-decks. She had no lights save the glow which hovered above her funnel or spread fan-shaped when the furnace-door was opened. Every timber in her quivered at the heightening speed. Not a man of the four aboard her but knew that this was a race for liberty—it might be for life. Yonder, through the northern darkness, lay freedom and reward; behind, where the guns made thunder of the night, were the prisons of Russia and the fields of Bondage.

Their course lay almost due west for a while and when they had been an hour at sea they could discern the lights upon the Finnish shore no longer nor the twinkling stars which spoke of villages on the Ingrian coast. The Gulf broadened so quickly that they stood almost at once in the heart of the widening sea, in the channel of ships steaming to Russia or labouring to make Helsingfors. At one time a great ironclad loomed above them suddenly and passed so close that they could hear men calling to one another upon her decks. Or, again, they passed a Norwegian barque lubbering in the swell in a vain effort to keep the great breakers from her decks. These shapes loomed out of the dark for an instant to be lost immediately. Scudding white mists hid the moon fitfully as though relishing a jest with those who sought light on the earth below. Storm-clouds began to gather in the south and to beat up warningly. The night fell bitter cold and the wind was as a whip upon the face.

"Come, let us go down," said Paul, who hitherto had been held to the deck as one chained there by the anticipation of advancing peril. " I have tasted no food since midday;

and you, little girl, I should be ashamed to keep you here."

"My place is at your side, Paul."

"Then my side shall be in the saloon. And you shall give me my supper there. It will be time enough to think of other things when we see the light of their ships."

"You think that they will follow us?"

"Is it possible not to think so?"

"They will send a cruiser?"

"Undoubtedly; but we shall not mind that. There is no ship in Russia which can catch the *Esmeralda* while she has coal in her bunkers; and we have coal everywhere. Oh, it will amuse you well when the fun begins."

He entered the saloon and switched on the electric lights. The veils for the ports were ready now, and when he had covered up the glasses with them he gave the girl hot wine.

"You must drink it at a draught," he said. "I want to see the colour in your pretty cheeks."

"Paul," she said earnestly, "how can I thank you? how can I tell you all I feel?"

"You can thank me by drinking the wine and afterwards by eating your supper. You must say how you like the *Esmeralda* and her cook. She is my other self, this little ship. We have been friends many years, but not the friends we shall be to-night."

The steward, a portly, good-humoured, but, above all, fatherly man, known in twenty ports by the name of Sal, by reason of his ability to perform all woman's work, now hurried into the cabin and set a steaming dish upon the table.

"A bit of beef, and cooked with my own hand, miss," he said. "I thought you'd be glad of it, and so I made bold."

She thanked him prettily.

"You come from London?" she asked.

A voluble man, her question was like oil upon his tongue.

"Indeed and I do, my miss. I was born at West 'Am, as my poor mother knows, and precious glad I shall be to see Hingerland again. It's a dreadful thing to feel as you're an ixile, miss. Fourteen years now it is since I clapped eyes on London. As for these Russians, I can't abide 'em."

Paul roared with laughter.

"Sapristi!" said he, "you're a fine fellow to sign for a Russian ship."

"A Russian ship? No, it ain't that, sir. I had the word of Reuben afore I come aboard. 'Where you like and when you like,' says I, 'but no foringers for yours truly.' And that's what we signed upon. 'As for the young gentleman,' says I, 'he's no Russian, or what's he doing with our lingo? You don't find Joshua Sill sailing with foringers willing.' Five times round the world, miss, I've been, believe me. But there ain't no place like the country we was bred to, indeed there ain't."

His patriotism choked him with emotion, and he withdrew, still shaking his head. His talk had led them away for a brief moment from the hour and the place, and the shadows passed from their faces. It was possible, down there in the warmth and brightness of the pretty cabin, to imagine that they, too, were already upon the seas of liberty and safety; to imagine that they had come to that kingdom of love and possession which they had sought in tears and tribulation and perils often. They began to talk with a new confidence; to promise each other what they would do when the sunny fields of Devon were theirs to roam and the white cliffs of England stood up for their defence. The spell of the warming wine worked upon them so that the man could tell himself that the reward was greater than the sacrifice; the girl, that love was at last born in her heart unquestionably, a love to endure, to overshadow all, to be the very sap of her life. Lying there in her lover's arms, the past, the future, the scene, the peril alike were forgotten. She lived in a present which was in itself an eternity—the eternity of love realised.

In this employment of supper two hours passed swiftly away. Paul lingered in the cabin because he knew that the deck might show him that which he feared to see—the lights of the cruisers sent out from Kronstadt or Helsingfors in pursuit of the *Esmeralda*. Trusting to the quick eyes and to the devotion of his servant Reuben, he knew that they would summon him when need was that he should go above. The quiver of the boards beneath his feet, the jar of the glass upon the table, spoke of the high speed maintained and of a smoother sea. Could they but keep the *Esmeralda* at such a speed she would out-steam any vessel which Stefanovitch could command. The danger lay ahead—in the warships at Helsingfors and at Revel. The telegraph could warn these that a launch was escaping from Kronstadt. The *Esmeralda* had yet to pass the neck of the Gulf, yet to outwit those who would strain every nerve to take her. Folly alone helped Paul to hope in the midst of dangers such as these. Despair whispered that the girl he loved was in his arms, but that he touched her lips for the last time.

"Let us forget, Marian, let us forget all," he would cry; "let us think only of to-night, and of each other."

"I could never forget," she answered with deep affection. "I am unworthy of the love you bestow upon me; I shall be your servant until my death."

"You shall be my wife!" he cried passionately. "I will hear your words all day. The days cannot be long enough. There shall be nothing to think of—no past, no future, but only the moment of our love. When to-morrow comes we shall be where no Russian ships can harm us. It will be yours then to repay me, dearest, to remember whose servant I have been and why I left Russia. You will be the friend of my country as I shall be of yours. You will forget all that you learnt and saw at Kronstadt."

"I have forgotten it already, Paul. Oh, I should be for ever guilty if I did not regret all that I have done and said, if I did not think of Russia as of my own country. How could it be otherwise since I love you?"

"They will tempt you," he said: "they will offer you money as they offered it before; and I am poor, I have no longer an employment. The home which I can give you must be one of your own cottages. My friends will not help me now; they will call me a traitor and forget my name."

She shrank at the words, for they rebuked her selfishness. She realised she had made him the partner of her guilt.

"Oh, no, no, do not say that!" she cried; "do not let me bring this shame upon you. Take me back to Russia, Paul; to-morrow it will be too late."

"It is too late now," he said with a bitter smile.

The door of the cabin opened as he spoke, and the face of Reuben, still wearing the bucolic grin, appeared unwelcomely. Paul rose at once.

"You have something to say to me, Reuben?"

"It is about the coal, sir."

"Then I will come immediately."

But to Marian he said—

"You must sleep now, little wife. To-morrow we shall be in the Baltic and sunset will bring us to Stockholm. You can begin to think of England then."

She raised her lips to his and clung to him with a new tenderness. The words he had spoken, that his friends would call him a traitor, echoed again in her ears. She thought of them still when he had left her, and they were an enemy to sleep. The gift of sacrifice cut her heart; it poisoned the cup of forgetfulness she had tasted so willingly.

But Paul hurried to the deck, and so soon as his feet had left the ladder he knew why Reuben called him. Away upon the port quarter a great arc of golden light was playing upon the sea. Now rising in a focus of dazzling beams, now skimming the water with a vast area of radiance, now shining full as a star new fallen from the heavens, the meaning of the light was not to be hidden from those on board the *Esmeralda*. The telegraph had done its work. A cruiser had put out from Helsingfors and was searching the Gulf for the yacht which sought to carry from Russian waters secrets of such price.

"God help my little wife!" said Paul when he saw the light—and that was all.

CHAPTER XIII.

AT THE ZENITH OF THE NIGHT.

THE yacht stood upon a course almost due west. The lamps in her saloons burned no longer; she carried no light and showed no glow of flame above her funnel. Save for the vibrations of her screw and the buffet of the seas upon her arched bows, no sound followed in her wake. She cut the gathering waves rather than breasted them; she rushed onward through the swell as some living thing come up for breath or to the pursuit of prey. Until this time the arc of light which lay upon the sea as a golden carpet had not spread so far that its rays were shed upon the yacht. She stood out of it to the northward. Her crew watched its path with an excitement not to be described. Men clenched their hands when the great lamp swung round and their eyes were blinded by its fuller radiance. But darkness continued to befriend them. Save in that place where the great lantern gave gold to the waves, night reigned upon the sea. And night might yet deliver the *Esmeralda* if destiny willed.

"They are standing for the south, sir," said old

John Hook, who was at the wheel. "It'll be in their heads that we're running for the German coast—perhaps for the Baltic port. You'll go by 'em yet with a handful of luck—I'm damned if you won't!"

Old John, who had shipped for the trip willingly when he heard that an Englishwoman was to be snatched from a Russian prison, trusted to pick up at Stockholm his own brig, then at anchor in Kronstadt harbour. The adventure was no more to him than an hour in the fog at the mouth of the Thames.

"Stop you, sir!" he had exclaimed. "Why, there ain't no ship in the Baltic as could catch yon bit of a kettle when she'd the mind to show her starn. And if so be as they do, why, ain't there such things as counsels for to talk to 'em properly and show 'em what's the colour of your flag? I'd spit on all the skippers in Roosher for a noggin of rum—damn me if I wouldn't."

With this proper contempt for all foreigners and their ships (and a bundle containing a lace handkerchief, a photograph and a dirty shirt), John had come aboard the *Esmeralda*. The race from Kronstadt to the open Gulf had been a joy to him. Nor did this sudden appearance of a warship upon the horizon terrify him at all. The yacht had the heels of her. If they were taken, the English

Consul at Kronstadt would shake his fist in the face of the Governor, he reasoned, and that would be the end of it. Paul shared nothing of such stolid optimism. The very darkness of the seas about him caused the great white light to stand out like some uncanny beacon set up to remind him that he was still in Russian waters; that Kronstadt knew of his flight and of his purpose.

"She is running to the south, John," he said gloomily, "but it will not be for long. For the matter of that she is going about now."

John touched the little wheel and spat emphatically.

"That's true, by thunder!" he cried; "but what of it, sir? It'll be a pretty steady hand that picks us off in this light; and we've the heels of her, all said and done. You take my word for it, if they're waiting to take us afore they turn in they won't finish this watch until the day of judgment."

Paul smiled.

"You English have a pleasant way of looking at things; we Russians are not so ready."

"Which is your misfortune, sir, a-begging your pardon. It don't do to be a Rooshian, not in these days—leastwise not when you can sail under a skipper who reads the noosepapers."

L

He touched the wheel again, and the little yacht rose on the crest of a great wave before plunging into the shining darkness of the hollow. The arc ceased to glow while the great ship went about; the curtain of the cloud was unlifted, save at one spot low upon the horizon where a little gate of light, like a wicket-gate to the heaven beyond the envelope, gave promise of a clear sky before the morning. For ten minutes the yacht raced in darkness toward the distant seas of refuge. Then the mighty beams shone out again, and their glory, surpassing the glory of day, fell once more upon the waters. Rippling as with a ripple of molten gold, the wave of radiance flowed on. It made jewels of the wind-tossed spindrift; it focussed upon the black sails of a fishing-boat and showed her labouring and sagging in the trough of the seas; it struck upon the dark hull of a distant steamer, and she stood out in it so that the very men upon her decks were to be counted: and it rested at last upon the *Esmeralda*, gathering her into its aureola, feeling her, as with fingers of light which touched prey and would torture it.

No man spoke in that supreme moment. The hand of old John was still upon the spokes of the wheel; Paul leaned spell-bound against the shrouds- and watched the quivering beams; Reuben showed his head above the engine-room hatchway, and the grin still hovered upon his face. Minutes passed and the enchantment was not broken. Full upon them the light rested, discovering every shroud and rope. And the men had no answer to it—no answer save the answer of the *Esmeralda*, which rushed onward toward her goal as though the race were a joy to her—a race from which she would yet reap victory.

Reuben was the first to find his tongue.

"She's the *Peter Veliky*, of Revel," he said quietly; "I could pick her out of a thousand. She carries four twelve-inch, and her speed's fourteen— in the books."

"To hell with the books!" cried John Hook. "The question is, what's her speed here, and when is she going to show it?"

Reuben's grin was yet broader.

"She is going to show it now, John; if you want to dance, there's the music."

A gun boomed out above the moaning of the wind, and its smoke hung for an instant, like an envelope of vapour above the decks of the *Peter Veliky*. Then a woman's voice was heard, and Paul turned quickly to find Marian standing at his side.

"I could not stay below," she said, "it suffocates me—and I saw the light, Paul."

She slipped her hand into his and stood with him. She feared no longer for herself, but for the

L 2

man who had risked life and honour that she might be free.

"You will never make a sailor, Marian," Paul answered; "you do not know how to obey."

"I have come here to learn, dearest; I could not stay down there with yesterday for my friend."

Paul pointed to the distant ship whose blinding lantern moved slowly across the spuming sea.

"There is our to-morrow," he said grimly. "I did not wish you to know that. I thought that you would sleep and wake where no one could harm you; but now—we shall dance, as Reuben says."

She laughed to conceal her excitement.

"Who can harm me here when you are with me?" she asked—and then, less heroically, "Did you not say that the *Esmeralda* was the fastest yacht in the Baltic?"

Paul took her face between his rough hands and kissed it.

"Little woman," he said, "if I had your heart! You give me courage always. Indeed, good luck goes with you, Marian; we are leaving them already."

The ships were abreast now, a mile of sparkling sea racing between them. But the *Peter Veliky* was no match for the yacht which Yarrow had built. The *Esmeralda* forged ahead from the first. She held her course unflinchingly even when the gun sent flame again across the water and a shell fell hissing into the waves behind her. She steamed on in the envelope of night, seeking to shake the light from her as quarry might shake a dog.

"To hell with the books!" cried old John Hook in the fervour of the moment. "There ain't a ship in Roosher which is going to catch her this night, a-begging your pardon for the expression, miss."

"Oh, it is true, it is true!" cried Marian, clasping her hands joyfully. "To-morrow we shall be at Stockholm. What a thing to tell little Dick!"

Her eyes blazed; the magic of combat, that inexplicable fever, which gives scorn of death had touched them. She stood entranced, a little slim figure, upon which the white beams fell picturesquely. When the man looked upon her he forgot all else but the morrow which should put her in his arms and dower him with her love while life was.

"We will tell the story together, little girl," he said; "but there is something else to say before then, and the music has not finished."

A second shot hissed above the sea and was swallowed up in a fountain of foam which rose up so close to the *Esmeralda* that the faces of her crew were wetted as by driven rain. It drew a curse from old John, but the girl laughed fearlessly. She could not realise the meaning of the tragedy which was being played. To her it was no more than some great set scene in a theatre where wondrous lights coloured the enchanted waters, and demons danced impotently before the gates of the house impregnable. She did not believe that anything on earth could harm a ship manned by English sailors and built in London city. And she had an abounding confidence in her lover. He would save her—that had been her thought from the beginning of the terrible days.

"Paul," she asked, turning to him with a gesture of love, " when shall we be in London ?"

"In four days' time, little one."

"And then——"

"And then—it will be your turn to command. I have no plans; I have not thought of it."

"There is no need to think, dearest. I shall make England a home to you indeed. We will live for that. We will talk of to-night often. You shall tell Dick how they fired at us. He will not believe, but it will be good to remember. You do not regret, Paul?"

" Regret—with you at my side, and the day

to dawn, and the little yacht to carry me—how should I regret?   It is life to look into your eyes, Marian!"

She answered with a half caress, and he led her to the poop, where together they watched the wake of water behind them aglow with phosphorescent brilliance and the jewelled spray of the white-capped waves.   For a moment the danger seemed to be passing.   The ships were no longer abreast; the great aureola scarce touched them; silence fell upon the sea, and the guns of the *Peter Veliky* ceased to speak.   Anon the yacht plunged into the welcome shadow, and all the pent-up gladness of those who had waged the fight so dauntlessly broke out and was not to be restrained.   A great cheer—an English cheer— went ringing across the sea.   It was the answer of the four to the four hundred aboard the *Peter Veliky.*

"Outsteamed, by God!" cried old John Hook. "I said there warn't no Rooshian as could touch her."

CHAPTER XIV.

THE TERRIBLE NIGHT.

THE echo of the cheer which rose up from the decks of the *Esmeralda* yet lingered upon the sea when the Russian answer to it was forthcoming. Even as the crew of the little yacht said that the danger was done with, and that an open sea now lay before them, a voice out of the darkness gave them the lie. So swift was it to come, so surprising, that the men stood mute and wondering and helpless. It was as though the avenger had risen from the depths before them — a phantom ship conjured up by the powers of ill to reckon with them. They thought themselves without consort in the heart of the Gulf, and while the thought was still with them the strange ship appeared. Her light shone full upon them from a point not two hundred yards distant. They could count the men upon her decks; could see the figure of her commander outstanding on the bridge; could follow the delicate contour of the great hull which now towered above them.

The strange ship lay motionless, for she had been awaiting the signal of the *Peter Veliky*, and so stood toward the centre of the Gulf that she might command the channel. It is possible that the *Esmeralda* would have slipped by her. in the dark but for the cheer of victory raised so foolishly. That triumphant cry was as the gun of a sentinel to those on board the Russian ship. Her lantern blazed out; voices of warning were raised on her decks; men roared to one another that the quarry had run into the snare, that the hunt was done. The beams of the great light fell upon the yacht and upon her crew, and the cheer froze on the lips of those who had raised it. Her men were powerless to think or act. The ultimate terror of defeat was upon them.

A man wearing the uniform of a naval lieutenant stood in the bows of the cruiser and was the first to hail the *Esmeralda*. His voice was like the roar of a bull; the wind carried his words so that none of them were lost. Already Reuben had shut off steam mechanically, so that the two ships lay rolling to the swell like swimmers who seek breath after the travail of a race. But no one gave answer to the hail of the lieutenant. Stupor possessed the crew of the yacht. The blow had been so swift to come; the shadow of the prison lay already upon the men.

"What ship?" roared the lieutenant, putting the question for the third time.

"She's the *Kremi*, of Helsingfors," said Reuben, who was again the first to reckon up the danger.

"An old ship," said John Hook in a giant's whisper.   "She might catch a hearse—leastwise I'd venture on it."

"Nine knots in the books, John."

"To hell with the books!   She carries her guns forward."

"Then they cannot fire at us as we pass them," exclaimed the girl excitedly.

Old John added to the wealth of the sea by a mouthful of tobacco juice.

"You've hit it on the head, miss!" cried he.   "If we drift past 'em they want five minutes to get her about, and where shall we be in five minutes, mates?"

Reuben ceased to grin.   Paul could not take his eyes off the cruiser.   They had drifted so close to her that they could see the faces of those who trod the great decks above them.   There was not a man on board the *Esmeralda* whose heart did not beat high, not one who did not tell himself that this was the hour of reckoning.

"C'est fini!" Paul exclaimed, drawing the girl into his embrace. "This is our to-morrow, little Marian. But I have done my best, God knows."

She kissed his lips and that was her answer.

Many men had come together to the port-bow of the *Kremi*, and they stood gaping at the stranger and at her crew. The lieutenant who had first cried out, asking "What ship?" gave the order that a gangway should be lowered; he did not doubt that it was the intention of the pursued to surrender without further effort. But those on board the *Esmeralda* were of one mind and purpose again. The grin broadened upon the face of Reuben; old John lighted his pipe with the deliberation of a man at his own fireside. Silently he waited while the crew of the *Kremi* flocked to the gangway, encouraged by the shrill, fife-like voice of a commander who plumed himself already upon his victory. Child's work, the Russian thought, to grapple with the impudent and perky cockle-shell which had defied so vain-gloriously the might of his country. He gave the order triumphantly. He came to the very edge of the bridge to watch the irons slipped upon the hands of Zassulic the spy and of the woman who had tempted him. When the *Esmeralda* did not stop at the gangway, but drifted on, he thought for the moment that it was clumsy seamanship; but when, with dramatic suddenness, she began to go full steam ahead, his anger was not to be controlled.

"Stand by to clear the guns!" he roared. "Are you going to lose her? Great God! she will cheat us yet!"

He foamed and raged like a madman, for the yacht shot into the darkness as a shell from a great gun. The terrible moment of waiting was past. Inch by inch the little ship had drifted, carrying men whose hearts quivered with excitement but whose spirit was unbroken. The terror of waiting was upon them no more. They had been within a boat's length of the ladder when John cried "Let her go!" Then all the courage of their despair fired them. As a horse champing at his bit, so was the *Esmeralda* sagging there in the trough of the sea. The rush of steam into her cylinders was the touch of the spur she asked. She bounded forward into the heart of the breakers, and a cloud of spray hid her from the enemy's sight.

"Below, below for your lives!" roared old John; "they're manning the machine-guns!"

"We cannot leave you here!" cried Paul, ashamed for the moment that it was not a fellow-countryman who spoke.

"SHE BOUNDED FORWARD INTO THE HEART OF THE BREAKERS" (p. 172).

"Then you stand to your death!" cried John Hook. "There ain't a gun in Roosher which I care a d—— for!—the Lord be my witness. Down there, sir, as you vally your life!"

The rattle of musketry and a sputter of bullets on the near sea cut short his honest bravado. Paul, needing no other argument, dragged Marian into the shelter of the scantling. The yacht, yawing in her course that she might avoid the hail of bullets, appeared to rush into the very bowels of the seas. Onward she flew, the foam frothing at her bows, the spray reeking upon her funnel, a great wake of quivering water behind her. Bullets struck her decks and sent chips of wood flying as though an adze cleaved them; the search-light followed her path as the light upon a stage follows the step of the dancer. Every minute was an eternity of suspense. The hearts of the men seemed to stand still. When at last the guns ceased there were tears upon the faces of the crew, but they were tears of joy.

"Down under again, by the Lord!" roared old John, who rolled with excitement. "Down under again, and the young lady thought of it. Glory be to God who made me an Englishman this night!"

He shook his fist defiantly at the distant light, for he knew that the hour of deliverance was at hand. The lumbering *Kremi*, which ventured rarely from her moorings in Helsingfors, was marked in the books as a ship which could steam at nine knots, but that was a fiction beloved of officials. Put to it now in the heavy swell of a fresh night, she strained and groaned like a derelict of the deep; she lurched over the seas, she smothered herself in them. The yacht ran from her as a hare from a bull. She fired her great gun again and again, but the shells found no other billet than the thundering breakers. When thirty minutes had passed she abandoned the pursuit and headed once more for the harbour she quitted so rarely. But first she shot a rocket high into the darkness and was answered by other rockets, blue and flaming on the far horizon. And at this sight old John ceased to laugh, and foreboding fell again upon the crew of the *Esmeralda*.

"You saw that, Reuben?" cried John Hook, pointing upward with his bony finger.

"I saw it, John."

"Then there ain't no need for me to speak."

"Speak or silent, it don't make no difference."

"If I've eyes in my head, that's the Baltic Fleet coming up the Gulf."

"It is so, John."

"The Baltic Fleet!" exclaimed Paul. "Then God help us! We shall never run by there."

"You speak gospel truth, sir."

The master of the *Esmeralda* paced the deck again in all the agony of uncertainty prolonged. He had persuaded Marian to lie down in her cabin so soon as the *Kremi* ceased to fire ; there she slept and dreamed of England. But for him there was no sleep. These recurring difficulties were to him as a sign from God rebuking his work. It had seemed so simple when he planned it at Kronstadt —the quick rush in the darkness, the friendship of surprise, the possibility of escape before the news was known. But now the truth would not be hidden. The flaming rockets spoke of a girdle put about him by the avenger. He realised what a task was that which a man set himself when he sought to pit his cunning against the might of Russia. His enemies would crush him as they would crush a worm. They would drag him from the woman whose lips he had kissed, whose love was all that remained to him in life.

"You think there is no hope for us, Reuben ?" he asked, suddenly stopping in his walk and facing the silent group.

"No hope out yonder, sir—leastways not to-night."

"You have no plan in your mind ?"

"None—unless you should run north, sir. There are always the islands."

"I had not thought of them," said Paul.

"I thought of them from the first," continued Reuben. "There are a hundred creeks which might hide us until the hunt is over. And we've the land behind us, sir, if it should come to the worst."

"Then to the islands let it be, and God help us if they know that we are still in the Gulf."

"Ay, ay, to that," said old John; and so the little ship went about, and heading straight for the coast of Finland, she began to race anew. But the hearts of the men were heavy. It was as though they turned her towards the gates of that prison which their minds had built for them during the hours of the terrible night.

CHAPTER XV.

UPON THE NAMELESS ISLAND.

IT was the afternoon of the day, and the *Esmeralda* lay at anchor under the lee of one of the rocky islets which abound upon the southern shores of Finland. They had warped her to the sheer rock, so that she lay snug and hidden and sheltered from the wind-driven tide which raced between the island and its neighbour. A loom of haze above her funnel alone spoke of life within her. Her crew had gone ashore to stretch their legs, and were to be discovered upon the beach in all those attitudes of repose which seamen court. The sun fell upon the barren rock and upon their faces, but did not wake them. They had kept the long vigil, and this was their hour of rest.

The day had been one of tempest since the dawn : and though it was now late in the afternoon and the rain had ceased to fall, there was a thunder of surf upon the outer islands of the archipelago and the open water frothed white with foam. But the creek into which they had moored the *Esmeralda* was sheltered both from the wind and seas. Sheer walls of granite towered above

M

the decks of the yacht; a girdle of tiny islets, stretching far out to the Gulf or back to the distant shore of Finland, was her defence against the breakers. She rode proudly at her moorings as though conscious of the victory which the night had given her.

This haven had been made at the dawn of the day by men who knew every channel and landmark in the Gulf. They had welcomed it, for therein they could think of food and sleep, and forget that the Russian was at their heels. Though the truce might prove but a truce of hours, it was a gift of God to those whose eyes ached with watching, whose limbs were cold with wet, whose tongues were parched with thirst. The gale which sprang up with the coming of the light was a befriending gale to them. They said that no ship of war would venture near them while the surf thundered, and the mist of spray made clouds above the land, and the west wind screamed in the Gulf. And so they slept, and the sunshine of the later day was a balm of light to their eyes, and welcome warmth suffused bodies that had been stiff and cramped with the bitter cold of the Baltic night.

Though Paul had gone ashore with his crew, it was not to sleep. The few hours of rest he had snatched in the earlier hours of the day sufficed for him. He, perhaps, of all the little company, understood most truly the malevolence of Fate in casting him back to the shelter of the island at an hour when he should have been in the great sea-road of the Baltic. The Land of the West, wherein liberty lay, seemed to have become a land beyond the horizon of his dreams. He looked out from the island upon the whitened billows and remembered that Russian ships, sent to the pursuit of him, were watching and waiting in the channel of the Gulf. The distant shore, high and rocky and barren, spoke of coast patrols and Finns who soon must learn that a strange yacht lay in the harbour of the islands; of peasants who would run to carry the news to Helsingfors that a few kopecks might be thrown to them. Scheme as he would, he could contrive no plan whereby the peril wrought of the gale might be turned. He must wait for a smoother sea and a fairer wind. And waiting was an agony of doubt scarce to be supported.

All this was in his mind when Marian awoke at midday and was rowed by old John Hook to the little patch of beach which permitted them to land upon the nameless island. He met her at the water-side and lifted her from the boat; but he would tell her nothing of his thoughts, for he saw that colour had come again to her face and that the great rings beneath her eyes had been washed out by the

M 2

waters of sleep. She was, indeed, almost the light-hearted pretty creature who had won his love at the Governor's house; and when he looked into her brightening eyes and heard her girlish laughter, love came surging up to compel forgetfulness of all else.

"I have been waiting for you," he said tenderly. "The hours were long."

"They will race now," she answered, as she locked her hand in his. "We shall see each other growing old, Paul. Oh, is it not good to breathe again? I could run, run, run to the world's end."

She dragged him on, hastening with joy of her freedom, telling him a hundred things at once, asking unfinished questions and waiting for no answer. When they had come to the high place of the rock she curled herself up on the ground and there she feasted her eyes on the panorama of whitened sea and whirling gull and desolate island. The man lay beside her, content that he had won her this hour of happiness.

"I cannot believe it," she said, while the spindrift freshened her face and the wind swept the curls from her little ears, "I cannot believe that we are here. How should a day make such a difference? How should our lives run so evenly through long years and then turn so swiftly, carrying us away from everything we have ever known to things we never dreamed of? A month ago I was a governess in the house at Kronstadt. I taught the twins to grow up in the way they did not want to go. But to-day, where am I? what am I? Why are these things hidden from us? And if it is so strange to-day, what will it be next year and the year after? Oh, if one could look even for a moment into the glass of life!"

"But you cannot," said Paul stolidly. "There is no glass except the glass of your mind and conscience. We cannot look; we can only act, Marian. And that is what we have been doing, you and I, though God knows what kind of a story we have written or where it will end. At this moment we are on an island near Hango, and we wait there until the wind and the sea go down. When that happens we shall go aboard the *Esmeralda* again, and to-morrow we shall come to Stockholm."

She clapped her hands, and regarding her environment wistfully, she cried—

"It is a world of islands, a world without life. There can be no spot on all the earth as lonely as this. And yet it is a city to me now. I could people it with the birds; the rocks should be the churches and buildings for me. Paradise lies on the broad road when one has been a month and has not seen the sun."

He stroked her face, encouraging her to forget that her freedom might depend upon the whim of the wind.

"You are glad to be free, Marian, as glad as I am! Some day, perhaps, we will remember this day and speak of it as the morning of our love. I do not think that they will follow us; there are few that can sail these seas. Even the fishermen come here reluctantly. It is a grave for sailors, as many a good fellow knows."

"And yet *you* come here?"

"It was the one thing left to do. We could not pass the ships they had sent out yonder; we could not go back; this was our only haven, unless we returned to the prison as they wished."

She shuddered and drew close to him.

"We shall never go back, dearest; you think that?"

He began to pick at the rocky stones and to throw them into the froth of the breaking waves.

"I do not know," he said after a long pause. "Who can say what the future will bring? But

I am a Russian no more. I have no country now. It does not concern me."

The infinite pathos of his words was not to be concealed from her. Never since he had carried her from the cell at Alexander had she understood so well the price he had paid.

"Oh, Paul, Paul!" she exclaimed bitterly, "what have I done? what crime have I committed that I should bring this upon you? Let me go back to Kronstadt. I am not worth your sacrifice. I can never repay. There is time yet."

The man laughed at her distress, and, blaming himself because he had spoken, he answered by taking her face into his hands and looking into her tear-stained eyes.

"The crime you have committed," he said, "is to be the sweetest woman on earth! The wrong which you have done is to make me love you so that without you there is no world for me! Why talk of repaying? Is there to be a reckoning between those who love? Have they not all things in common? Who hurts you hurts me. When you are content I am content. I lose a country to gain the whole world. If I am no longer a Russian, shall I not be the husband of Marian? Let us not talk of these things; it is ingratitude while we have the bread of life so abundantly. When that bread fails we will complain. To-morrow, if the wind goes down, we shall be at Stockholm. I shall leave the yacht there and take an English steamer for London. It will then be your turn to forget that you are an Englishwoman; you will be the wife of Zassulic; you will be the friend of Russia. All that you have learnt at Kronstadt will be forgotten; the friends who tempted you will be strangers to you henceforth. We will begin life again, pilgrims in a strange country. But we shall walk the way of life together, and so the journey will be easy."

The shadow of regret passed from his face while he went on to speak of all he would do in London; how that he hoped much from his kinsman and from his own training as an engineer. Marian, in her turn, listened with smiling face, though she was telling herself all the time that she must prevent the sacrifice must compel him to return to his work and his country; if possible, to return, not as one disgraced, but a man who had wrestled with a great temptation and had vanquished it. As for herself, she did not doubt that her wits would find a way whereby she might reach her own country. The present danger she was in,

the peril of almost immediate discovery by the
Russian ships, was not real to her. She could
run again and see the sky and breathe the fresh
air. She felt herself adrift upon the ocean or
circumstance, and the voyage was not without
its measure of excitement.

"You must go back, Paul," she said very firmly
when he had done speaking; "we must find a way
and an excuse."

"A way, Petite, when you have been seen upon
my ship, and the Sergeant has told them that I
took you from the fort? Oh, yes, that would be
easy enough; they are such simpletons at Kronstadt; they will believe me when I say, 'The
prisoner escaped: it was an accident'; they will
reward me—with a file of soldiers and lead for
medicine. The day when I can return to Russia
will be the day when stars fall at our feet and
there is no longer any sun in the sky. It is foolish
to talk of it. Henceforth you shall make a country
for me; it shall be a country of the heart; the
house will be the house of our affections. We
shall laugh then to remember of what little worth
are all those material things which at one time
seemed so much to us; we shall laugh at to-day,
and tell how we cheated old Bonzo after all."

It was a brave effort to conceal from her the
apprehension he felt; but the woman's instinct

rightly interpreted the words. When next he looked into her face she was gazing over the storm-tossed waste to the distant field of the open sea, where the west wind still blew with hurricane force and banks of gathering cloud were the gloomy heralds of the night to come.

"The wind befriends us," she said thoughtfully, "but the wind will die away presently, and then——"

"And then the darkness will take its place, little woman. Even if they think we are here among the islands, they must spend days before they discover upon which island we are. While they are looking for us we shall be snug in the harbour at Stockholm. We must steal from harbour to harbour until we see that no ships follow, and then the little yacht will do the rest. There is no ship in Russia that can outsteam her with a clear sea before us. We shall wait for the clear sea and all will be well."

They had left the grassy knoll at this time and had come up to the headland, wherefrom they could overlook the strange haven into which destiny had cast them. Marian beheld again the world of islands, vast, interminable, stretching as far as the eye could see away toward the Baltic or back to the Russia they had left. The gloom of water and sky, the cold gray light, the haunting solitude, the wash of the waves, the shrill note of the gull, oppressed her anew with a vast sense of her own loneliness. She thought that she was an outcast from the world. She pictured herself flying from man to the desolate places of the earth. A hundred years of time seemed to lie between her and the life she had lived. She reproached herself bitterly that she had rewarded so great a love with so terrible a gift—the gift of men's slander and the insult of evil tongues, the brand of dishonour and the exile's lot.

And this thought grew upon her, that she must save Paul from himself and go alone upon the way to which her folly had carried her.

CHAPTER XVI.

ALONE.

THE westerly gale held throughout the day, and was still at its height when the men of the *Esmeralda* turned into their bunks. They had watched unceasingly during the afternoon for any sign of ships upon the horizon or for token of life upon the neighbouring shore of Finland. But the sea continued to run mountains high in the broad of the Gulf, and there was a haze of mist and spray over the land which served them well in those anxious moments of waiting. They argued that the Baltic Fleet would not attempt to weather such a gale, but would be already snug and sheltered at Helsingfors or at Revel. As for the fishermen of the neighbouring isles, the circumstance of the day accounted for them and for their ships. No little craft could live in such a gale; no peasant would patrol the shores while the west wind swept up the Gulf and the breakers thundered upon the outer reef. To-morrow the wind would fall away and the calm would come. To-morrow they would begin to live again.

The night fell dark and misty and threatening,

so that there was no need of any watch upon the decks of the little ship. Guarded by the breakers without and the towering crags for sentinels within, the haven befriended her beyond hope. No lights shone from the ports of the *Esmeralda* upon the swirling waters of the channel. Her men went to and fro silently as though afraid to speak. They welcomed the hours of truce, for therein they could sleep and rest. Marian alone kept a vigil of the night. For her sleep had become a fitful friend. There were terrors of her dreams which no waking argument could shake off. She slept to imagine herself once more in the cell at Alexander; she awoke to ask herself if she would ever come to England again. She remembered that she was an outcast and had struck at the honour of the man she loved in her fall.

Old John Hook and Reuben, the engineer, went ashore several times during the night to see if there was any abatement of wind or sea; but when at four o'clock they found the gale still blowing, it was evident to them that the necessity for watchfulness existed no longer—at least until the day dawned. They were sound asleep in their bunks when Marian dressed herself in the darkness at four o'clock and left the cabin wherein sleep had brought her so many terrible dreams. She had no set purpose in quitting her bed other than the desire to breathe the fresh air of morning. The gray beams of light shining behind banks of sullen cloud were welcome to her after the darkness and confinement of her little cabin. Silently she trod the steps of the companion, and ran to the bow of the yacht to stand there and hear the water lapping monotonously upon the face of the cliff. The nameless islands around began slowly to shape themselves in a vista of spray and haze. Strange birds went screaming from crag to crag; but of human life there was no sight or sound.

It had been an impulse which brought her to the deck, but this was to prove a morning of impulses. Ever present through the weary night of waiting had been the desire to save the man she loved from the consequences of her folly. Just as at Kronstadt, in the hour of her necessity, a woman's weakness had cast her upon his pity and devotion, so now was she convinced that she must rely upon that pity and devotion no longer. She told herself, but with the vaguest notions of reasoning, that if Paul were alone, it would be easy for him to return to his own country with some story that would convince Bonzo and old Stefanovitch of his fidelity. And she must not deny him that pportunity. He had given all; her gift should not be less.

"I will save him from himself," she said again

and again. "They shall not find me upon his yacht. He will go back to Russia and forget. I have been alone so many years; it is nothing that I am alone until the end."

She repeated the words while she stood at the bow of the *Esmeralda* and watched the sea racing in the narrow of the channel. To save the man who had lost all for her, to give him back country, friends, honour—she cared not at what cost—that must be her purpose. All the happiness of his love which had come into her life must wither and die. If God willed, she would still have the love of the child. Her unbroken courage suggested that she would find the way to England when once she was alone. Half-formed schemes of a place of hiding in the hut of a peasant, of flight in a fisherman's ship, helped her resolutions. She remembered that she had rowed a boat often upon the river Dart, and that weeks of imprisonment had still left much of her girlish strength. And so the great idea took finite shape and was resolved upon.

Quickly, silently, with deft hands, she drew the yacht's boat, then lying at the stern of the ship, to the gangway, which had been left down during the night. A feverish haste characterised all her movements. She was afraid that they would come and rob her of success; she feared that someone would awake to prevent her emprise.

Her great love for Paul surged up in her heart, yet did but quicken her steps. A rebellious anger urged her on to a war against circumstance: a war she must wage alone and without friends.

Stealthily the little gray-clad figure moved in the morning light. Hither and thither, pitiful in the agony of a farewell she could not speak, tears falling upon her cold hands, anger (she knew not why) in her heart, the girl bent down to kiss the deck beneath which her lover was sleeping.

"God bless you, Paul, my love! God bless you for your love of me!"

And so the voyage began, and the pilgrim was alone again, and the curtain of the mist shut the yacht from her sight.

*　　*　　*　　*　　*　　*

They awoke the master of the *Esmeralda* and told him of her flight. He did not answer them, but stood long peering into the mists which enveloped the island seas. When Reuben spoke to him at last he turned quickly and fell senseless upon the deck of the silent ship.

CHAPTER XVII.

FORSAKEN OF ALL.

THERE were oars in the yacht's boat, but the current ran so swiftly that Marian was unable to fix them in the rowlocks before the tide caught the little ship in its embrace and swept it out towards the open sea. So rapid was the race that the panorama of crag and headland about her seemed to be hidden in a moment from her sight. Turn where she would she espied an horizon of fog and vapour. The searching white mists of morning lay upon the sea in billows of chilling cloud. No breath of wind stirred to sweep the Gulf and roll up this veil which hid the world from her sight. Calm —the calm that those upon the *Esmeralda* had wished for—had come at last. But the very silence of it was a terror to the helpless girl cast adrift at the whim of impulse, the martyr to a woman's logic and a woman's love.

Swiftly the current ran, but silently, so that no sound broke the stillness save the lap of the water upon the prow. Minutes were numbered, but were hours for her. She heard bells

N

ringing strangely through the curtain of the fog, and wondered if they were the bells of a town. Anon the sound of waves breaking upon some strand spoke either of the coast of Finland or of the shore of a neighbouring island; but she could make out no land looming through the haze, and though she tried to row the boat in the direction of the bells, the current mastered her, and she was borne on, she knew not whither. It seemed to her that Fate was carrying her out to the death of the veiled sea. While the mist benumbed her hands and drenched her clothes, and the spray sparkled upon her face, an anger of impulse still drove her on, she cared not to what end if her lover might thereby be saved. He had suffered that she might be free; she would suffer that his country might be given back to him.

"I will save him!" was her cry, oft repeated, while she used her oars desperately and shut her lips firmly as though to help the resolution. "They will find him alone, and he will be able to make some excuse. He will say that I am dead."

At other times she would laugh aloud, asking herself what she must look like with her hair drenched and dank, and her face white and pinched, and her gown bedraggled. She said that old Stefanovitch would make love to her no more if he could see her at such a moment. She ceased to row a little while that she might recall all his leers and amorous antics—how long ago it was since they had been a part of her daily life! Or she would gaze wistfully at the barrier of fog, as though seeking beyond it a lamp of destiny which should show her the course. Death itself must be like this solitude; the stillness of the grave could bring no greater terror than the terror of one drifting in the loom of mists, far from friends and from men.

"I must not think," she said, beginning to row again with new energy. "There will be sunshine presently, and then it will be different. I shall put ashore on some island, and the fishermen will give me food and take me across to Sweden. Paul will go back to Russia. I have done right, and have only myself to blame."

She longed for sunshine as the sick long after the vigil of a night of waking. The folly of putting out to sea in a boat which carried neither food nor drink became more apparent to her every hour. There were moments of regret, when she began to wonder if Paul would follow her, when she hated the obscurity of day, which was her shield against pursuit.

N 2

Hunger now began to forewarn her of added suffering to come. The biting air of morning and the labour of the oar were foes to the little reserve of strength which had nerved her to flight. She said that none but a woman would have done so foolish a thing, and laughed at herself because she had done it. When she found herself able to row no more than a dozen strokes at a spell, when her head began to swim and all nature cried out for food, she laughed no more, but bit her lips again, and remembered that it was for her lover's life. And so day came up at last out of the sea, and the curtain of the mist was rolled back.

Gradually, as though a hand from the ether was stretched out to scatter it, the fog lifted. A golden sea shone beneath, rippling, sparkling with jewels of light. Farther back, and yet farther, showing new glories of the mirror of waters, the curtain was drawn. Marian beheld the red disc of the sun like a mighty globe hanging in the east; she saw a new world rise up out of the dissolving fog. Jagged crags of rock stood suddenly in the path of the current. Shapes as of cliffs and domes of granite were formed against the white background. A new warmth suffused the whole air softly ; the out-posts of the night were rolled back until day triumphed and all the sea was glorious with its radiance.

For some little while the girl sat entranced at the spectacle. The current, which had borne her vessel to this new scene, no longer raced toward the open sea. The tide was on the turn, and the boat rested in the slack of the water. Far away, beyond many a reef and boulder, lay the greater waters of the Gulf. She spied out the shape of a vessel lying at anchor there, and her first thought was that a Russian ship had come to the islands in pursuit of the *Esmeralda*. She said that it would find Paul alone. As for herself, there was no longer need to fear. Islands lay all about her. Here and there she perceived smoke rising from some cot or village ; the friendly sea brought her almost to the very beach of an islet green and ripe with spring grasses. She rowed to its sandy shore, and dragging the boat as far as her strength would permit up on a ridge of shingle, she set out to discover upon what kind of a haven she had fallen. Never did woman set foot upon land more gladly. Wet and cold and miserable, knowing well that she stood alone in the world, conscious that the Russian guarded the gate by which she must pass to England, nevertheless the sunshine was as wine to her,

the warmth of morning as a gift of God.
Impulsively, with a child's joy, she ran to the
higher places of the island; she wrung her wet
clothes and bound her unkempt hair again.
There would be fishermen's huts upon the other
side, she said; they would give her food for
charity's sake; she would make them understand, it would be fun to do so. But when she
stood upon the high place of her little kingdom
she found that it was desolate as the other
isles had been. No hut or cottage spoke of
life awaking, or of men still at their sleep. The
shrill note of the whirling birds, the splash of
the sea upon the golden sands, were the voices
of the sanctuary. Marian listened to them a
little while as one who hears the tidings of
surpassing ill. Then with a bitter cry of woe
she ran down to the beach again.

She had thought to find her boat where
she had left it, washed by the lips of the
waves, but the tide had ebbed back a little
way—for there is always a suggestion of tide
in the Gulf—and the little ship lay high and
dry upon a bed of oozy sand. Nor could all
her strength move it again, even so much as
a foot, from its resting-place. When she was
sure of this, when she knew that she was
alone upon that desolate isle, her courage for-

sook her for the first time since she had left Kronstadt, and she sank upon the sands weeping bitterly.

"Paul, Paul," she cried, "come to me—do not leave me here alone!"

So she cried for her lover. A gull screaming above her head answered with a mocking note. Only the life-giving sunshine befriended one whom all the world had forsaken.

CHAPTER XVIII.

A STRANGE FIGURE ON THE SHORE.

THE fit of weeping passed when reason had come to her own again, and Marian sat a long while gazing wistfully over the rippling sheen of the sunlit sea. Once she thought she heard a gun fired in the distance; and this spoke to her of a life being lived around her, of other isles near by, wherein men's voices were heard and the laughter of children. She began to argue that she had but to wait for the flood of the tide to put off her boat and come at some neighbouring shore which should offer more welcome harbourage. Weary and faint as she was, with hope dimmed and courage broken, despair was not for such an hour. She had the idea to go up to the cliff and there to drink at the spring which she had seen jetting forth from the face of the rock. Thereafter she would sleep, and night would bring her food and friends.

While she knew nothing of her situation, of the land upon which she was cast, or of its environment, she was in reality upon that place

known to the Finns as the island of the Holy
Well. In circuit perhaps the third part of a
mile, this speck of land lay five miles from
that other isle which had harboured the *Esmeralda*
from the storm. But it was a kindlier shore,
for the cliff reared its head only on the west-
ward side, and elsewhere silver sand made a bed,
as of the dust of jewels, for the gentle seas
which fell upon it. A few sickly trees stood
sentinels about the spring, and heather-like bushes
thrived and flourished in the path of the water.
Marian sought the scanty shade of these trees
so soon as it was plain to her that she must
await the will of the sea. She drank long
draughts of the fresh water and bathed her
face and hands in the translucent pool. Now
that the sun shone gloriously upon the island
her heart was lighter and her hope returning.
She perceived other isles, distant more than a
mile, and she could distinguish the cottages of the
fishermen. Night should find her sleeping in
one of those huts, she argued. She would
sleep the sounder because of the sacrifice, because
she had found strength to give as it had been
given unto her.

"I shall live my life with little Dick," she
said. "There is always a living in England for
those who will work. We will face the world

together, the child and I, and God will show us the road. I must forget that it has ever been otherwise. Paul will marry a Russian woman, and yesterday will be scored out of the book."

She was tearing at the grass vindictively when she said this, and the sheen of the pool glowing radiantly, she beheld her own face in it—a face white and drawn and pitiful, with curls run wild and eyes shining from black rings. Ill as the picture pleased her, a little vanity helped to recall the faces of the Russian women she had known; and therein she found a great content. It was good to tell herself that Paul's wife would have the face of a Japanese; that her figure would be flat like a board; that her skin would be parched and brown, and that her dresses would come from Paris and would not fit her. She said that she hated all Russian women; but the woman who was to be his wife she hated already with a hatred which, when she reflected upon it a little while, compelled her to laugh. She was still laughing when she saw the apparition on the beach.

So intent had she been upon her occupation of gazing into the pool that for the time being she lost all memory of the island and of the silent seas about her. When she looked up again and came back to remembrance, her first thought was of the boat lying down there upon the silver sand below her. Quickly her eyes sought it out; but she could scarce trust them when she beheld a strange figure, come, she knew not whence, to stand by the seashore and watch her vain employment.

The figure was the figure of a man garbed in a flowing robe of brown cloth girdled at the waist with a coarse knotted rope. Huge in stature, the monk, for such he seemed to be, stood motionless as a pillar of rock. His long waving hair fell upon his shoulders abundantly and was caught by the gentle breeze, which tossed it over his haggard face so that his features were hidden. The glowing eyes shone cadaverously with a light of fasting and of faith. So old were the leather sandals he wore that they permitted the sharp rock to cut his feet, the sea to wash them. Strange and forbidding, like some wild man of the woods, the apparition stood with folded arms to watch the girl, while she in turn, speechless with fear and dread of the mystery, crouched upon the grass and found herself unable to utter a word or stir a step from the place. Never in all her life had she been so conscious of that ultimate terror of the unseen, which surpasses the terror of death itself. Sure as she was that no human thing had moved upon the island when she first trod it, this apparition seemed to have risen up before her from the very heart of the rock. Her impulse was to cry out, to flee the place as an abode of dreadful images, but her limbs did not answer to her will. The cry she would have uttered froze upon her lips; she shook with the beating of her heart. For some little while indeed the trance of fear passed to oblivion. She fell in a swoon, and when consciousness returned to her the apparition had vanished.

Marian had never known, until she came to Russia, what the meaning of a nervous system might be. Though her nerves had been shattered by the terrors of Alexander and by days and nights of dreadful contemplation, she was still able to recover quickly from panic and to laugh at it. When she found herself crouching upon the grass, and was conscious of a great glare of sunlight in her eyes, she did not, upon the instant, recall why she had swooned. The island about her was as desolate as when first she set foot upon it. The sea droned its lazy song as though welcoming the restful spring; the beach showed no sign of human thing. She watched it dreamily for a little while and then recalled the terror.

"It was a dream," she said, though she shuddered again at the memory. "I must have been asleep. How could there be anyone here? Or if there is, why should I be afraid of him? What nonsense to think of such things!"

Consoling herself thus, she sprang up lightly and ran down to the shore. Her boat was just as she had left it; but when she turned to examine the sand thereabout she discovered unmistakably the imprint of a sandalled foot; she could trace the steps to the border of the grass, but thereafter they were lost. And at this she stood spellbound again, not fearing because a man was with her upon the island, but because he hid himself thus from her, and his place of habitation was not to be discovered by her eyes. She had heard, it is true, of fanatical hermits who build pillars for themselves upon these lone rocks of Finland, but the traditions did not help her reasoning. She thought that she could never rest until she had seen and spoken to the unknown. The terrible hunger from which she suffered drove her rather to desire a meeting with him. She must know that he was human. Calling out with all her strength, she began to run across the island. She searched the beach and all the little caves and crannies cut out in the heart of the rock. She stood to listen for the sound of steps, but the dreadful silence was unbroken. No dwelling place nor other trace of man, save those footsteps upon the shore, was to be discovered. It was an awful thought for her, this thought of mystery and concealment; it was more dreadful to think that night might come and trap her still on the haven.

The sun had passed the meridian by this time. It was nearly three in the afternoon. Hunger, relentless and increasing, became an added punishment of her pilgrimage. She had the strength to walk no more, yet feared to sleep. She knew not what might happen to her if she lost consciousness and the apparition should stand over her while she dreamed. Her place of refuge was a ledge of rock raised ten feet above the sand, and so narrow that anyone coming up to her must awake her in the act. Here she was sheltered from the sun; a great boulder of granite hid her from the view of anyone who might pass on the beach below. At the very moment when she said that she would not close her eyes, nature prevailed above her resolution and she fell into a sound sleep. When she awoke, the sun was dipping into the sea and the chill of a spring sunset was upon the island.

The West was aflame then with mountains
of crimson light merging at the crown of the
arc into orange and purple and the finer shades
of yellow. The monitive stillness of the coming
night lay heavy upon the waters. There were
gray shadows everywhere and darkness in the
glens of the rock. Marian sat up, blaming herself
that she had slept so long. Her brain burned
and her hands were hot and dry. She had
never known that hunger could be such a cruel
foe. It seemed to her then that she would
have given half her years for a drink of milk
and a cake of bread.   All the dainties she
loved were shaped in fancy before her eyes;
she could have eaten the very grass. Slowly
and painfully she rose, determined to go up
again and drink a little water at the spring,
but no sooner was she upon her feet than
she cried out with joy and clasped her hands
as a child that hears of a holiday.

While she slept someone had set a rough
earthenware dish at her side. She opened the dish
to find that it contained a loaf of coarse brown
bread with a mess of meat and vegetables, and
close by there was a bottle of red wine, rough
and sour, but more sweet to the little wanderer
than all the vintages of Champagne.

"A miracle! a miracle!" she cried gladly,

while she took the black bread in her hands and drank a long draught of the wine. "The ghost has been here while I slept, and I share his dinner. Oh, how good it is to eat and drink!"

The wine warmed her as a strong cordial. Blood suffused her cheeks; there was a nervous pulsation in all her limbs. She feared the apparition no more, for she knew that some wandering priest must be with her upon the island and that he had set the food at her side. All her thought then was to get her boat into the water and to set off for that unknown port which should be to her a port of safety. She would not delay another hour upon the desolate isle, for the flood was now surging upon the beach and the heralds of night were winging in the East.

Strong in the desire to quit the lonely scene, she ate her food quickly and ran down to the beach; but there she stood once more irresolute, for a ship lay in the offing, and it was one of the most curious she had ever seen.

CHAPTER XIX.

THE QUEST OF THE WOMAN.

It was midday and the *Esmeralda* lay at anchor in the shelter of some outstanding rocks which girdled an island distant three miles from that haven which had witnessed the flight of Marian. Two men of the four who had accompanied her master from Kronstadt were to be seen upon her decks; but so well chosen was her place of hiding, and so wonderfully did the boulders of rock shield her, that her crew were indifferent alike to the presence of a Russian cruiser which lay at anchor in the distant offing, and to the eyes of the neighbouring fishermen whose boats dotted the unruffled surface of the sea.

Of the two upon the deck, one was old John Hook, who leaned heavily upon the bulwarks and exposed his brawny arms and matted hair to the welcome warmth of the spring sun; the other was Reuben, the engineer, who squatted wearily upon a coil of rope.

"Eight bells," said Reuben, filling a pipe with a seaman's deliberation, "eight bells, John.

o

By gosh! I'd like to know where we shall be at eight bells to-morrow."

"To hell with the bells!" replied John Hook, spitting vindictively into the sea. " I'm damned if all you chaps don't think you're sky-pilots! It'll want something more than a Death's-head Rooshian to put a white choker round me, as sure as my name's John Hook!"

Reuben continued to cut his tobacco methodically.

" Women are rum-uns, I'm blessed if they're not," said he after a spell. "To think as she should have turned it up, in the middle of the night too! Why, if she'd have held on another twelve hours, we'd have put her into Stockholm before morning. What was in her head, that's what I want to know?"

"Common-sense, that's what was in her head, mate. She's a rare plucked 'un if ever I sailed with one! Why, think of a little bit of goods like that, not more'n you could crush in your 'and easy, a little bit of goods like that agen all Rooshia and agen all the world! Where's she now?— ask yerself. Starvin' meybe, meybe in one o' them ground-floor hells they call a prison in these parts. And why's she dun it? Why, so as they shan't find her along wi' him. It's a cruel thing, mate, a bit of a gal all alone on a shore like this. I'm derned if I wouldn't sign for a twelvemonth, if that would bring her back agen!"

Reuben lit his pipe and got up to watch the distant warship.

"Well," said he, "wishin' ain't goin' to bring her back, John, and as for that I'd take my dinner more easy if yon lot would weigh. Supposin' they've no news of us, what are they doing there? Is it to see a fisher fleet? A shilling sail wouldn't swallow that."

"Who's asking of you to swallow it?" asked the other testily. "Of course they've got the news; but having the news and sighting us through ten feet of rock's a different story, ain't it? Who's to tell 'em we're lyin' here? Are we goin' to run up a fleg? or is one of them swabs a-fishin' out there goin' to beat in a mile to spy us out? Damned if you don't talk like a babe and sucklin'!"

Reuben smoked angrily and crossed to the other side of the ship.

"I wish the guv'nor was aboard," said he; "there ain't no good to be done over yonder, I'll swear. It's eight hours since she went now. You want a good eye to spy out eight hours, John."

"That's so, mate, always rememberin' as tides

o 2

don't go on like women's tongues, for ever and ever. If she ain't gone ashore afore this, she's somewhere in the flow of this channel, and there we'll find her. It'll take more than the skipper of Petersburg to stop me when it's an English lady that's between us. I'm derned if I wouldn't pull his nose for a shilling!"

He added to the volume of the sea again; but Reuben continued to gaze wistfully at the island upon which his master had landed in quest of the little fugitive. Paul had known no resting hour since she was gone. He understood that he had played for the great stake and had lost. He saw himself branded as a traitor by the men who had known him and loved him; cast out from the career of his ambition to these desolate islands; utterly alone at a moment when, with all his heart and soul, he yearned for the love which destiny had robbed him of.

"My little wife!" he had cried when they brought him the news. "I cannot lose you. God help me, I cannot live alone again!"

Haggard and worn and weary with grief, the man, who had dared all for a woman's love, learned that love was to come no more into his life. The cup had been snatched from his lips at a moment when he had first tasted the sweetness of the draught. He began to remember all that Marian had meant to him. He recalled her tenderness, her prettiness, the delight of that hour when he had whispered his love in the shadow of the bastions of Kronstadt. He swore to God that he would never see the sun again if she were not given back to him; he raged against his destiny; a voice whispered that the woman had left him to carry the plans of the great fortress to England, and there to sell them as she had first intended. To this voice he would not listen; and when the paralysis of despair had passed, a new activity, the activity of the quest, possessed him as a fever. "He would find her," he said, "though he lived and died on that desolate shore!"

One boat remained to the *Esmeralda*, the dinghy which she carried midships. He ordered them to lower it that no haven or creek or channel might remain unsearched. Reckless, defiant, caring nothing for prudence or pursuit, his voice was raised pitifully in many a rocky harbour and upon many a shore. The moan of the wind alone answered him. The desolate sea was unpitying.

At midday the yacht made an island, prominent amongst the others by reason of a curious girdle of outstanding rocks which defended it. It was here that the men first observed the Russian cruiser lying far out at sea. They warped their ship to one of the boulders of the rock, while their master, headstrong and not to be restrained, went ashore to see if the heights of the new land would help him to discover the missing boat and the little wanderer, whose purpose in flight was now becoming more clear to him. But the journey was fruitless. He looked out from the heights upon a sea dotted with crags and isles; often shining in still lagoons of sunlit water; showing here and there the hulls of fishing boats, but giving no other answer to his question. A great fear—the fear that Marian had, indeed, been taken by the cruiser—began to give place to the supposition that she had found a refuge upon the shore. Nevertheless, he continued to watch and to wait, and would not return to the yacht until the quick eyes of his companion perceived the danger of the place and of the scene.

"They have put out a boat, sir," said the man; "what's more, that's a signal gun."

A puff of white smoke floated up from the deck of the distant cruiser, and anon the muted roar of a gun was to be heard. Paul delayed no longer upon the island, but hastened to regain his ship and there to consult with those who, in their rough way, offered him so precious a sympathy.

"Well!" cried old John, merrily, when the dinghy came to view. "Ye have news, sir?"

Paul shook his head.

"The cruiser is putting off a boat; that is my news, John."

"To hell with the boat! What's a boat got to do with us?"

Paul laughed sadly while he swung up on to the deck of the *Esmeralda*.

"You are good fellows," he said, "and you have been true friends to me. It is no good to deceive you any more, and it would be wrong to bring trouble upon you. I am the one to answer for this business, and I am ready to answer. What happens now is nothing to me. But you, my friends, you must all go ashore and leave me to make my answer alone."

John Hook thrust his hands deep into his trousers' pockets.

"Look here, sir," he said determinedly; " if it's questions, I'm on that job. And let me arst you this—am I a Britisher or am I a furringer?"

He looked appealingly to the others, who said knowingly—

"Ay, ay; that's the question, John."

Paul laughed again.

"I do not care what you are," said he; "it is sufficient that you have been my friends."

"And friends we'll remain. Leave you here alone! Is my name John Hook? Is my port Swansea, or ain't it? Am I goin' ashore because a lot of lubbers cruise round and fire off a popgun? I'm derned if I don't blush like a gal to hear you say so, sir!"

Paul held out his hand and shook the great rough paw of the English seaman.

"I wish you were my countryman," he said. "If you will not go ashore, you shall stay with me to the end, and it shall be as God wills. I have few friends now. I have no longer a country."

His voice failed him, and he turned away, pretending to watch the coming boat which was now being rowed rapidly toward the shore. It was as though the messenger of destiny winged across the sea. The hand of Fate appeared to be thrust out towards him. There was sunlight for his eyes to-day, but to-morrow there would be darkness—the darkness of the pitiless reckoning. He saw himself carried back to Kronstadt in ignominy. He would stand alone, he said. The little head, which should have nestled upon his shoulder, was to comfort him no more. And he had no longer a reproach upon his lips. The friendship of the stout hearts that sailed with him was a thing precious to him beyond words.

The *Esmeralda* had been warped to a rock sufficiently high to conceal her mast from any passing ship. The hands clambered upon this rock when the dinghy was hauled up; and therefrom they watched the long-boat which the Russian warship had lowered. Phlegmatic as they were in word and deed, the steady approach of the strange craft set their hearts beating with suppressed excitement. They could not turn their eyes away; they watched her foot by foot as she drew toward them. Some even whispered schemes for their defence; others spoke of the skipper's pistol and of their own good knives. John Hook alone cried out upon such an idea, and his word prevailed.

"There's twenty men yonder if there's one," said he doggedly; "supposing as this is their port, do you think they're bringing umbrellas with them? My eyes and limbs, that's a woman's notion! And who's goin' to sit here for a Rooshian swab to play marbles with him? Not me, by thunder! But I'll tell you what, mates, if we cast off, and back out while they're coming round, there'll be three hundred yards between us before they wake up to it. And there won't be nobody on deck besides me for them to play at pigeons with. It's for the guv'nor to say; but I know what I should do if old Death's-head yonder was coming down my street."

" Ay, ay; John's right," cried the other.

" I leave it to you," exclaimed Paul, indifferently; " I care no longer. The time for that has passed."

They cast the ship free at the words and stood with boat-hooks to steady her. So great was the silence of doubt and expectancy that the sound of the men breathing was like a whisper of voices. Yard by yard the strange craft crept into the bay. They could see the cutlasses her men carried, could read the name upon her prow. The agony of doubt was scarce to be endured when the lieutenant in charge of the boat cried an easy, and his crew ceased to row. Then indeed Paul said that the hour was at hand, that the dream was done with.

For twenty seconds, perhaps, the long-boat lay still upon the lagoon. The men, watching and waiting upon the decks of the *Esmeralda*, shut their eyes and stood like figures of bronze. But that was the supreme moment; and when they had counted twenty, their hearts began to quicken with a tremulous hope. For the oars were dipped again ; and going about suddenly, the Russian boat made off towards the further side of the island. The sigh of relief from the watchers was almost a nervous titter. Paul found that his forehead was wet and cold with icy perspiration.

"It is not for us after all. I do not understand," he said.

"But I do," cried John Hook excitedly. "Look yonder, sir. D'ye see that white barge with three masts? It's a leper ship, I reckon. The monks aboard 'em load with lepers as we load with coal. They go from island to island until they've took a cargo, and then they head north for the 'orspital. That's what brings old Death's-head this way. He must have a patient for 'em."

It was as he said. The cruiser's boat was rowed straight to a lumbering barge-like ship which had appeared suddenly in the centre of the lagoon. Twenty minutes later the small boat was but a speck in the offing, and the men of the *Esmeralda* were at dinner.

CHAPTER XX.

THE SHIP OF THE GOLDEN CROSS.

THE strange craft which Marian had seen from the beach of her island lay, perhaps, a quarter of a mile from the shore. It had three masts, whereof two were very short, while the third was lofty and capped with a great golden crucifix which shone glitteringly in the crimson light of the setting sun. A brown jib, half lowered, flapped to the fitful breeze; and a vast mainsail, resembling in many ways the lateen sails of the South, half hid the decks from view. Marian observed that the colour of the vessel's hull was a dull white, ornamented with many crimson crosses and with that which she thought must be an inscription, though her eyes could not read the lettering. At the same time she could make out the figures of many men standing together upon the poop of the ship; and a long white boat, which had carried four of its crew to the beach, now lay with its bow upon the sands and its stern rolled by the breaking waves. Of the four men who rowed the boat, three sat still at their oars, but the other stood in close talk with the recluse whom Marian had watched and feared earlier in the day. She could see that the two men were asking the meaning of her visit to the island, for they pointed often to her own boat and walked a little way to examine it more closely.

Her first thought was to go out and speak with them, telling, if she could, of her condition, and begging them to give her passage to some more friendly shore. But a subtle instinct, which spoke of the unfathomable superstition of the Finns and of their cruelty when those superstitions were aroused, held her a little while to her place of shelter behind the great boulder, and therefore she watched the men. Much to her surprise, she perceived that the recluse was no old man, as she had thought, but one still in the springtime of life. His long flowing locks of black hair, and the coarse robe which clothed him, deceived her. She had never imagined a young monk. As for the other, he also wore the rough habit of brown stuff, but his hair was short and crisp, and his face was the face of an intelligent man. That he read the story of the visit aright she could not doubt. He pointed often towards the distant Gulf with a gesture which seemed to tell her that the secret, not only of her presence upon the island, but also of her flight from Kronstadt, was known to him; and this sent her back to the shelter of the higher rocks, where she stood trembling with a vague dread, not so much of the discovery as of the men.

The last of the day was ebbing at this time; the fitful dusk of northern latitudes gave gray hues to all things about her, so that the men upon the distant ship were as figures moving in shadow. A haze of night floated above the waters. She seemed to be the habitant of a strange world, an unreal world of fear and fantasy. The visit of the cowled friars to her shore accentuated her loneliness. She crouched upon the rocks and cried despairingly for her lover, as though some miracle would wing her voice across the sea. Never until that moment had she realised how this love had grown about her heart protectingly, so that without it the very fount of life ebbed and was dried up.

"Paul, my husband," she cried. "Come to me—I am alone—alone!"

Voices answered her, but not the voice of him she called. She raised her pretty head to listen, and she heard sweet, melodious music floating to her from the distant ship. It rose and fell as a song of the placid sea; a harmony of many voices united in the evening hymn. The rocks gave it back in lingering echoes. It was as though nereids had come up from the depths to hymn the setting sun, to greet the darkness and the hour of their amours. When the last note died away she continued still to hunger for those sweet sounds; but other singers raised their voices in turn to chant a dirge-like litany, and this was a true hymn to the darkness, so weird, so mournful, so full of the suggestion of death and after.

Marian shuddered at this new song, for it carried her back to the place of shadows. When she had listened to it a little while, the harmonies became more clear, the note of the sonorous voices deeper. She awoke to the fact that the singers, whoever they were, had left the ship and were coming to shore. Lanterns now cast their yellow light upon the pulsing swell. A flame of torches illumined weirdly the rugged faces of a company which seemed to have voyaged from some monastery of the ultimate seas. Anon, three boats touched the sands, and a band of men, all garbed in the pilgrim's dress, began to gather upon the shore and to congregate about some dark object which the shadows hid from the watcher's eyes. She perceived, to her surprise, that an acolyte in a cassock and cotta carried a brazen crucifix on high. Torch-bearers walked at his side. Thurifers swung censers, from which an odorous smoke floated perfumingly on the still air. Presently a procession was formed and began to wind its way to the cliff of the island. The dirge-like chant arose again. The burden which the men carried was no longer hidden from the watcher's eyes. She saw that it was a coffin. The monks had come ashore to bury their dead.

The procession advanced slowly, for the thurifers turned often to cense the coffin and the priest to sprinkle it with holy water. Solemnly and deliberately the singers set out for the grass plateau by the well from which Marian had drunk earlier in the day. She on her part stood white and trembling in the shadow of the cliff. Though it was plain to her that the men had not come to the island in quest of her, she feared the visitation as she had never feared anything in all her life. The hour, the misty twilight, the brown habits, tortured her imagination. She did not ask herself wherefrom such strange voyagers had come; her thought was to escape them, even at the risk of discovery. But escape was not to be. So close to her did the procession pass that she could have touched the cross-bearer with her hand. She beheld the faces of the monks and read in them the visual record of fasting and of an emaciating faith. One by one they passed her; here an old man bent with the penance of years, there a youth

"THE PROCESSION ADVANCED SLOWLY"

whose eyes were aflame with the light of visions; here a face that spoke of the withered flesh, there lips which had fed upon the luxuries of life and still hungered for them. And when the monks were gone up, others followed in the grim train—old men hobbling, women weeping, even children. Marian looked at the faces of these, and her heart seemed to be stilled. The mission of the ship was a mystery to her no more.

"They are the lepers!" she cried, and so tried to draw back from them, as though God would open the rocks behind her and hide from her terrified eyes the awful sights they looked upon.

CHAPTER XXI.

ACHERON OF THE WATERS.

THE procession passed slowly, for many stragglers followed the priests. The minutes of waiting were as hours to the terrified woman. Often the lantern's light flashed in her very eyes; she felt the hot breath of the lepers upon her cheeks; she thought their dreadful hands would touch her. Whence they had come, whose ship it was, she did not know. The story of the monks of the Northern seas and of their mission to the outcasts of the islands was unknown to her. She saw rather a visitation of spirits; the dirge was a sound as of the woe of life; the graves had given up their dead to haunt her. While she had the impulse to flee, to seek, if it must be, the refuge of the waves, the ghostly shapes still held her to the rock. Moaning voices of the lagging sick mingled with the melancholy song of the billows. She beheld the fanatical carousals of the desperate, who laughed like imbeciles, or cast themselves foaming upon the grass, or shrieked to heaven for the mercy of death. Far above on the heights the monks were digging a grave for him who had died at sea. Their litanies echoed as sweet interludes to the cacophonous cries below. She repented bitterly that she had not gone down earlier in the day and spoken with the recluse of the well. She remembered that she was a woman, alone with this rabble, upon whom God's curse seemed to have fallen.

At this time, no memory of the peril of the island troubled her. She thought no more that she might be left alone upon it; nay, she prayed that the sick might return speedily to their ship and leave her to the silence and the night. Hours seemed to pass before the monks came down from the heights again. She watched the lanterns dancing upon the hillside as a mariner watches a beacon of the shore. Often she said to herself, " They are coming now; I hear them." Then the litanies would begin anew; the garish yellow stars would be still again; the hoarse laughter or the weeping of some leper near to her would crush her hope. Childlike, she fell to counting, and said that when she had numbered a thousand the ship would sail. But of that employment she soon wearied; and, impatiently, she crept out a little way from her place of shelter and stood for a moment that the breeze of the sea might blow upon her heated face.

P 2

In that instant a leper observed her and sprang up with a loud cry to seize her by the wrist and drag her toward the open of the beach. It was as though the ultimate horror had gripped her, had come out of the darkness to embrace her in a loathly and indescribable embrace.

She dared not to look upon the man's face, but vaguely, for speech was choked and all her limbs were benumbed, she perceived that he wore a tattered green uniform and carried a knife stuck in a worn girdle. She heard a torrent of words poured into her shrinking ear; but had not Russian enough to interpret them. Once she thought that the man would have crushed her in his lusty arms, and then she knew that he said, "Thou art such as I have lost." When release of tongue came, she raised her voice again and again in shrieks of uncontrollable fear, and at this other lepers ran up to the place. Soon a rabble surrounded her, and the cry was uttered that she was a spy. From twenty throats she heard the fierce accusation, "The Englishwoman: kill her! into the sea with her!"

Women, ragged and blear-eyed, forced their way to the heart of the throng; young girls laughed hysterically and tried to strike her down; old men raised their sticks to beat her bloodless

ON TOWARD THE SEA HE BORE HER

face. She was carried on, she knew not whither;
countless eyes, shining with the fire of disease,
looked into her own; fleshless claws ripped the
dress from her shoulders; they would have torn
her limb from limb but for the strong arm of the
man who first had gripped her. But he, roused
to some dream of the days before the curse, never
once released his hold of her. He bore her
high above the throng; he answered their curses
with a madman's laughter; the blows fell upon
his own face; they were as a flagellation of straws
to him; women struck him; he forced them
back and trampled upon them. On toward the
sea he bore her. He had the strength of ten
men, the passions of the maniac aroused, the
maniac's purpose. They stood from him at last
terrified; the devils of their own superstitions
possessed him; the cries ceased, their sticks were
lowered; he was alone when he dragged the
woman into her boat and thrust it from the
shore.

Marian had shut her eyes when the crowd
first pressed upon her; she thought that this
was the moment of her death; she waited for
some blow which would still the life within her
and permit her to rise up in spirit above these
horrid sights and sounds. Strong as her desire
was for insensibility, for a trance of the mind,

she did not swoon, nor lose her sense of time and place, and of the peril. She heard distinctly the fervid ravings of the madman who defended her; his hot breath was upon her cheek; his loathly touch was a torture. But still she would not look at him. While the blood surged in her ears, and her brain whirled, and her limbs were paralysed, she had no wish for life or freedom, no hope but that death would be quick to come. When she felt the grip released and sank helpless from the man's arms, she was conscious still that he was beside her. She opened her eyes at last to discover that the boat was already some way from the shore. She could see the lanterns dancing on the hillside, could hear the voices of the priests above the clamour of the rabble. The man had saved her life, though whither he carried her, or to what Acheron of the night, she dare not think.

The leper was huge in stature and of great strength. He plied the oar with a giant's arms, so that the yacht's boat shot out quickly toward the broad of the lagoon. For the time being he appeared to have forgotten the woman at his feet. His words were incoherent and unceasing; he chattered horribly. Presently the island was but a blot upon the sea; the lanterns were twinkling stars. No longer were voices to be heard; the stillness of the night lay like a cloak upon the waters. Marian said that she was being carried out of the world. She shivered with the cold and the spray cast upon her face. Gradually there crept upon her a new dread—dread of him who had saved her. She feared to move, lest, moving, she might remind him of her presence. When he ceased to row she could hear her own heart beating.

For a spell the man stood gazing with wistful eyes to the shore he had left. Then suddenly he turned and uttered a great cry, for he had forgotten the woman; forgotten why he was in a boat at all, and how he had been driven from his companions. But now the impulse which had led him to clasp her in his arms was re-born. He sank upon his knees and whispered wild endearments; he stroked her hands gently as one strokes an animal; he pushed her wet hair from her forehead and held back her head that he might look into her eyes. The name by which he called her was, she imagined, the name of one who had been dear to him long years ago. When she would have drawn back from him shudderingly, the words of love gave place to threats and ravings; he seized her by both wrists, and would have kissed her upon the lips. She screamed with fear, and rolled from his embrace.

Long minutes passed before either moved. The leper had risen again and once more looked out into the night. Marian was sobbing hysterically.

"Paul," she moaned; "O my God! Paul, come to me!"

Faintly across the sea the answer came. She thought at first that she heard it in her sleep. But the madman listened with ears erect and hand stayed. Once, twice, the cry was raised; the hail of English voices. When the little wanderer understood that it was no dream, but that someone upon the sea had answered her, she seemed to hear the music of heaven itself. Courage came back to her in that supreme moment. She leaped up from the bows of the boat and sprang into the waters. A loud demoniacal laugh followed her as the spurning sea closed over her head. It was the laughter of the leper, who had forgotten her again.

The sea was still as a lake in summer; the moon, new risen, cast a glow of silvery light upon the sleeping lagoon. Marian felt the water cold and sweet upon her face. She had been a swimmer since her childhood; she swam now as one hunted in the seas. Onward toward the cry of English voices! God would not drag her down, she said; she thought already to feel her lover's embrace. Life might be before her yet—the life with him she had left. To-morrow she might nestle on his shoulder again and tell him that nothing now should carry her from his side. Though her clothes were soaked and weighty, though the gentle waves rolled often over her mouth, she swam on with courage unbroken. "I go to Paul," she said. "O, God help me — I cannot die here!" The nether world seemed open to receive her; but the stars shone above; the gate of heaven was her lamp in the sky. A future of love and affection was imagined by her awakened brain.

"Paul," she cried, "come to me—I will not die!"

There was a pathos of an eternity of suffering in the prayer; but the night of her life was at an end, and the God-given day was about to dawn. Even as she cried out, and thought that cold hands were dragging her down to the icy depths below, a boat shot out from the loom of the darkness; strong arms gripped her; she saw her lover bending over her, she saw the star-lit heaven; warm lips kissed her forehead; she was crushed in a close embrace

—the embrace of a man who held her to him as though never more in life should she escape his arms again.

"Beloved, it is I—Paul. Oh, God be thanked, she lives, she lives!"

Swiftly he bore her to the *Esmeralda* and to her cabin. She had no strength to speak to him, but holding both his hands, she fell into a sweet sleep, and the gardens of England were opened for her while she slept.

At dawn of the day the *Esmeralda* sighted in the far distance one of the warships of the Baltic Fleet. But old John hitched up his breeches at the spectacle, and expressed himself as he was wont to do.

"To hell with that," said he; "they're the wrong side of us this time, mates. We'll be in Stockholm by eight bells."

Old John spoke a true word.

CHAPTER XXII.

PRISONER OF LOVE.

ON the morning of the fifteenth day after the flight from Kronstadt, Paul sat at the open window of his apartment in the Strand. The bells of St. Martin's at Charing Cross had just chimed half-past nine; the streets below his window were alive with the hum of voices and the echo of steps. He had visited London once or twice in his days of tutelage; but this spectacle of massed humanity, of countless men surging towards the East in quest of the daily wage, was new and wonderful to him as when first he beheld it. That vast multitude, looking neither to the right hand nor to the left, what tragedies and comedies of life it played every day! All the notes of the social scale seemed written upon that human score. Spruce stock-brokers lolled in hansom cabs on their way to 'Change; sleek barristers thrust themselves through the press as though the briefs they had waited for these long years lay to-day upon their tables; clerks from the suburbs passed with slow step or fast, as the office hours dictated;

smart girls carried themselves proudly, buoyed up with consciousness of sex and environment; 'buses lumbered by with a harvest of human grain heaped upon their roofs; only the clergy dallied before the shop-windows or sauntered contentedly in the sunlight.

Paul had heard of London as an abode of gloom, a city without a sky, a mighty capital of fog and mists. This morning of a glorious spring gave the lie to the reproach. Notwithstanding that April had many days still to run, the sun shone warmingly: the air was fresh and sweet as though blowing upon the city from a perfumed garden. And to the sweetness of morning was added the comfort of the English rooms he had engaged for himself and his "sister" Marian. It had been a solemn compact between them that she should not communicate with her English friends, should not even see them, until that future they loved to speak of was something more than the dream of lovers. And she had respected the understanding as though it were a law to her.

"I owe my life to you," she had said; "I will see no one, speak to no one, until you wish it. But I must write to Dick."

"And tell them that you are in England!" he exclaimed, a little anxiously. "If you write, they will come here; they will ask you for your secrets. I know that you will tell them nothing; but I do not wish you to see them; I do not wish to meet the man who tempted you."

"I will not see him, Paul, dearest; God knows, if you asked me, I would never see him again."

She had begun to understand her lover wholly at this time; to understand him with that intimate appreciation of moods which nothing but the magnetism of one mind for another can make clear. Great as was his love for her, the thought that she carried in her clever head those secrets, of which he had been the guardian, haunted him now that she was in England, a free agent beyond the reach of the Russian. A soldier's creed of honour was ever upon his lips. "I will not betray my country," he said always. He knew that marriage would seal her lips for ever. But until they stood before the altar together he must rely absolutely upon her promise. What their future was to be, he scarce dared to think. The son of a Russian noble, he knew not how to serve. A stranger in a strange country, what miracle should give him livelihood? If he married at once, it would be to cast himself blindly upon the sea of life, trusting that some wind of destiny would carry him to a friendly shore. A great sympathy for her prevailed even above his passionate longing to call her wife.

"We are two children drifting," he said. "God alone knows where the journey will carry us; but we will be together always. You wish it, Marian?"

She put her arms about his neck.

"We shall not drift while I have a home in your heart," she said.

That was upon the day after they had arrived in London. They had gravitated toward the city; drawn there by no impulse that was defined, but only by the hope that London would befriend them. Much as Marian desired to see her child-brother again; yearn as she might for the lanes and villages of Devonshire, she did not speak of these desires to her lover. Had he asked her, she would have gone with him, on the day of their arrival, straight to some church, and there have given herself to him for ever. She welcomed the remembrance that it was hers now to play the strong part. She would help him and compel him to forget. For her sake he had cut himself off from friends and fortune. His courage, which had saved her at Kronstadt, here moved her to pity. A child lost in a maze of streets could not have been more helpless than the man she loved, cast out by fortune to this city of exile. She began to plan that she might work for him, might build the home of her promise. The desperate task did not affright her.

"If I had my health, if I could have the child near me, it would be easy," she thought. "These are the days when a clever woman earns a living for herself in London, and I have brains."

The ambition was well enough, but the execution lagged. They had come from Stockholm straight to this apartment by Charing Cross, and there, passing as brother and sister—no difficult achievement, since Paul spoke English fluently— they waited for the light. She obeyed his wish that her arrival should be kept a stern secret. Of her few friends in London, none knew that she had left Kronstadt. She did not write to the child; she never left her rooms. Paul, in his turn, remembered that one who had been a comrade of his student days, Feodor Talvi of Novgorod, was now at the Russian Embassy in Chesham Square. He wrote to him, and to his kinsman Prince Tolma, telling them of his condition and of his purpose. "I am no traitor to Russia," he wrote. "I am here to keep her secrets, not to betray them."

The letters were despatched, but many days passed and no answer was returned. On the fifteenth day, when Paul sat at his window waiting for Marian to come down to breakfast, he began to tell himself that his friends would be friends to him no more. He had thought his kinsman, Tolma, to be a man of broad mind and generous impulses, one who had lost a Russian's creed in the teaching of many cities. But the earnest appeal he had despatched to Paris remained unanswered. He said that the Prince was not in the city; he was at Monaco, or cruising in his yacht. Paul would not believe that one who had loved him as a son would desert him in this hour of misfortune. He shrank from the truth, and would not reckon with it.

Marian entered the sitting-room while he was still musing at the window. She crossed it with girlish step, and bent down quickly to kiss his cheek. Regardless of time or place, he sprang up and took her in his arms.

"Dear little one!" he said, "you bring me back to earth again. And you have roses on your cheeks to-day. There is no doctor like one's own country. You have slept, Marian?"

She would not tell him of her night of waking; nor had he eyes to see that the flush upon her cheeks was a flush of weakness.

"I sleep always," she answered, with a little laugh; "you must not worry about that."

He pushed her back from him, still holding her hands.

"Oh," he said, "and that is our new dress! Am I not a good modiste, little one? Is it not splendid? I shall open a shop here, and you will make my fortune."

She kissed his hands, and turned to the breakfast-table.

"I shall send you to buy my dresses when we are married," she exclaimed. "You won't mind them laughing——"

"I mind? Sapristi! Did I mind yesterday when I bought the 'triumph,' and twelve young ladies fitted it on for me, and the boutiquier himself carried it to the cab? Nom de Dieu! it was a procession, and I was the flag. You must lose your clothes again, and get another cold, Marian. It will amuse me to buy your dresses."

He had shopped for her on the previous day; for she carried no dresses from Russia, and Stockholm had furnished her with a poor wardrobe. Her promise not to go abroad in the streets of London she kept faithfully, as much from will as from weakness. The chill and horror of her night at the island of the Holy Well had eaten into her little store of strength. She feared that some dangerous illness would overtake her, and that he would be alone to wage the unequal fight.

Q

"You have letters, dear?" she asked him, while she poured out his tea and busied herself with his breakfast.

He shook his head a little sadly.

"Feodor Talvi cannot be in London; I shall hear from him the day he arrives. We were as brothers; he must listen to me at least. As for Tolma, it will be sooner or later. He is not a man of this city or of that. He makes the world his home, and wherever the sun shines, there is his fireside. But I know that he will help me when my letter reaches him. He cares nothing for other people's stories. He has called me his son since I was twelve years old. I wrote to him as to a father. While we wait for their help, we have two hundred pounds—your English pounds—to spend. When we have spent those, there is the *Esmeralda* to sell. I shall order her to the Island of Wight, where all your yachting people go, and she will bring us twenty thousand roubles at the least. They will give us time to think and to plan. I have thought a little already, and the way seems clearer to me. After all, a strong man does not starve when he is willing to work. I can teach the Russian language if the worst comes, and box the ears of little boys who will not learn."

He laughed merrily at the idea, and passed his cup for tea. She would not tell him that she could not share his hopes; her face wore a bright smile when she lifted it to look at him.

"You are making a home of England already," she said; "I am happy to think it is so. It will all come right by-and-bye, when I am strong and can work again. You must not forget me when you speak of your plans. I could not be an idle woman; I should go mad."

"You shall be the mistress of my house," he answered, with a touch of the old pride. "I am the heir of Tolma, and I shall know how to find a home for you."

"Yes, but while we wait, dear—there is no dishonour here in England because a woman works. You were not born for the things you speak of; you do not know the difficulties. It is I who have learnt how to face the world and not to fear what people call independence. Your friends may write to you, or they may not. But it will help us both if there are no drones in the hive. You will be happy because I am happy, and I shall come to forgive myself then."

"There is nothing to forgive," he said tenderly. "God knows, it is happiness enough to hear your voice all day, and to tell myself that I shall kiss you when the morning comes. By-and-bye I shall not wait for the morning—that will be when the priest has spoken. You understand, little one?"

They had risen from the table and stood together in the shadow. He drew her to him winningly and kissed her white face again and again.

" I understand, dearest—a little," she said, with a new flush upon her cheeks.

" A little—is it not more than that? You still ask yourself questions as you did at Kronstadt."

" Certainly, I ask myself questions—but not the questions of carnival."

" You want to run away again?"

" Oh, yes—when I am strong enough."

He looked into her eyes questioningly. The love of jest was written there.

" Arrivons!" he said; " where would you run to, here in London?"

"To the church," she whispered, and so hid her head upon his shoulder.

A knock upon the door of the room put them apart. She turned to the glass to straighten her hair while he tore open a telegram, which the slut of the house delivered triumphantly, as though she carried letters of gold.

"For the gentleming," she said, with great satisfaction, "and he's a-waiting."

Marian looked over Paul's shoulder to read the message.

"Is it from your friends, dearest?" she asked anxiously.

"It is from Feodor Talvi," he answered, while the hand which offered her the paper shook with pleasure and excitement. "I am to go to him at once. I told you that we were as brothers; read that, and write the answer for me. I will see him to-day—now. There are no more troubles, thank God!"

He began to search about for his hat and gloves; he did not see the shadow of doubt which flitted upon her face. When the message was written, she gave him instructions for his momentous journey to South Audley Street, where the house of Talvi was.

"You must take a cab, and it must wait for you," she said determinedly; "I have a good mind to pin a card inside the flap of your coat —or you will forget where we live. Do not let him keep you long, dearest."

"He shall not keep me an hour; he shall come here to be presented. We will all go to the great hotel to dine together. I told you that my friends would not desert me."

He babbled on incessantly while she picked threads from his new frock-coat and pinned in his buttonhole a spray of the lilies he had bought for her. When they had said good-bye for the tenth time, she watched him from the window, a manly figure, broad and confident, in the throng below. Many turned to look at one who carried himself with such a fine air; but he saw nothing save the white face at the window—the face for which he had dared all and had brought himself to this land of exile.

"She shall be my wife before the week has run," he said to himself as he went. "I forget the rest when she is near me!"

* * * * *

The hour of his promise passed swiftly, and found Marian still waiting for the sound of his steps upon the stair. A second hour was numbered, and a third. She began to count the minutes; she took her stand at last by the open window and scanned the faces of all who came eastward. But his face was not among them. When six o'clock struck, and the throngs were hurrying home again, and Paul did not return, there came to her suddenly the thought that some peril had overtaken him. That the hand of the Russian is everywhere active had

long been known to her. She began to blame
herself that she had permitted him to leave her.
Since that night of nameless horror upon the
sea, her shattered nerves were quick to bring
foreboding upon her.

"O my God!" she said at last; "if they
have trapped him here in London!"

Dusk succeeded to the sunshine of the day;
night loomed over the city; but Marian continued to watch at her window, and to pray
God that no ill had befallen the man she loved.

CHAPTER XXIII.

THE UNFORESEEN.

PAUL rested his gloved hand upon the doors of his cab; he smoked contentedly. For the first time since he had set foot in London the streets and the people were without interest to him. A boyish readiness to accept the possible for the actual had already carried him in his mind to the realisation of fine schemes. He was sure that fate would work some miracle of surprise for his particular benefit.

"I shall tell the truth; it is no good to conceal anything," he thought. "Feodor will write to the Prince at Petersburg and say that I am here in London protecting the secrets of my city. If they had kept Marian at Alexander, there would have been trouble with the English Government; possibly, they would have been compelled to release her, and then she would have returned here with all those plans in her head. I do not see why it should be so great an affair. I have done them a service, and they know that I am not a traitor. Granted that they will not restore me to my regiment, there is other work for a clever man to do. I might even go to the Balkans and serve Ferdinand or the Austrians. When they learn how small my offence is, they will not be too hard upon me. And I shall marry the little girl I love, and take her where these English fellows will not trouble her. Ma foi! what crowds, and not a soldier among them all!"

He was passing the Criterion at the moment. The crowd of idlers, the youth of bars and stage-doors, the sleek dandy, the hastening clerk, moved him to a fine contempt for their stooping bodies and undrilled gait. A soldier's blood had run in his veins from his birth. To wear gold lace and to carry a sword, to strut in the market-place, to serve the Czar—what other career was open to an honest man? Merchants and traders—he regarded them as so many licensed thieves. Priests were necessary to minister to the superstitions of the people and to pray for the sins of the army. Professions were all very well for little men and knaves; but they were not a career. As for himself, he had inherited wits above the ordinary; but it never dawned on him that they could be used to other ends than those of his regiment. There was no better scholar in Kronstadt, no more promising officer of artillery, but that, he said, was his good fortune. His wits would never have been awakened but for the music of the great guns and the clash of steel. Whatever lay before him, he determined to work to one end—the right to carry a sword once more, once more to be the master of the guns.

The cab, bumping roughly against the kerb, brought him back from the success of thought to the broken baskets of reality. He saw that they were in a narrow street before the doors of a large but ugly house, which had no ornaments for its windows and little paint for its railings. He paid the cabman the money which Marian had put into his hand, and rang the bell of the house timidly. A moment later he stood in a hall furnished with such exquisite taste, and so richly, that he could hardly believe it to be the hall of the house before which the cabman had set him down. But the man who opened the door was a Russian, and that reassured him.

"Count Feodor—is he at home?"

"He expects you. He is waiting."

Paul entered the house confidently. The magnificence of the ante-chamber astonished him, for he had lived his life in barracks; and such splendour of habitation as he had known was the splendour of palaces at Petersburg or of hotels at Paris. When he followed the footman up a broad flight of stairs and through a conservatory upon the first floor, the same richness of decoration and of ornament testified to the luxury with which Feodor Talvi had surrounded himself. The apartment into which he was shown at last, though of limited extent, was draped with exceeding taste. Dainty watercolour sketches gave brightness to the silk-panelled walls; lounges cunningly contrived were the emblems of ample leisure; flowers stood upon many little tables; a stained glass window hid from the eyes the ugly stone wall which bounded the garden of the mansion. Paul put his hat upon a sofa and sat down with a great air of content.

"These diplomatists," he said to himself, "they talk all day and dance all night. They are paid twenty thousand roubles a year for telling their neighbours that black is white. When there is any work to be done, they go home. Fichtre! it should be easy to tell lies for twenty thousand roubles a year. And Feodor has no need of them; he was rich always. He must be very rich now."

The footman left him when he had given his name, saying that the Count would be disengaged presently. Paul took up a Russian paper and read it through. It was a pleasure to be carried in spirit back to Petersburg and his home. He found himself thinking about his friends of yesterday—old Stefanovitch who had loved him, and Bonzo whom he had feared and never understood. Karl, too, and Sergius and the others—had one among them taken pity upon him and remembered that he had been a friend of the old time? The pathos of memory was very bitter. He was as a child shut out from his old home. Imagination kindled for him a fire burning redly upon the hearth; the rays shone upon the unpitying faces of those who had been brothers to him.

This occupation of regret carried him away from the house of Feodor Talvi, so that he forgot where he was and upon what errand he had come. When the little gilt clock upon the mantelshelf struck one, he put the paper down quickly and remembered with amazement that he had been an hour in the room. That rascal of a lackey must have forgotten to speak to the Count, he said. Impatiently he pressed the button of an electric bell, and it was answered immediately, not by the Russian who had brought him to the boudoir, but by an English servant, who seemed astounded to find a stranger in the place.

"You are waiting for the Count, sir?"

"If I am waiting!" exclaimed Paul, turning on

the man as he would have turned upon a default-
ing corporal, "I have been here an hour! Is your
master out, then?"

"I don't know, sir; I will ask, if you like—that
is, if you wish it, sir."

Paul stared at the man with astonishment. If
he had been in Russia, he would have laid his cane
sharply upon the shoulders of the rogue; but he
was not in Russia, and the English barbarians did
not permit a man to flog his servants. He was still
seeking a word when the lackey shut the door and
left him to reflect upon a state of civilisation so
monstrous.

The little gilt clock struck a quarter past one;
the man had not returned. There was no sign of
Feodor. Paul went to the door of the room and
threw it open. The house was silent as one of his
own cells at Alexander. He could hear a great
clock ticking in the hall below; there was a rumble
of passing carts from the street without, but of
human life within the house no evidence. He
returned to the boudoir and rang the bell for the
second time. To his amazement the Russian
answered him, and began at once to apologise.

"We expect the Count every moment," he said
stolidly; "my master is sorry to keep you waiting.
He has been called away. We are to offer you
lunch, Excellency."

Paul assented indifferently.

"It is a peep-show," he said with scorn: "first the English rogue and then you. I shall speak to the Count, and tell him that he has made a mistake. You should both dance in a booth—to the music of the whip."

The Russian listened without changing a muscle of his face—he was accustomed to a *rôle* of servility. When Paul had finished, the man set to work to clear a little table and to get the lunch ready. Then he disappeared once more, and another quarter was struck upon the bell.

"Sacré nom!" said Paul, pacing the room angrily; "the servants lie better than the master! If this is the house of a diplomatist, to the devil with the twenty thousand roubles!"

"My dear fellow!" cried a voice at the door, "do you know that the chair you are kicking was once the property of Napoleon?"

He turned and stood face to face with the intruder. A spectator would have said that the two men resembled each other as brothers of a house. Both were tall and finely built; both had flaxen hair and blue eyes; both held themselves as those trained in the school of the world. If the newcomer was slightly shorter than the captain of artillery, if his face was less sunburnt and more furrowed, that was to be set down to the life of the city and the Court.

"Paul—it is you then ?"

"Feodor—my friend !"

"You have been waiting here ?"

"A century !"

"The devil ! It is that rogue Demetrius again. You are hungry; *tais toi*, we shall lunch and talk afterwards. I have a thousand things to say; you have a thousand things to tell. I become a boy again at the sight of you !"

He talked, indeed, with a boy's enthusiasm, but said nothing of that great and engrossing subject which Paul desired so earnestly to broach. For the moment they might have been students together—students enjoying such a rare day of fortune that they ate the dishes of princes and washed them down with the wine of kings. Paul wondered, in the moments of silence, if he had, in truth, branded himself as an outcast and a traitor. For if that charge were true, how came it that he ate and drank with Feodor Talvi and was called brother by him ? He could not believe in such good fortune. "He does not know," he thought; "he will not call me brother when I tell him."

The dishes were many before luncheon was done ; champagne foamed in long Venetian glasses ;

the dainty manner of the service was beyond question. When the cloth had been cleared, Demetrius carried cigars and liquors to a little bower of palms in the conservatory. Paul found himself reclining indolently upon a sofa, while the Count curled himself up in a basket armchair which Sleep herself might have designed. For the first time since they had met, an embarrassing interlude of silence gave the men opportunity for recollection. Paul made up his mind that this was the time to speak; but before he could open his lips Feodor asked him a question.

"The young English lady—is she well?"

The question was astonishing, bewildering. Paul opened his eyes very wide, for he thought it was a jest.

"Oh, she is very well," he stammered; "that is to say—you know about her?"

The Count answered sympathetically—

"I know your story, Paul, my friend; I read it in a despatch four days after you left Kronstadt."

Paul took heart.

"If you know my story, you know also that I am no traitor to Russia; you know that I am here in London to guard her secrets."

"Exactly, or how could I receive you at my house? It was all clear to me from the first.

A pretty face, a clever little head, a bribe from the English Government; my old friend falls in love with the pretty face, and persuades the woman to deliver up to him all the plans she has stolen. He comes here to give me those plans, and to tell me that the woman may go to the devil, while he goes back to Russia."

The smile left Paul's boyish face. He stood up awkwardly against the mantelshelf.

"You do not understand," he said gravely. "It is not that, Count; there are no maps to be given up. Marian has none. I am convinced of it. When I left Russia it was to make sure that she did not see any of her friends—that she did not betray us. It is true that her father and mother died some years ago; but she has relations in London—the Englishman who tempted her. I did not wish her to meet those people. Judge me as you will for what is past, I have this to say, that, by God's help, I will never leave her side again!"

Feodor, no longer the diplomatist, but the man of the world, laughed good-humouredly.

"Oh," he said, "we are still in that stage, then. It is the second stage, I think. When I was the bel ami of 'La Superbe' in Paris, I took a course. You begin with a bad appetite and end by buying a pistol. Convalescence dates from

R

the moment when you present your pistol to your
brother at school and go out to dine at Voisin's.
Complete recovery is to hear with equanimity
that she, for whom you would have died a
thousand deaths, has married the leader of the
orchestra. Possibly, in your case, if you had
stayed in Russia, you would have been well by
this time ; but a change of air fosters these
complaints.   A month, even two months, may
be necessary now. And pity is a factor. Send
the girl back to her relations, since you know
that she has brought no luggage with her, and
enjoy London for a month. I can recommend
nothing better."

Paul took up his cigar and lit it. His hand
trembled undisguisedly. The love creed, chanted
by the man of the world, was a thing he had
ever despised. He knew well the impossibility
of convincing this dandy of a dozen cities of
the reality of his love or of the nature of it.
He would not try, he thought; he feared that
mockery might cast a false light on the name
so dear to him.

"Do not let us speak of Marian," he said
after a moment of silence; "you do not understand me, and I do not understand you. No
man has a right to say to another, you shall
love here or there. If you are my friend, you

will help me at home. You must tell me what they are saying there. God knows, I dare not ask myself that question. Have I any longer a name in Russia? Is there any friend of mine to speak a word for me? These are the questions I ask myself while I lie awake at night and remember Kronstadt. The night is punishment enough—believe me, Feodor."

The Count, who disliked emotion of any kind, looked foolishly at the fire of his cigar.

"My dear fellow," he exclaimed in the tone of the candid friend, "it is no good exciting yourself. And it would be absurd to tell you any lies. How can I know what they are saying now at Petersburg. Am I likely to find the expression of any sympathy in official documents? When a man runs away from his regiment without leave, and takes with him a young lady who has been occupied for a month or more in stealing the plans of his fortress, he must expect his friends to open their eyes. How could it be otherwise? We judge men by their deeds. As the thing stands, you, in the eyes of the authorities, share the woman's guilt; we, who are your well-wishers, cannot stoop to help you with the expression of false hopes. That you will ever return to Kronstadt I do not believe. The thing is out of the question. Discipline

R 2

would suffer and you would suffer. But I will not say that influence at Petersburg might not, at some distant day, restore you to the Emperor's service. It depends upon yourself and upon the course you take here in London. You will not expect us to join with any enthusiasm in a scheme for your benefit as long as you utter this ridiculous nonsense about marrying the Englishwoman and constituting yourself her protector. Oh, my dear Paul, do you not see that she is the soubrette of your opera, and that her tears are shed only while the curtain is up? By-and-bye she will be supping with the leading tenor, while you are back in your own country and are ready to thank Heaven that you have done with her."

Paul bit his lip. He was within an ace of losing his temper and of quitting the house.

"It is a lie!" he said doggedly; "there is no better woman breathing. If you knew her, Feodor—if you were my friend, you would not say these things. I came here thinking that you would help me; I am sorry now that I came."

The Count sank deeper into the cushions of his chair.

"Du calme, du calme!" he cried, with the air of one who is much amused. "We are at the third stage now, and these are the symptoms. While I knew 'La Superbe,' I had not a friend in Paris. There was not a man whose throat I did not wish to cut. See, mon ami, how these diseases resemble each other. As I live, you will fight me before dinner-time!"

"No, indeed," replied Paul very quietly; "I cannot quarrel with you, Count. If your creed of life is not mine, I do not complain of that. We will talk of it no more, for I am going home. It was a promise to her. She will be waiting. I said that I would be away an hour, and three have passed."

A shadow of anxiety crossed the Count's face.

"Oh, you must not talk about going," he exclaimed earnestly, "and you must not think me unfriendly. What has passed is nothing. We will talk of serious things presently, and you shall meet one better able to advise you than the mere diplomatist who sees everything through the glass of office. If you think that mademoiselle will be anxious, write a little letter and the man will take it. You will find pens and ink in the library on the next floor. I am going to smoke here until you return. It would be folly to go away now, at the beginning of it."

Paul stood irresolute, but the Count touched

a gong at his side, and the Russian appeared once more.

"Demetrius, show the way to the library. His Excellency will give you a letter; see that it is delivered at once."

The library was a small room furnished prettily, with many books chiefly in French. Paul wrote his letter quickly—a letter of love and hope. He had met Feodor; the Count was his friend still; he was waiting for another to help him to some position of honour and emolument—all this he honestly believed as he wrote it. Never for a moment did it dawn upon him that he was the victim of a trick. He was convinced that the note would be delivered at once. He did not know that Demetrius would carry it so far as the kitchen of the house and there burn it in the stove. When he returned to the conservatory a smile of content was upon his face. It was good to have found a friend again. He determined to show a greater gratitude to the Count; but the words he wanted would not come to his lips. Nor was the reason far to seek. When he descended the stairs, whom should he see with Feodor but old Bonzo himself—the Bonzo of Kronstadt; the Bonzo whose name had struck terror into his heart so often; the Man of Iron whom all feared.

The Colonel sat upon a basket sofa. He wore a black frock coat with flowing skirts; his trousers were grey; his tie was a tremendous bow in the French fashion, *négligé* and ample. He smoked a black cigar and sipped a glass of absinthe. When he saw Paul, confused and hesitating, upon the threshold of the conservatory, his little eyes twinkled merrily, and he held out a great paw, as though to give the younger man confidence.

"Le voici!" he exclaimed boisterously, "le voici! the renegade, the traitor, who has brought me all the way from Petersburg!"

Paul shook the outstretched hand timidly. The room seemed to dance before his eyes.

"You here, my Colonel—you?" he repeated, with broken words. "You have come to London to see me?"

"If I have come to London to see you! Do I make the Cook's Tour then? Am I here to visit the Westminster Abbey—have I the tourist's suit? Look at me—Bonzo—and ask why I come?"

He put the question in a voice of thunder— the voice Paul had heard so often on the ramparts of Kronstadt. But the note of jest mingled with a deeper chord, and the two who listened to him laughed when he laughed.

"I should not call it a tourist's suit," said the Count, surveying the tremendous proportions of Bonzo's coat; there is too much cloth in it. They don't make a fortune out of you, Colonel—those tailors."

Bonzo nodded his head approvingly. He was a stranger to civilian dress, and his new appearance amused him.

"Behold!" he said, "it is a coat for my son and for my son's son. I have worn it twice in fourteen years. It is only a barbarous people that would wear a coat like this. Sit down, my friend, Paul, and see how I degrade myself for you."

He thrust a low chair forward, and Paul sat down, hoping he knew not what, afraid to ask why the Man of Iron had followed him to the land of exile.

"You are well, my Colonel? You had a good passage?"

"I am very well, my son."

"You stay in London long?"

"Until I hear that a foolish young man has come to his senses again."

Paul flushed. There came upon him irresistibly the impulse to appeal to this strong man's pity.

"Oh," he said, "you do not think me guilty,

Colonel? You do not believe that I am a traitor to my country?"

"Du tout, du tout, my son; you are no traitor—you have not the brains."

Paul stopped as though one had shot him. The eloquence of pity, which had inspired him in thought, deserted him at the first word of that ironical response. As well ask mercy of the tomb as of the Man of Iron.

"It was not a question of brains!" he blurted out presently. "I am not clever, my Colonel, I know that, but I am no traitor to Russia."

"Pah!" said old Bonzo, a little severely; "traitors do not run off with chorus-girls and then say they could not help it. You are a fool, my son; you have not the wisdom of the boy! What, when you had the woman in Alexander, when she was alone with you, when you could have made love to her all day, you bring her back here to her friends, you cut yourself off from those who love you, and then say that you did it for us! Oh, it is a story for a fairy-book."

Bonzo spoke with a strong man's contempt for the folly of the child. Paul shuddered at his words. The horrible suggestion—for he knew well what the other meant—fired his blood. He could have struck the speaker on the mouth.

"Colonel," he asked in a low voice, "you knew Mademoiselle at Kronstadt, and yet you are ready to say these things of her!"

"Certainly I am ready. Would you have me cry that she is of noble birth? Shall I raise my hat when I mention the name of Stefanovitch's governess, the daughter of an English *batushka*, a village priest at fifteen hundred roubles a year? What, a woman who played with you as I play with this leaf; who brings you to England to draw for her the maps which she had not time to draw when she was with us; who will laugh in your face presently and tell you to go to the devil—is this the one that Tolma's heir would marry? Pah! I have not the patience to speak of it!"

Paul picked up a cigarette and began to roll it in his fingers. He was unable to answer such an argument. Bonzo, he made sure, would never understand him; the hopes he had placed in his friends were shattered at last; they did not know Marian; they would never know her. He was still searching for his reply to the accusation when the Colonel spoke again, but with less heat.

"À la bonne heure!" he said, "I am not

here to scold you. We will say good-bye to this day of folly, for it is done. To-morrow you will leave London for Paris, my son. It will be the beginning of your journey to Vienna, where you will stay until this madness is forgotten. After that we shall appeal to the Emperor. His clemency may find for you some duty in the East. If you have suffered, those who love you have suffered too. Even I—Bonzo—could I hear of this, and forget that, of all at Kronstadt, you alone were a son to me? You shall be a son to me once more—when you have left England."

Paul stood up as the speaker continued. An undefined dread of some calamity about to overtake him prompted him to speak.

"Colonel," he said, "I cannot go to Paris with you to-morrow. I cannot leave England. Mademoiselle is waiting for me now. I thank you with all my heart for your promises, but the day for them is past. I think of Russia no more. I shall find a home here. Some day you will understand me."

Bonzo waved his arm dramatically.

"Sit—sit," he said; "this is not a theatre, Captain Paul. You are in Russia here. This house is our house. It is the Emperor's house Your English friends may come, but we shall not let them in. Be reasonable, and make up your mind that mademoiselle must wait a little longer."

Paul looked from one to the other with dazed eyes. Count Feodor had risen, and stood with his back towards the window; the Colonel's face was not to be read.

"I do not understand!" he exclaimed excitedly. "You would not keep me here against my wish, Colonel?"

Bonzo laughed ironically.

"For a few days," he said, with a gesture of indifference, "until you come to your senses, Captain. Meanwhile, if mademoiselle is waiting, send another little note."

In that moment the truth flashed upon Paul. He stepped backward as though seeking a way of escape; there was the look of a hunted animal in his eyes when he turned to the master of the house.

"My God!" he cried, "you would not do this, Count! You have no right to do it. I must go back to my house. I tell you that she is waiting for me."

Bonzo answered him by striking a gong at his side.

"My son," he said sternly, "she will wait many days yet. It is the duty of your friends to save you from yourself."

"SILENTLY, DETERMINEDLY, THEY FELL UPON THE FUGITIVE, AND THREW HIM
TO THE GROUND" (p. 300).

The deep note of the gong echoed through the silent rooms of the house like an alarum. The three men—for all had risen—stood facing each other. They knew that the time for words was past. As for Bonzo, he had ceased to smile; anger and determination were to be read in his eyes. He looked around him with the air of one who has planned everything, and whose plan is to be put into execution.

"You are mad, Captain Zassulic, and we shall cure you," he repeated triumphantly. "To-morrow we set out, but not for Vienna. The fortress of St. Peter shall be your hospital. Fool that you were to pit your wits against mine."

He raised his hand to point threateningly, and, as if in instant answer to the signal, the conservatory was filled with troopers in the uniform of the Russian service. Silently, determinedly, with great strength, they fell upon the fugitive and threw him to the ground. So sudden was the attack, so swift had been the sequence of word and of event, that Paul was a prisoner in their arms even while the thought of escape was shaping in his mind. For a moment he struck at them with the strength of ten men. Agony and despair gave him courage. The whole bitterness of life seemed to be his portion.

"Marian!" he cried. "O my God, let me go

to her—you kill me—I suffocate—let me go to her
—let me go——"

A strong arm, the arm of a giant, stifled the
broken cries. The whole landing seemed to be full
of men. Though the captive struck right and left,
clutching at this object and at that, they carried
him swiftly from the place up and still up to the
prison of the garrets. He beheld other landings
and the interiors of bedrooms poorly furnished,
the stairs were stairs of marble no longer, the light
of the fuller day fell upon his face through a
frosted dome of glass. When they flung him down
at last, with blood upon his hands, and torn clothes,
the light was shut swiftly from his eyes. He lay
in utter darkness, and he thought it the darkness
of hell. For he knew that the unpitying hand of
the Russian had fallen upon him even in England
—the England for which she whom he loved had
longed so earnestly.

CHAPTER XXIV.

TOWARD THE LIGHT.

MARIAN awoke from a troubled sleep when the clock of St. Martin's Church was striking a quarter past four of the morning. She had not meant to sleep at all, but weakness prevailed above her misery, and for an hour she was carried in her dreams back to Alexander and to the nameless horror of her cell below the sea.

When she awoke she was still sitting in her low chair by the window, but the cold of dawn had stiffened her limbs, and the burden of the night and its weariness lay heavy upon her heart. Nor could she bring her mind at the first to remember why she was not in her bed, or how it came to be that she looked down upon the silent streets at such an hour. When memory helped her, it was swift and terrible. She rose to her feet and opened the door of their little sitting-room. Had Paul come back to her? she asked herself. Why did he wait? What new ill had overtaken him? God, if he should be dead!

A tortured, helpless woman, worn with suffering and doubt, she crept along the darkened passage until she stood at his bedroom door. It was wide open. She could see the bed, but no one had slept in it. Scattered here and there were the few things he had purchased since they had been in London—a pair of slippers, a little dressing-case, a writing-desk. A bunch of violets he had worn when shopping for her two days ago stood on his washhand-stand. She took it up and kissed the faded flowers; she knelt at his bedside and prayed, a woman's prayer, that the day might bring him back to her.

It was strange, at this time, how her sense of dependence upon the man was magnified and made real to her. A year ago the truth that she stood alone in the world would have been a matter of indifference to her. But that day had passed. While she had no exaggerated notions of Paul's cleverness, while she knew him, heart and mind, he remained the idol of her dreams and of her love. She had trembled when he held her in his arms. Her first waking thought had been for him; she had won sleep often with his name upon her lips. The past years of loneliness, of struggle, of poverty, seemed removed by ages from her present life. If there had come to her sometimes the reflection that this whirl of events was unreal and false, that she was deceiving herself, that the reckoning must be paid, she brushed the thought aside. She was a woman, and she had learned to love.

The house was quiet with the stillness of the hour before the dawn. Without, the steely gray light fell upon shuttered windows and silent streets. Even great London nodded. Her gaudy ornament of gold and garish painting had become subdued and shabby; immense buildings loomed up as though the sun had shaped them from the mists. Save for the passing carts, or the rumble of a wagon on its way to market, or the fleeting figure of some ragged and homeless creature awake once more to the hopeless life of thousands, she might have looked down upon a city of the dead. Those who had passed and repassed while the sun shone—whither had they gone to sleep? What change of fortune had they known since yesterday? Who among them would rejoice with the day? How many would know the day no more? The very emptiness of the city awed her. She was afraid of the stillness. Not one in all those millions would stand at her side to help her. She remembered the child, and thought of him sleeping in a house

S

of sunshine and of flowers, but the remembrance was bitter, for her courage was broken. The old way of life was closed for ever. She would go hand in hand with little Dick, but there would be tears upon her face.

Seven o'clock struck, and the sun shone upon the city. People flocked to the great railway stations ; cabs began to loiter by the pavements ; she heard the scream of whistles and the cry of the newsboys. It was a relief to her, this surging of the stream of life. She began to reckon with herself as she had not reckoned since she left Kronstadt. If Paul did not return during the morning, she resolved that she would go to Scotland Yard and tell his story, in so far as it could be told without the surrender of her promise. A woman of clear and quick thought, she scouted the trivial suggestions which desire to deceive herself had prompted. Taking new courage of the morning, she refused to believe that her lover was dead or that an accident had overtaken him. An echo of the truth dinned in her ears. "It is the hand of his own countrymen," she thought, "he has been lured from here by a trick." And then she remembered that these things were not to be done in England. A glad pride in the might of her own country quickened her heart.

" I will save him!" she said; "I will go to them
and learn the whole story."

Her course would have been easier if she
had known Paul's intentions when he left her.
It was in her mind that he had gone to the
Russian Embassy; she remembered that he spoke
of South Audley Street, but could not recall the
number of the house.

She said that she would get her breakfast and
go afterwards to the Embassy in quest of news.
If none was to be had there, it would be time
to consult with the people at Scotland Yard.
True, she had given Paul her word that she
would not go out alone; but the promise was
made for a set of circumstances other than these.
His liberty, his very life, might depend upon her
breaking that promise. A great desire to be up
and away at once took possession of her. It was
hers now to play the strong part. Nevertheless,
the hope that she might hear his step on the
stair before the clock struck again held her to
the place.

" He has stayed at the Count's house all night,"
she argued childishly; " it was necessary, and he
is among friends."

At eight o'clock she dressed herself, wearing
the pretty blouse that he had bought for her,
and coiling up her wealth of brown hair

s 2

picturesquely above her white face. She sighed often when she looked into the shabby glass, and asked herself how it came to be that a man had cast off country and friends for her sake. Very few in the world cared whether she lived or died. She did not wonder at that. Her life had been one long battle with circumstances; the smile her face had worn during the years of childhood was but the cloak which hid the scars of mental ill and oftentimes of defeat. Yet here was one to stand among the multitude and to say " Thou art the woman." The mystery of love baffled her.

It was nine o'clock when she finished her cup of tea and found herself ready to go out. She had but a few shillings in her pocket; their little store of gold was locked in Paul's trunk, yet she would not stop to reflect upon that new trouble which lack of money must bring to her presently. Glad in her way to escape the confinement of the stuffy room, rejoicing that her errand was for her lover's sake, she descended the stairs with quick step. But at the street door she stood irresolute; and when she had looked about her an instant, she returned hastily to her room, and went to the window to watch.

A carriage drawn by a pair of magnificent grey horses was the secret of her irresolution.

It stood before her house at the moment she would have begun her errand. She saw that the master of the carriage, a white-haired old man, slight and slim, but with the face of an aristocrat, was about to send the footman to her door. Instinct told her that here was one of Paul's friends. When the footman waited in the street below, she had the impulse to run down, fearing that the carriage would be driven away before she could tell Paul's friend what had happened. She was still wavering when the slut of the house entered the room, holding in her dirty fingers the card of Prince Tolma.

"It ain't for you; it's for the gentleming," she said, wiping a smut from her forehead. "I told 'em as he'd gawn out to supper, and hadn't come back yet."

Marian brushed her aside and ran down the stairs with the step of a schoolgirl. Care for her own dignity was forgotten. She arrived in the street breathless and with flushed cheeks. It was in her mind that this stranger would save her lover.

"Paul is not here," she said excitedly; "he left me yesterday to visit Count Talvi, and has not returned. I fear that something has happened. He would not leave me without a word. I am Marian Best, and I have heard your name so often. If I might speak to you for a little while——"

She stood panting and expectant, while the old man regarded her with wondering eyes. Apparently the spectacle pleased him, for, of a sudden, he grunted like an animal and called to the footman.

"John, I am going to get out."

With great pomp and ceremony, after the unwrapping of rugs and laborious changes of posture, the Prince wormed himself from his seat.

"My dear," he said apologetically, "you must give me your hand. I am an old man—and your English wines do not love me. Is it far to mount? —there are many stairs?"

Marian blushed.

"We are not rich," she said diffidently; "we feared to go to an hotel——"

"Du tout, du tout," said the Prince; "we must find another apartment for you. The sun up there will scorch that pretty face. Ma foi, we go to heaven itself!"

A friendly banister and the strong arm of the footman dragged the burden to the heights. Marian followed with a sense of relief such as she had scarce known in all her life. It was as though a strong hand had been thrust out to her from the shadows of the great city. The tone, the gesture, the kindly eyes of this old man, the easy air of command and authority—these won upon her confidence.

The Prince entered the shabby little room and waddled to an arm-chair. He sank in it with a pathetic sigh of gratitude. Drops of sweat stood upon his bald forehead. He mopped them up with a tremendous handkerchief; his breathing was stertorous and rapid.

"It is a vapour bath," he exclaimed between his gasps; "you shall send for a shampooer, my dear. Or if you will not do that, you shall give me a little of the red wine I see upon the buffet there."

A flask of Australian wine stood upon the sideboard. Marian half filled a tumbler, and diluted the wine with soda-water. She had not noticed the poverty of her surroundings before. The coming of the aristocrat, his spotless clothes, his grand air, showed them in all their nakedness.

"I am sorry," she said, moving about with girlish activity; "I fear our stairs are dreadful. If it had not been that I knew you were Paul's friend——"

"Tut, tut," replied the Prince, taking the tumbler in his hand; "it is a recompense to see you in the room. There is no other ornament necessary, my dear—your eyes and the sunshine. If I were a young man, I would come here every day to see you. We do not count the rungs of the ladder which leads up to Paradise."

He swelled with gallantry, remembering the days which had carried him, hungering for love, to many a garret of old Paris. When he had emptied his tumbler and put it down, he began to speak again, leaning forward heavily upon his gold-mounted cane and staring so hard at his little hostess that her cheeks flushed crimson,

"So you are Mademoiselle," he said, nodding his head cunningly, "and you have brought my boy to England, and it is for you that he has forsaken his friends and turned his back upon his country. Well, my dear, I should begin by scolding you. I meant to scold you when I came here. But I am helpless, you see—so come and sit by me and we will talk a little while."

He pointed to a little stool, and she obeyed him, sitting almost at his feet. Never in her life had she met one whom she would have trusted so implicitly. Her own father—long dead—the man of dusty books and monotoned sermons, had awakened in her but pity. The fine face of this noble Russian, his soft and winning voice, his kindly gesture, inspired her to ask herself what her own life would have been if such a man had brought her into the world.

"You are very kind to me," she said simply; "it is a long time since I have found a friend. I think sometimes that I shall never find another. I cannot call Paul my friend; he is more than that. But then, he has left me here——"

Her cheeks reddened and she paused. Tolma patted her arm encouragingly.

"Do not be afraid to speak to me," he said. "I know your story, but it comes prettily from these pretty lips. You do not call Paul your friend; he is more than that. Ma foi, I would disown him if he were not!"

"I love him," she answered, taking courage of herself; "whatever he may do here, I could not blame him. He has given up everything for me— God knows how much I regret it if it is not for his good. Yet how can a woman answer such a question? How is she to read the depths of a man's love? If you and his friends wish him to leave me, if you think it is in his interest to do so, I have no right to stand between you. It would be happiness to know that he is happy."

Tolma moved restlessly in his chair. He had come to carry his heir from the trap into which he believed that he had fallen. He had come to convince Paul that the woman was a charlatan, an

impostor, the tool of the English Government.
When he hastened back from Paris, it had seemed
to him that his mission was the easiest in the
world. He flattered himself that no man knew
women as he knew them. He thought that he
would find his nephew with some notorious servant
of the spies of Europe—a chorus-girl, the wife of a
chevalier d'industrie gone bankrupt, the partner
of a baron snapping up unconsidered trifles. Ten
words with her shattered that hypothesis. "She
is an English lady—she is honest," he said to
himself; "we shall have trouble."

"You are a pair of children," he exclaimed,
cutting Marian short in her protests; "it is all a
play to you—the ships and the armies of Russia
are your toys. And yet, like your elders, you can
think of the money."

She was silent at the rebuke.

"Yes," he went on very seriously, "you can
think of the money, children that you are. What
you have done, mademoiselle, is a great crime
toward my country. If I did not believe the story
which Paul has told me, if I did not say that there
are excuses which must suffice when a woman is
the offender, nothing would keep me in this room
even for an hour. But I am not like those others.
I know men. I know women, vous savez. To
me they are the pieces upon the board. I have

seen so many put in the box; a few years more or less and destiny will have done with me. You are young, and your life is before you. I shall see that it is a pleasant life. You will live here in your England. Paul will go with me to be my companion in Paris. I like young faces; I am lonely in age. If it rested with me alone, I might make other promises for the future. But I must win a way for Paul to return to his country, and to return with honour. Do not think me harsh. I speak as the friend of you both. It cannot be otherwise: it is the only way."

Marian sat very still and white and silent. She thought herself in that instant to be abandoned of God and man. And yet she did not turn from the sacrifice.

"It is for Paul," she cried bitterly. "If there is no other way, let it be so, and God help us both!"

Tolma abhorred the spectacle of a woman distressed unless his were the hand to wipe away the tears. The fair, girlish figure at his side, so slight, so pitiful, created for him a boyhood to be lived again in an instant of thought. He drew Marian's head upon his knee and stroked the curls through which the hardly checked tears glistened.

"My child," he said gently, "if an old man

could work a miracle, assuredly it should be worked to-day. But what would you? If we wish Paul's name again to be known in Russia, shall not we make this sacrifice gladly? While he is with you—when he is your husband—they will say, 'Ah, she loves him for what he is worth to her.' They will declare that you have not all the maps you want to sell to your English Government, and that Paul will make them for you. By-and-bye you will laugh at him, and find another officer of artillery and another Kronstadt. That is what they will say."

Marian smiled through her tears.

"Poor Paul," she said; "if he had to live by making maps of Kronstadt, we should starve, Prince."

Tolma looked at her searchingly.

"You do not think that he is clever?"

"Oh, yes, he is clever, but not in that way. He would laugh if he could hear you. I do not believe he sleeps at night for thinking that I should tell someone the things that I know. He came here at first to be quite sure that the memory he says I am cursed with should not do Kronstadt any harm. He feared that I would draw the maps."

"The maps? But you have not got any maps; they were all burnt. He told me so."

"He told you the truth; but you cannot burn

the memory. I could draw Kronstadt now, this instant. I could place every fort and every gun. If I did not love Paul, my drawings would make me a rich woman, Prince."

Tolma sat very still. He was debating quickly a hundred possibilities The girl had struck every weapon from his hand. If her tale were true, she had struck every weapon from the hands of her enemies in London.

"It may be so," he said, with the politest possible suggestion of doubt, "it may be so, my child; but who will believe a story like that?"

"I ask no one to believe it. Why should I? What have I to gain?"

She drew back from him, and, rising, went and stood by the window. The sun of morning flashed upon her white face and gave threads of gold to her tumbled hair. Tolma saw the child no more; a woman, self-reliant, proud, and beautiful, now answered him.

"What have I to gain?"

She repeated the question with just a *soupçon* of mockery in her tone. She did not forget that she was in England. The strong arm of her own country stood between her and the Russian. The man on his part was ready to appreciate the drama of the moment and to act up to it.

"Mademoiselle," he said, struggling to his feet and posing threateningly, "you have a husband to gain."

"A husband! Oh, Prince, you jest."

The woman of Kronstadt spoke—the woman who had been willing, before love weakened her hand, to strike a blow at the Russian in his very holy of holies.

"You jest, Prince," she said again, with the air of a grand dame; "what is more, you do not believe me."

Tolma answered her by banging the table with his cane.

"Mademoiselle," he exclaimed, "I jest so little that if you will prove your story I will make you Paul's wife to-morrow."

It was her turn now to open her eyes in wonderment. But he continued without pause—

"Do you not see that they have taken him from you because they believe you want his secrets? Prove to them that the secrets are yours, not his, and they will move heaven and earth to shut your lips. A child would understand that. You are a free woman in your own country; who can prevent you speaking where you will? But the wife of Paul Zassulic—will she betray Russia! Ma foi, the boy's eyes are better than ours now! He will cheat Bonzo yet and I shall be there to enjoy it. And he will be the husband of a clever woman, mademoiselle. Do not contradict me; I, Tolma, say it, and I am never wrong. You shall be my daughter. You shall live in Paris with me—when you have proved the story."

Lack of breath alone put a curb upon his eloquence. Marian listened to him as she would have listened to one who spoke of miracles. It had been upon her lips to tell him of her promise to Paul, her promise to keep the secrets to the day of her death; but love working in her heart silenced her. She could not shatter the cup raised so unexpectedly to her lips.

"I will prove my story when and where you will," she said with dignity. "Give me time to get pen and ink, and I will prove it now."

Tolma raised his hand.

"Not here," he said, with a gesture of an actor; "to-night, at the house of Count Feodor. My carriage shall fetch you. Fear nothing; you have the word of Tolma."

He waddled down the stairs, calling loudly for "John." Marian stood as one in a trance; but it was a trance of joy.

CHAPTER XXV.

THE WORD OF TOLMA.

IT was the evening of the day. Three men waited in the great drawing-room of Count Talvi's house in South Audley Street. The silver clock upon the mantelshelf had just struck nine. Its ticking was the only sound to be heard.

Of the three who waited, Tolma alone sat at his ease. He lounged in a great chair and smoked Russian cigarettes incessantly. A glass of Chartreuse at his elbow went often to his lips. There was a complacent smile upon his face, the smile of a man who has played a great card and waits for his opponents. He looked ever and anon at Bonzo, the second of the three, moving in and out of the shadows which the dim light of shaded candles cast in dark patches upon the heavy carpet. But Bonzo was unconscious of the Prince's gaze. His hands were linked behind his back. He did not smoke. He paced the room restlessly. If he had eyes for anything, it was for a white sheet of paper spread out upon a writing-table in the alcove of the window. There his glance rested often, as though some wonder would be wrought by an unseen hand. He feared that lines would appear upon the paper.

Count Feodor, the third of the men, sat upon a sofa near the door. He had a Russian newspaper in his hand, but he did not read it. His eyes turned often toward the silver clock. He seemed to be waiting for someone who should break the silence of the room. When, at five minutes past nine, a carriage was heard at the door below, he rose with a little sigh of relief. At the same moment, Bonzo stood quite still and uttered an exclamation of satisfaction.

"Ha," he said, "they have come then."

"You mean that *she* has come," said Tolma, with a slight emphasis for the pronoun.

"I wait and see," replied Bonzo diplomatically; "I expect nothing, Prince, from a woman."

"And yet you owe everything to one, my dear Colonel."

Bonzo resumed his sentry duty, but at the door he stopped suddenly. A lackey was there to announce a guest.

"Mademoiselle Best," cried the fellow in a loud voice.

Marian entered the room upon his heels.

T

She wore a black French hat, becoming and unobtrusive. The cape, which Paul had bought for her, sat well upon her shoulders. Her gown was new and rich and in excellent taste. Tolma chuckled when he saw it, for he had caused it to be sent to her that very day. He said to himself that, gowned thus, this English girl might hold her own in any room in Europe. There was about her a dignity of presence, a sweet graciousness which no mere childish prettiness of face could rival. She seemed born to command. Nor did she betray the fear which had dogged her steps when she set out for the house of Feodor Talvi. She had been ready to take the word of Tolma, and he would answer for her safety.

"Bravo! bravo!" he cried, struggling painfully to his feet; "I said that you would come, mademoiselle. I told them that you would not be afraid."

"Why should I be, Prince?" she asked, with a pretty laugh. "Am I not among friends?"

Again it was the old Marian who spoke, the Marian of carnival, the light of the Governor's house.

"Certainly you are among friends," repeated the Prince, while he raised her hand to his lips with an Eastern courtesy; "you have the word of Tolma."

"And the knowledge that I am in England," she said with simple pride.

Bonzo laughed harshly.

"Mademoiselle prefers the English police," he cried with iron gaiety; "assuredly she is among friends here."

Marian turned her great eyes upon him and looked him full in the face.

"Monsieur," she said with a gaiety to which she had long been a stranger, "you have helped me to my preference."

"Arrivons!" exclaimed Tolma, "we are not here to write histories. What has been has been; let us forget it."

"No woman could forget Colonel Bonzo," said Marian jestingly, with a laugh, "at least, if she had shaken hands with him."

Bonzo's great face flushed angrily, but while he was still seeking a clever answer, Count Feodor slipped out of the shadows.

"Colonel," he said, "we forget the business upon which Mademoiselle Best has been good enough to come here to-night. Is it not time for that?"

"Sans doute," exclaimed Tolma. "To the affairs. Why do we wait? Mademoiselle is ready, I am sure."

Marian looked from one to the other with

T 2

anxious eyes. Then she perceived the table upon which the white paper was spread.

"I am quite ready," she said, though her heart began to beat quickly, "when you tell me what you wish me to do."

Bonzo advanced to the table and set it straight.

"Mademoiselle," said he, "we have been so long away from Russia that we forget our own country. You, they tell us, have a better memory. If you will make a little map upon that paper, it is possible that you will have no cause to regret the trouble we shall put you to. It would be a map of Fort Constantine, mademoiselle."

He watched her as he spoke. She drew off her gloves with trembling fingers. The hour stood supreme among all the hours of her life. If she had forgotten! If her memory failed her now! It was for Paul's sake, she said to herself again and again. It was that she might be his wife. The lights danced before her eyes. The figures of the men were blurred to her sight. She lived in a room of shadows. The white paper seemed to spread out until it became a mighty scroll upon which her own doom or her own joy was to be written. "God," she prayed in her heart, "help me, hear me!"

"A map of Fort Constantine? Oh, that is easy, Colonel!"

She sat at the table, guiding herself thereto with shaking fingers. Minutes passed and she could not find the pen. Tolma put it at last into her hand.

"Du courage," he whispered; "it is for his liberty, his life. He is a prisoner in this house."

She took the pen; her hand ceased to tremble. Quickly she drew the outline of the fort. The scratching upon the paper, the ticking of the silver clock, were the only sounds in the great drawing-room. Those who watched her breathed with an effort. The figure of old Bonzo seen in the shadows was like a figure of bronze.

Fifteen minutes passed. The woman had forgotten where she sat. She drew upon the paper with the skill of a trained draughtsman. She lived again under the shadow of the mighty fortress. Kronstadt arose above the sea of white waves. Line by line she conquered it; alone she went into the chambers of the secrets; the living death came near but could not touch her.

"There is your map," she said.

The three were about her chair now. The paper was in Bonzo's hands. He laid it side by side with another map and compared the two. For ten minutes no word escaped him. Then he drew himself up erect and delivered his judgment.

" Mademoiselle," he said, " there are few in Russia who could draw a better map than that."

She did not answer him nor the others as they exclaimed upon the excellence of her handiwork. Rather she asked herself again if they had mocked her; had brought her to the house to charge these things against her. And while she stood, doubting and fearful she knew not of what, the folding doors which divided the great room from a smaller one behind it were thrown open by one of the servants, and she beheld a little room fitted up as a chapel, and an old priest standing before a shrine, upon which many candles were burning.

CHAPTER XXVI.

THE EVENING OF THE SECOND DAY.

PAUL heard a clock strike eight, and remembered that he had been nearly thirty hours a prisoner in Talvi's house. It seemed to him that a century of hours had passed since he kissed Marian's pretty lips and told her that he would return to her without delay. He was sure that he would never look upon her face again; that he would live his life alone in dishonour and in exile. The lamp, which they had set in his room, wounded his eyes with its garish light. He wished for darkness that he might accustom himself to the thought of unending captivity. He did not believe that any power on earth could snatch him from the relentless hand of his own countryman which had, in treachery, struck him down. They would send him to the fortress of St. Peter and St. Paul. She, whom he loved to call his little wife, would look for him and look in vain. He dared not ask himself how she would face the world alone. Self-reproach would endure while life was: the unanswered question would remain the surpassing punishment of his folly.

The room in which they had locked him was one of the garrets of the house. A dormer window stood out upon a sloping roof, high above the surrounding roofs. But the window was boarded up, and iron bars, newly fixed, forbade any hope of it. He saw that Talvi had foreseen the need of such a room when he sent the telegram. They had made up their minds to get the spy out of England at any cost; friendship would count for nothing with a Russian who believed that he was serving his country. Even if Marian went to her English friends and told them her story, he doubted that those friends could help him. False charges would be made; his extradition would be demanded by a Government powerful to enforce its wishes. They would brand him as a criminal and carry him back to the unnameable horrors of the fortress of the Neva. And Marian—he clenched his hands when he remembered her. She would be standing at the window waiting for him. He pictured her to himself—the wan face, the great thoughtful eyes, the quick girlish movements, the gestures he had loved, the gold-brown hair, the winning voice. He would hear that voice no more. It must be to him but a memory through eternity. The way of pilgrimage was before him still; but the hand which had been locked in his would never touch his own again.

There was a little furniture in the room, a basket chair, a shelf of books, a mahogany table, a camp bedstead. He had been there but a very short time when the Russian servant brought a lamp to permit him to see these things. He did not speak to the man nor question him, for he knew well how little that would help him. When the servant was gone, he resented the light which had been left. The gable of the roof was dark and ominous above him. He moved in ghostly shadows, for they had robbed him even of the day. So still was the place that he could hear a clock ticking in the room below. No sound came up from the distant street. The roar of the city's life was as a falling of great waters heard afar.

It was near to five o'clock of the afternoon then, he remembered. Marian must have begun to ask herself what mischance had overtaken him. Rightly, he could hope nothing from the friendship of a helpless girl; and yet there were moments when he hoped much. She would tell the English police that he had gone to Talvi's house. The police would begin to ask questions.

It was possible that the whole of his story would be made known, and then—and then! He dreamed even of liberty won by her. She would not rest day or night in her quest of the truth. She might save him even yet from the hand of the Russian.

The weary night dragged on, but the man neither slept nor ate. The supper they had put upon his table reminded him of the short days of content he had known in London. What a gift of the joy of life it had been to sit by her side all day, to hear her morning words of greeting, her pretty good-night, to hold her in his arms, and to say that therein was the place of his abiding rest! But for the thought that in some way—he knew not how—a miracle would bring her to his side, even in that house of darkness, he would have lost his reason. The impulse to beat upon the door of his prison, to cry aloud for mercy, was scarce to be controlled. The hope that she might yet come alone empowered him to play the man. He listened for her footstep through the long watches of the terrible night, and laughed at himself for the fancy. At dawn he fell asleep, and sleeping, he dreamed that her arms were about his neck.

It was a quarter past nine o'clock on the

evening of the second day before any message came to him from the outer world. He had eaten a little dinner, and was asking himself all the old questions when a sound upon the stair without brought him quickly to his feet, and he stood with heart a-quiver, wondering who came. For a spell, brought down to earth suddenly from the giddy clouds of dreamland, the thought lingered that it might be Marian's step. He was still laughing at himself for so foolish a notion when the door swung back upon its hinges, and Count Feodor stood before him.

The Count was in plain evening dress; his face was flushed, for he had run up the stairs; he was boisterous as a lad who carries good news. He had regretted, with a friend's regret, the indignity put upon Paul by those whom he served. He was glad with a friend's joy that those indignities were soon to be forgotten.

"Paul, mon vieux, c'est fini," he gasped, while he held out both his hands to the prisoner, "you are to remain here no longer; they have discovered their mistake, they know all; they have sent for her—she is here!"

Paul staggered like a drunken man.

"She is here? Oh, my God!"

"It is Tolma's work," continued the Count, with a child's pride of his words. "He discovered that she could make the maps. He is downstairs with her now. You are to go there. They want you—at once."

"They want me at once?" repeated the dazed man. "But look at me—my face, my hands, my beard."

"Ivan shall see to that; he will not be ten minutes. There is no time——"

Paul stood quite still. He seemed to read in that instant the moment of Talvi's words.

"For what should there be time?" he asked very quietly.

"For the priest to marry you to the little lady who knows so much about Kronstadt."

Paul reeled out into the light. He was sobbing like a child.

CHAPTER XXVII.

AT MIDNIGHT.

A CANDELABRUM set before the altar in the chapel of Count Talvi's house cast a soft light upon the face of the old priest and upon the little group around him. Huge and unwieldy, like some broken pillar, was the figure of Bonzo back in the shadows. But the Man of Iron thought and planned no longer. The difficult mission which had carried him to England was accomplished. For the rest he cared nought. Kronstadt had lost a good soldier, but her secrets were safe. The clever little woman, who knelt before the altar with the light of love awakened in her eyes, would betray the citadel no more. Everything else was indifferent to the servant of the Gate. Love was the recreation of children. He had never loved.

Near to the Man of Iron sat old Tolma. There was upon his face a look of sly triumph and of elation. He had crossed swords with Bonzo of Kronstadt and had defeated him. The pretty English girl would bring sunshine into his house in Paris. Paul should become a son to him in deed and act. This strange marriage, at night in a house of Western

London, appealed to an insatiable appetite for romance. He recalled the faces of all the women to whom he would willingly have given himself under similar circumstances. What a roll-call it was! The subjects of his amours would have numbered a battalion.

The remaining witness to this strangest of strange marriages was the master of the house. Count Talvi showed how much his old friend's happiness meant to him. He came often to Paul's side; he whispered words of congratulation to him. Hither and thither he moved with silent step, now to help the priest, now to give orders to the lackeys. He was a servant of Russia still, but this was his holiday.

The priest raised his hands to bless those whom God had joined together in the holy mystery of marriage. For one long moment Paul held his wife's burning face close to his. Then all rose and passed to the great dining-room below.

Here lights from many electric lamps shone down upon Talvi's guests. Lackeys were busy at the tables laid for supper. It was the moment for congratulations.

"You forgive me?" cried old Bonzo, holding out both his hands to the trembling girl. "You forgive an old soldier for making you a Russian?"

Marian turned laughing eyes to his.

"I don't know what I am or where I am," she said bewilderedly; "I cannot believe that any of you are real."

Bonzo laughed his great laugh, which filled the house with a tumultuous sound.

"Fichtre!" he roared. "I—Bonzo—I am not real! Oh, c'est bien drôle! Will you not kiss me, my child, and see if I am real?"

Tolma, waddling laboriously, put his arms round the girl's neck and kissed her on both cheeks.

"You must eat and drink, little girl," he said; "you must remember that you are the daughter of Tolma. It is ten o'clock, and the train is at midnight."

"The train?" she asked wonderingly.

"Yes, the train to your Devonshire. It is there you will go until the house in Paris is prepared for you."

"To little Dick," she said, and the words were his reward.

* * * *

The mail rushed on towards the West. By sleeping villages, through silent towns, above dark swirling rivers, away to the gardens of England it carried the man and the woman who had suffered. But the day of suffering was forgotten already.

In the corner of their carriage Paul held Marian in his strong arms. A rug was wrapped about them. The wan light of the feeble lamp fell dimly upon their happy faces.

"It is good to rest," she said, as his arm closed about her and she laid her pretty head upon his shoulder.

"The rest shall be for ever," he answered.

THE END

PRINTED BY CASSELL & COMPANY, LIMITED, LUDGATE HILL, LONDON, E.C

20.498

A SELECTED LIST

OF

CASSELL & COMPANY'S

PUBLICATIONS.

6G—3.93

Illustrated, Fine Art, and other Volumes.

Adventure, The World of. Fully Illustrated. Complete in Three Vols. 9s. each.

Adventures in Criticism. By A. T. QUILLER-COUCH. 6s.

Africa and its Explorers, The Story of. By Dr. ROBERT BROWN, F.R.G.S., &c. With about 800 Original Illustrations. *Cheap Edition.* In 4 Vols. 4s. each.

American Life. By PAUL DE ROUSIERS. 12s. 6d.

Animal Painting in Water Colours. With Coloured Plates. 5s.

Animals, Popular History of. By HENRY SCHERREN, F.Z.S. With 13 Coloured Plates and other Illustrations. 7s. 6d.

Architectural Drawing. By R. PHENÉ SPIERS. Illustrated. 10s. 6d.

Art, The Magazine of. *Yearly Volume,* 21s. *The Two Half-Yearly Volumes for* 1897 *can also be had,* 10s. 6d. *each.*

Artistic Anatomy. By Prof. M. DUVAL. *Cheap Edition,* 3s. 6d.

Astronomy, The Dawn of. A Study of the Temple Worship and Mythology of the Ancient Egyptians. By Sir NORMAN LOCKYER, K.C.B., F.R.S., &c. Illustrated. 21s.

Ballads and Songs. By WILLIAM MAKEPEACE THACKERAY. With Original Illustrations by H. M. BROCK. 6s.

Barber, Charles Burton, The Works of. With Forty-one Plates and Portraits, and Introduction by HARRY FURNISS. *Cheap Edition,* 7s. 6d.

Battles of the Nineteenth Century. An entirely New and Original Work, with Several Hundred Illustrations. Complete in Two Vols., 9s. each.

"Belle Sauvage" Library, The. Cloth, 2s. (*A complete list of the volumes post free on application.*)

Beetles, Butterflies, Moths, and other Insects. By A. W. KAPPEL, F.L.S., F.E.S., and W. EGMONT KIRBY. With 12 Coloured Plates. 3s. 6d.

Biographical Dictionary, Cassell's New. Containing Memoirs of the Most Eminent Men and Women of all Ages and Countries. *Cheap Edition.* 3s. 6d.

Birds' Nests, British: How, Where, and When to Find and Identify Them. By R. KEARTON, F.Z.S. With nearly 130 Illustrations of Nests, Eggs, Young, &c., from Photographs by C. KEARTON. 21s.

Birds' Nests, Eggs, and Egg-Collecting. By R. KEARTON, F.Z.S. Illustrated with 22 Coloured Plates of Eggs. *Enlarged Edition.* 5s.

Black Watch, The. The Record of an Historic Regiment. By ARCHIBALD FORBES, LL.D. 6s.

Britain's Roll of Glory; or, the Victoria Cross, its Heroes, and their Valour. By D. H. PARRY. Illustrated. 7s. 6d.

British Ballads. With 300 Original Illustrations. *Cheap Edition.* Two Volumes in One. Cloth, 7s. 6d.

British Battles on Land and Sea. By JAMES GRANT. With about 800 Illustrations. *Cheap Edition.* Four Vols., 3s. 6d. each.

Building World. In Half-Yearly Volumes, 4s. each.

Butterflies and Moths, European. By W. F. KIRBY. With 61 Coloured Plates, 35s.

Canaries and Cage-Birds, The Illustrated Book of. By W. A. BLAKSTON, W. SWAYSLAND, and A. F. WIENER. With 56 Facsimile Coloured Plates. 35s.

Cassell's Magazine. Half-Yearly Volumes, 5s. each; or Yearly Volumes, 8s. each.

Cathedrals, Abbeys, and Churches of England and Wales. Descriptive, Historical, Pictorial. *Popular Edition.* Two Vols. 25s.

Cats and Kittens. By HENRIETTE RONNER. With Portrait and 13 magnificent Full-page Photogravure Plates and numerous Illustrations. 4to, £2 10s.

China Painting. By FLORENCE LEWIS. With Sixteen Coloured Plates, &c. 5s.

Choice Dishes at Small Cost. By A. G. PAYNE. *Cheap Edition,* 1s.

Chums. The Illustrated Paper for Boys. Yearly Volume, 8s.

Cities of the World. Four Vols. Illustrated. 7s. 6d. each.

Civil Service, Guide to Employment in the. *Entirely New Edition.* Paper, 1s.; cloth, 1s. 6d.

Clinical Manuals for Practitioners and Students of Medicine. (*A List of Volumes forwarded post free on application to the Publishers.*)

Cobden Club, Works published for the. (*A Complete List on application.*)

Colour. By Prof. A. H. CHURCH. *New and Enlarged Edition*, 3s. 6d.

Combe, George, The Select Works of. Issued by Authority of the Combe Trustees. *Popular Edition*, 1s. each, net.
The Constitution of Man. Moral Philosophy. Science and Religion. Discussions on Education. American Notes.

Conning Tower, In a; or, How I Took H.M.S. "Majestic" into Action. By H. O. ARNOLD-FORSTER, M.P. *Cheap Edition.* Illustrated. 6d.

Conquests of the Cross. Edited by EDWIN HODDER. With numerous Original Illustrations. Complete in Three Vols. 9s. each.

Cookery, Cassell's Dictionary of. With about 9,000 Recipes. 5s.

Cookery, A Year's. By PHYLLIS BROWNE. *New and Enlarged Edition*, 3s. 6d.

Cookery Book, Cassell's New Universal. By LIZZIE HERITAGE. With 12 Coloured Plates and other Illustrations. 1,344 pages, strongly bound in leather gilt, 6s.

Cookery, Cassell's Popular. With Four Coloured Plates. Cloth gilt, 2s.

Cookery, Cassell's Shilling. 135*th Thousand*. 1s.

Cookery, Vegetarian. By A. G. PAYNE. 1s. 6d.

Cooking by Gas, The Art of. By MARIE J. SUGG. Illustrated. Cloth, 2s.

Cottage Gardening. Edited by W. ROBINSON, F.L.S. Illustrated. Half-yearly Vols., 2s. 6d. each.

Countries of the World, The. By Dr. ROBERT BROWN, M.A., F.L.S. With about 750 Illustrations. *Cheap Edition.* Vols. I. to V., 6s. each.

Cyclopædia, Cassell's Concise. With about 600 Illustrations. 5s.

Cyclopædia, Cassell's Miniature. Containing 30,000 Subjects. Cloth, 2s. 6d. ; half-roxburgh, 4s.

Dictionaries. (For description, see alphabetical letter.) Religion, Biographical, Encyclopædic, Concise Cyclopædia, Miniature Cyclopædia, Mechanical, English, English History, Phrase and Fable, Cookery, Domestic. (French, German, and Latin, see with *Educational Works*.)

Diet and Cookery for Common Ailments. By a Fellow of the Royal College of Physicians and PHYLLIS BROWNE. *Cheap Edition.* 2s. 6d.

Dog, Illustrated Book of the. By VERO SHAW, B.A. With 28 Coloured Plates. Cloth bevelled, 35s. ; half-morocco, 45s.

Domestic Dictionary, The. An Encyclopædia for the Household. Cloth, 7s. 6d.

Doré Don Quixote, The. With about 400 Illustrations by GUSTAVE DORÉ. *Cheap Edition.* Cloth, 10s. 6d.

Doré Gallery, The. With 250 Illustrations by GUSTAVE DORÉ. 4to, 42s.

Doré's Dante's Inferno. Illustrated by GUSTAVE DORÉ. *Popular Edition.* With Preface by A. J. BUTLER. Cloth gilt or buckram, 7s. 6d.

Doré's Dante's Purgatory and Paradise. Illustrated by GUSTAVE DORÉ. *Cheap Edition.* 7s. 6d.

Doré's Milton's Paradise Lost. Illustrated by GUSTAVE DORÉ. 4to, 21s. *Popular Edition.* Cloth gilt, or buckram gilt, 7s. 6d.

Earth, Our, and its Story. Edited by Dr. ROBERT BROWN, F.L.S. With 36 Coloured Plates and nearly 800 Wood Engravings. In Three Vols. 9s. each.

Edinburgh, Old and New, Cassell's. With 600 Illustrations. Three Vols. 9s. each ; library binding, £1 10s. the set.

Egypt: Descriptive, Historical, and Picturesque. By Prof. G. EBERS. Translated by CLARA BELL, with Notes by SAMUEL BIRCH, LL.D., &c. Two Vols. 42s.

Electric Current, The. How Produced and How Used. By R. MULLINEUX WALMSLEY, D.Sc., &c. Illustrated. 10s. 6d.

Electricity, Practical. By Prof. W. E. AYRTON, F.R.S. *Entirely New and Enlarged Edition.* Completely re-written. Illustrated. 9s.

Electricity in the Service of Man. A Popular and Practical Treatise. With upwards of 950 Illustrations. *New and Cheaper Edition*, 7s. 6d.

Employment for Boys on Leaving School, Guide to. By W. S. BEARD, F.R.G.S. 1s. 6d.

Encyclopædic Dictionary, The. Complete in Fourteen Divisional Vols., 10s. 6d. each ; or Seven Vols., half-morocco, 21s. each ; half-russia, 25s. each.

England and Wales, Pictorial. With upwards of 320 beautiful illustrations prepared from copyright photographs. 9s. Also an edition on superior paper, bound in half-persian, marble sides, gilt edges and in box, 15s. net.

England, A History of. From the Landing of Julius Cæsar to the Present Day. By H. O. ARNOLD-FORSTER, M.P. Fully Illustrated, 5s.

England, Cassell's Illustrated History of. With upwards of 2,000 Illustrations. *Library Edition.* Ten Vols., £5.

English Dictionary, Cassell's. Containing Definitions of upwards of 100,000 Words and Phrases. *Cheap Edition,* 3s. 6d. ; *Superior Edition,* 5s.

English History, The Dictionary of. Edited by SIDNEY LOW, B.A., and Prof. F. S. PULLING, M.A., with Contributions by Eminent Writers. *New Edition.* 7s. 6d.

English Literature, Library of. By Prof. H. MORLEY. In 5 Vols. 7s. 6d. each.

English Literature, Morley's First Sketch of. *Revised Edition.* 7s. 6d.

English Literature, The Story of. By ANNA BUCKLAND. 3s. 6d.

English Writers from the Earliest Period to Shakespeare. By HENRY MORLEY. Eleven Vols. 5s. each.

Æsop's Fables. Illustrated by ERNEST GRISET. *Cheap Edition.* Cloth, 3s. 6d. ; bevelled boards, gilt edges, 5s.

Etiquette of Good Society. *New Edition.* Edited and Revised by LADY COLIN CAMPBELL. 1s. ; cloth, 1s. 6d.

Fairy Tales Far and Near. Retold by Q. Illustrated. 3s. 6d.

Fairway Island. By HORACE HUTCHINSON. *Cheap Edition.* 2s. 6d.

Family Doctor, Cassell's. By A MEDICAL MAN. Illustrated, 10s. 6d.

Family Lawyer, Cassell's. An Entirely New and Original Work. By Barrister-at-Law. 10s. 6d.

Fiction, Cassell's Popular Library of. 3s. 6d. each.

Tiny Luttrell. By E. W Hornung.

The White Shield. By Bertram Mitford.

Tuxter's Little Maid. By G. B. Burgin.

The Hispaniola Plate. (1683—1893.) By John Bloundelle Burton.

Highway of Sorrow. By Hesba Stretton and * * * * * * *, a Famous Russian Exile.

King Solomon's Mines. By H. Rider Haggard. Illustrated.

The Lights of Sydney By Lilian Turner.

The Admirable Lady Biddy Fane. By Frank Barrett.

List, ye Landsmen! A Romance of Incident. By W. Clark Russell.

Ia: A Love Story. By Q.

The Red Terror: A Story of the Paris Commune. By Edward King.

The Little Squire. By Mrs. Henry de la Pasture

Zero, the Slaver. A Romance of Equatorial Africa. By Lawrence Fletcher.

Into the Unknown! A Romance of South Africa. By Lawrence Fletcher.

Mount Desolation. An Australian Romance. By W. Carlton Dawe.

Pomona's Travels. By Frank R. Stockton.

The Reputation of George Saxon. By Morley Roberts.

A Prison Princess. By Major Arthur Griffiths.

Queen's Scarlet, The. By George Manville Fenn.

Capture of the "Estrella," The. A Tale of the Slave Trade. By Commander Claud Harding, R.N.

The Awkward Squads. And other Ulster Stories. By Shan F. Bullock.

The Squire. By Mrs. Parr.

A King's Hussar. By Herbert Compton.

Playthings and Parodies. Short Stories, Sketches, &c. By Barry Pain.

Out of the Jaws of Death. By Frank Barrett.

Fourteen to One, &c. By Elizabeth Stuart Phelps.

The Medicine Lady. By L. T. Meade.

Leona. By Mrs. Molesworth.

Father Stafford. By Anthony Hope.

"La Bella," and others. By Egerton Castle.

The Avenger of Blood. By J. Maclaren Cobban.

The Man in Black. By Stanley Weyman.

The Doings of Raffles Haw. By A. Conan Doyle.

A Free Lance in a Far Land. By Herbert Compton.

Field Naturalist's Handbook, The. By Revs. J. G. WOOD and THEODORE WOOD. *Cheap Edition,* 2s. 6d.

Figuier's Popular Scientific Works. With Several Hundred Illustrations in each. 3s. 6d. each.

The Insect World. | Reptiles and Birds. | The Vegetable World.
The Human Race. | Mammalia. | Ocean World.
The World before the Deluge.

Flora's Feast. A Masque of Flowers. Penned and Pictured by WALTER CRANE. With 40 pages in Colours. 5s.

Flower Painting, Elementary. With Eight Coloured Plates. 3s.

Flowers, and How to Paint Them. By MAUD NAFTEL. With Coloured Plates. 5s.

Football: the Rugby Union Game. Edited by Rev. F. MARSHALL. Illustrated. *New and Enlarged Edition.* 7s. 6d.

For Glory and Renown. By D. H. PARRY. Illustrated. *Cheap Edition.* 3s. 6d.

Fossil Reptiles, A History of British. By Sir RICHARD OWEN, F.R.S., &c. With 268 Plates. In Four Vols. £12 12s.

Franco-German War, Cassell's History of the. Complete in Two Vols., containing about 500 Illustrations. 9s. each.

Garden Flowers, Familiar. By F. E. HULME, F.L.S., F.S.A. With 200 Full-page Coloured Plates, and Descriptive Text by SHIRLEY HIBBERD. *Cheap Edition.* In Five Vols., 3s. 6d. each.

Gladstone, The Right Hon. W. E., Cassell's Life of. Profusely Illustrated. 1s.

Gleanings from Popular Authors. With Original Illustrations. *Cheap Edition.* In One Vol., 3s. 6d.

Gulliver's Travels. With 88 Engravings. Cloth, 3s. 6d. ; cloth gilt, 5s.

Gun and its Development, The. By W. W. GREENER. With 500 Illustrations. *Entirely New Edition*, 10s. 6d.

Guns, Modern Shot. By W. W. GREENER. Illustrated. 5s.

Health, The Book of. By Eminent Physicians and Surgeons. Cloth, 21s.

Heavens, The Story of the. By Sir ROBERT STAWELL BALL, LL.D., F.R.S. With Coloured Plates and Wood Engravings. *Popular Edition*, 10s. 6d.

Heroes of Britain in Peace and War. With 300 Original Illustrations. *Cheap Edition.* Complete in One Vol., 3s. 6d.

History, A Footnote to. Eight Years of Trouble in Samoa. By R. L. STEVENSON. 6s.

Home Life of the Ancient Greeks, The. Translated by ALICE ZIMMERN. Illustrated. *Cheap Edition.* 5s.

Horse, The Book of the. By SAMUEL SIDNEY. With 17 Full-page Collotype Plates of Celebrated Horses of the Day, and numerous other Illustrations. Cloth, 15s.

Horses and Dogs. By O. EERELMAN. With Descriptive Text. Translated from the Dutch by CLARA BELL. With Fifteen Full-page and other Illustrations. 25s. net.

Houghton, Lord : The Life, Letters, and Friendships of Richard Monckton Milnes, First Lord Houghton. By Sir WEMYSS REID. Two Vols. 32s.

Hygiene and Public Health. By B. ARTHUR WHITELEGGE, M.D. Illustrated. *New and Revised Edition.* 7s. 6d.

India, Cassell's History of. In One Vol. *Cheap Edition.* 7s. 6d.

In-door Amusements, Card Games, and Fireside Fun, Cassell's Book of. With numerous Illustrations. *Cheap Edition.* Cloth, 2s.

Iron Pirate, The. By MAX PEMBERTON. Illustrated. 5s.

Khiva, A Ride to. By Col. FRED BURNABY. *New Edition.* Illustrated. 3s. 6d.

King George, In the Days of. By Col. PERCY GROVES. Illustrated. 1s. 6d.

King Solomon's Mines. By H. RIDER HAGGARD. Illustrated. 3s. 6d. *People's Edition.* 6d.

Kronstadt. A New Novel. By MAX PEMBERTON. With 8 Full-page Plates. 6s.

Ladies' Physician, The. By a London Physician. *Cheap Edition, Revised and Enlarged.* 3s. 6d.

Lady's Dressing-Room, The. Translated from the French by Lady COLIN CAMPBELL. *Cheap Edition.* 2s. 6d.

Letts's Diaries and other Time-saving Publications are now published exclusively by CASSELL & COMPANY. (*A List sent post free on application.*)

Little Huguenot, The. *New Edition.* 1s. 6d.

Lobengula, Three Years with, and Experiences in South Africa. By J. COOPER-CHADWICK. *Cheap Edition.* 2s. 6d.

Locomotive Engine, The Biography of a. By HENRY FRITH. 3s. 6d.

Loftus, Lord Augustus, P.C., G.C.B., The Diplomatic Reminiscences of. First Series. With Portrait. Two Vols. 32s. Second Series. Two Vols. 32s.

London, Cassell's Guide to. With Numerous Illustrations. 6d. Cloth, 1s.

London, Greater. By EDWARD WALFORD. Two Vols. With about 400 Illustrations. *Cheap Edition*, 4s. 6d. each. *Library Edition.* Two Vols. £1 the set.

London, Old and New. By WALTER THORNBURY and EDWARD WALFORD. Six Vols., with about 1,200 Illustrations. |Cheap Ed., 4s. 6d. each. *Library Ed.*, £3.

Manchester, Old and New. By WILLIAM ARTHUR SHAW, M.A. With Original Illustrations. Three Vols., 31s. 6d.

Mechanics, The Practical Dictionary of. Three Vols., £3 3s. ; half-morocco, £3 15s. Supplementary Volume, £1 1s. ; or half-morocco, £1 5s.

Medical Handbook of Life Assurance. By JAMES EDWARD POLLOCK, M.D., and JAMES CHISHOLM. *New and Revised Edition.* 7s. 6d.

Medicine, Manuals for Students of. (*A List forwarded post free on application.*)

Mesdag, H. W., the Painter of the North Sea. With Etchings and Descriptive Text. By PH. ZILCKEN. The Text translated from the Dutch by CLARA BELL. 36s.

Modern Europe, A History of. By C. A. FYFFE, M.A. *Cheap Edition in One Volume*, 10s. 6d. ; *Library Edition, Illustrated*, 3 vols., 7s. 6d. each.

Music, Illustrated History of. By EMIL NAUMANN. Edited by the Rev. Sir F. A. GORE OUSELEY, Bart. Illustrated. Two Vols. 31s. 6d.

National Library, Cassell's. Consisting of 214 Volumes. Paper covers, 3d. ; cloth, 6d. (*A Complete List of the Volumes post free on application.*)

Natural History, Cassell's Concise. By E. PERCEVAL WRIGHT, M.A., M.D., F.L.S. With several Hundred Illustrations. 7s. 6d.

Natural History, Cassell's New. Edited by P. MARTIN DUNCAN, M.B., F.R.S., F.G.S. *Cheap Edition.* With about 2,000 Illusts. Three Double Vols., 6s. each.

Nature and a Camera, With. Being the Adventures and Observations of a Field Naturalist and an Animal Photographer. By RICHARD KEARTON, F.Z.S. Illustrated by a Special Frontispiece, and 180 Pictures from Photographs by CHERRY KEARTON. 21s.

Nature's Wonder-Workers. By KATE R. LOVELL. Illustrated. 2s. 6d.

Nelson, The Life of. By ROBERT SOUTHEY. Illustrated with Eight Plates. 3s. 6d.

New Zealand, Pictorial. With Preface by Sir W. B. PERCEVAL, K.C.M.G. Illust. 6s.

Novels, Popular. Extra crown 8vo, cloth, 6s. each.

Grace O'Malley, Princess and Pirate. By ROBERT MACHRAY.
Cupid's Garden. By ELLEN THORNEYCROFT FOWLER.
A Limited Success. By SARAH PITT.
The Wrothams of Wrotham Court. By FRANCES HEATH FRESHFIELD.
Ill-gotten Gold : A Story of a Great Wrong and a Great Revenge. By W. G. TARBET.
Sentimental Tommy. } By J. M. BARRIE.
The Little Minister. }
From the Memoirs of a Minister of France. } By STANLEY WEYMAN.
The Story of Francis Cludde. }
Kronstadt. }
Puritan's Wife, A. } By MAX PEMBERTON.
The Impregnable City, }
The Sea-Wolves. }
Young Blood. }
My Lord Duke. } By E. W. HORNUNG.
Rogue's March, The. }
Spectre Gold. } By HEADON HILL.
By a Hair's-Breadth. }
The Girl at Cobhurst. }
Story Teller's Pack, A. } By FRANK STOCKTON.
Mrs. Cliff's Yacht. }
The Adventures of Captain Horn. }
Treasure Island. }
The Master of Ballantrae. }
The Black Arrow. } By ROBERT LOUIS STEVENSON. } Also a *Popular Edition*, 3s. 6d. each.
Kidnapped. }
Catriona : A Sequel to "Kidnapped." }
Island Nights' Entertainments. }
The Wrecker. By ROBERT LOUIS STEVENSON and LLOYD OSBOURNE.
Loveday. A Tale of a Stirring Time. By A. E. WICKHAM. (*Also at* 3s. 6d.)
What Cheer ! By W. CLARK RUSSELL.
Lisbeth. By LESLIE KEITH.

Nursing for the Home and for the Hospital, A Handbook of. By CATHERINE J. WOOD. *Cheap Edition*, 1s. 6d. ; cloth, 2s.

Nursing of Sick Children, A Handbook for the. By CATHERINE J. WOOD. 2s. 6d.

Our Own Country. With 1,200 Illustrations. *Cheap Edition.* 3 Double Vols. 5s. each.

Painting, The English School of. By ERNEST CHESNEAU. *Cheap Edition*, 3s. 6d.

Paris, Old and New. Illustrated. In Two Vols. 9s. or 10s. 6d. each.

Peoples of the World, The. By Dr. ROBERT BROWN, F.L.S. Complete in Six Vols. With Illustrations. 7s. 6d. each.

Phrase and Fable, Dr. Brewer's Dictionary of. *Entirely New and largely increased Edition.* 10s. 6d. Also in half-morocco, 2 Vols., 15s.

Physiology for Students, Elementary. By ALFRED T. SCHOFIELD, M.D., M.R.C.S. With Two Coloured Plates and numerous Illustrations. *New Edition.* 5s.

Picturesque America. Complete in Four Vols., with 48 Exquisite Steel Plates, and about 800 Original Wood Engravings. £12 12s. the set. *Popular Edition* in Four Vols., price 18s. each.

Picturesque Australasia, Cassell's. With upwards of 1,000 Illustrations. In Four Vols., 7s. 6d. each.

Picturesque Canada. With about 600 Original Illustrations. 2 Vols. £9 9s. the set.

Picturesque Europe. Complete in Five Vols. Each containing 13 Exquisite Steel Plates, from Original Drawings, and nearly 200 Original Illustrations. £21. *Popular Edition.* In Five Vols. 18s. each.

Picturesque Mediterranean, The. With a Series of Magnificent Illustrations from Original Designs by leading Artists of the day. Two Vols. Cloth, £2 2s. each.

Pigeons, Fulton's Book of. Edited by LEWIS WRIGHT. Revised, Enlarged, and Supplemented by the Rev. W. F. LUMLEY. With 50 Full-page Illustrations. *Popular Edition.* In One Vol., 10s. 6d. *Original Edition*, with 50 Coloured Plates and numerous Wood Engravings. 21s.

Planet, The Story of Our. By Prof. BONNEY, F.R.S., &c. With Coloured Plates and Maps and about 100 Illustrations. *Cheap Edition.* 7s. 6d.

Polytechnic Series, The. Practical Illustrated Manuals. (*A List will be sent on application.*)

Portrait Gallery, Cassell's Universal. Containing 240 Portraits of Celebrated Men and Women of the Day. Cloth, 6s.

Portrait Gallery, The Cabinet. Complete in Five Series, each containing 36 Cabinet Photographs of Eminent Men and Women of the day. 15s. each.

Poultry, The Book of. By LEWIS WRIGHT. *Popular Edition.* Illustrated. 10s. 6d.

Poultry, The Illustrated Book of. By LEWIS WRIGHT. With Fifty Exquisite Coloured Plates, and numerous Wood Engravings. *Revised Edition.* Cloth, gilt edges, 21s. ; half-morocco (*price on application*).

"Punch," The History of. By M. H. SPIELMANN. With nearly 170 Illustrations, Portraits, and Facsimiles. Cloth, 16s. ; *Large Paper Edition*, £2 2s. net.

Q's Works, Uniform Edition of. 5s. each.

Dead Man's Rock.	The Astonishing History of Troy Town.
The Splendid Spur.	'I Saw Three Ships,' and other Winter's Tales.
The Blue Pavilions.	Noughts and Crosses.
The Delectable Duchy. Stories, Studies, and Sketches.	Wandering Heath.

Queen Summer ; or, The Tourney of the Lily and the Rose. Penned and Portrayed by WALTER CRANE. With 40 pages in Colours. 6s.

Queen Victoria, The Life and Times of. By ROBERT WILSON. Complete in 2 Vols. With numerous Illustrations. 9s. each.

Queen's Empire, The. First Volume, containing about 300 Splendid Full-page Illustrations. 9s.

Queen's London, The. Containing Exquisite Views of London and its Environs, together with a fine series of Pictures of the Queen's Diamond Jubilee Procession. *Enlarged Edition*, 10s. 6d.

Railway Guides, Official Illustrated. With Illustrations on nearly every page, Maps &c. Paper covers, 1s.; cloth, 2s.

London and North Western Railway.	Great Eastern Railway.
Great Western Railway.	London and South Western Railway.
Midland Railway.	London, Brighton and South Coast Railway.
Great Northern Railway.	South Eastern Railway.

Abridged and Popular Editions of the above Guides can also be obtained. Paper covers, 3d. each.

Railways, Our. Their Origin, Development, Incident, and Romance. By JOHN PENDLETON. Illustrated. 2 Vols., 12s.

Rivers of Great Britain : Descriptive, Historical, Pictorial.
Rivers of the West Coast. With Etching as Frontispiece, and Numerous Illustrations in Text. Royal 4to, 42s.
The Royal River : The Thames from Source to Sea. *Popular Edition*, 16s.
Rivers of the East Coast. With highly-finished Engravings. *Popular Edition* 16s.

Robinson Crusoe. *Cassell's New Fine-Art Edition.* With upwards of 100 Original Illustrations. *Cheap Edition*, 3s. 6d. or 5s.

Rogues of the Fiery Cross. By S. WALKEY. With 16 Full-page Illustrations. 5s.

Ronner, Henriette, The Painter of Cat-Life and Cat-Character. By M. H. SPIELMANN. Containing a Series of beautiful Phototype Illustrations. 12s.

Royal Academy Pictures. With upwards of 200 magnificent reproductions of Pictures in the Royal Academy. 7s. 6d.

Russo-Turkish War, Cassell's History of. With about 400 Illustrations. *New Edition.* In Two Vols., 9s. each.

Sala, George Augustus, The Life and Adventures of. By Himself. *Cheap Edition.* One Vol., 7s. 6d.

Saturday Journal, Cassell's. Illustrated throughout. Yearly Vol., 7s. 6d.

Scarlet and Blue; or, Songs for Soldiers and Sailors. By JOHN FARMER. 5s. Words only, paper, 6d. ; cloth, 9d.

Science for All. Edited by Dr. ROBERT BROWN, M.A., F.L.S., &c. *Cheap Edition.* With over 1,700 Illustrations. Five Vols. 3s. 6d. each.

Science Series, The Century. Consisting of Biographies of Eminent Scientific Men of the present Century. Edited by Sir HENRY ROSCOE, D.C.L., F.R.S., M P. Crown 8vo, 3s. 6d. each.

> Michael Faraday, His Life and Work. By Professor SILVANUS P. THOMPSON, F.R.S.
> Pasteur. By PERCY FRANKLAND, F.R.S. and Mrs. FRANKLAND.
> John Dalton and the Rise of Modern Chemistry. By Sir HENRY E. ROSCOE, F.R.S.
> Major Rennell, F.R.S., and the Rise of English Geography. By Sir CLEMENTS R. MARKHAM, C.B., F.R.S., President of the Royal Geographical Society.
> Justus Von Liebig: His Life and Work. By W. A. SHENSTONE.
> The Herschels and Modern Astronomy. By Miss AGNES M. CLERKE.
> Charles Lyell and Modern Geology. By Professor T. G. BONNEY, F.R.S.
> J. Clerk Maxwell and Modern Physics. By R. T. GLAZEBROOK, F.R.S.
> Humphry Davy, Poet and Philosopher. By T. E. THORPE, F.R.S.
> Charles Darwin and the Theory of Natural Selection. By EDWARD B. POULTON, M.A., F.R.S.

Scotland, Picturesque and Traditional. By G. E. EYRE-TODD. 6s.

Sea, The Story of the. An Entirely New and Original Work. Edited by Q. Illustrated. Complete in Two Vols., 9s. each. *Cheap Edition*, 5s. each.

Shaftesbury, The Seventh Earl of, K.G., The Life and Work of. By EDWIN HODDER. Illustrated. *Cheap Edition*, 3s. 6d.

Shakespeare, Cassell's Quarto Edition. Edited by CHARLES and MARY COWDEN CLARKE, and containing about 600 Illustrations by H C. SELOUS. Complete in Three Vols., cloth gilt, £3 3s.—Also published in Three separate Vols., in cloth, viz. :—The COMEDIES, 21s. ; The HISTORICAL PLAYS, 18s. 6d. ; The TRAGEDIES, 25s.

Shakespeare, The England of. *New Edition.* By E. GOADBY. With Full-page Illustrations. Crown 8vo, 224 pages, 2s. 6d.

Shakespeare, The Plays of. Edited by Prof. HENRY MORLEY. Complete in 13 Vols., cloth, in box, 21s. ; also 39 Vols., cloth, in box, 21s. ; half-morocco, cloth sides, 42s.

Shakspere, The Leopold. With 400 Illustrations, and an Introduction by F. J. FURNIVALL. *Cheap Edition*, 3s. 6d. Cloth gilt, gilt edges, 5s. ; roxburgh, 7s. 6d.

Shakspere, The Royal. With Exquisite Steel Plates and Wood Engravings. Three Vols. 15s. each.

Sketches, The Art of Making and Using. From the French of G. FRAIPONT. By CLARA BELL. With Fifty Illustrations. 2s. 6d.

Social England. A Record of the Progress of the People. By various Writers. Edited by H. D. TRAILL, D.C.L. Complete in Six Vols. Vols. I. (Revised Ed.), II., and III., 15s. each. Vols. IV. and V., 17s. each. Vol. VI., 18s.

Sports and Pastimes, Cassell's Complete Book of. *Cheap Edition*, 3s. 6d.

Star-Land. By Sir ROBERT STAWELL BALL, LL.D., &c. Illustrated. 6s.

Story of My Life, The. By the Rt. Hon. Sir RICHARD TEMPLE, Bart., G.C.S.I., &c. Two Vols. 21s.

Sun, The Story of the. By Sir ROBERT STAWELL BALL, LL.D., F.R.S., F.R.A.S. With Eight Coloured Plates and other Illustrations. *Cheap Edition*, 10s. 6d.

Sunshine Series, Cassell's. In Vols. 1s. each. (*A List post free on application.*)

Taxation, Municipal, at Home and Abroad. By J. J. O'MEARA. 7s. 6d.

Thames, The Tidal. By GRANT ALLEN. With India Proof Impressions of 20 Magnificent Full-page Photogravure Plates, and many other Illustrations, after original drawings by W. L. WYLLIE, A.R.A. *New Edition*, cloth, 42s. net.

Things I have Seen and People I have Known. By G. A. SALA. With Portrait and Autograph. 2 Vols. 21s.

Three Homes, The. By the Very Rev. Dean FARRAR, D.D., F.R.S. *New Edition.* With 8 Full-page Illustrations. 6s.

To the Death. By R. D. CHETWODE. With Four Plates. 5s.

Treatment, The Year-Book of, for 1898. A Critical Review for Practitioners of Medicine and Surgery. Fourteenth Year of Issue. 7s. 6d.

Trees, Familiar. By Prof. G. S. BOULGER, F.L.S., F.G.S. In Two Series. With Forty Coloured Plates in each. 12s. 6d. each.

Uncle Tom's Cabin. By HARRIET BEECHER-STOWE. With upwards of 100 Original Illustrations. *Fine Art Memorial Edition.* 7s. 6d.

"Unicode": The Universal Telegraphic Phrase Book. Pocket or Desk Edition. 2s. 6d. each.

United States, Cassell's History of the. By EDMUND OLLIER. With 600 Illustrations. Three Vols. 9s. each.

Universal History, Cassell's Illustrated. With nearly ONE THOUSAND ILLUSTRATIONS. Vol. I. Early and Greek History.—Vol. II. The Roman Period.—Vol. III. The Middle Ages.—Vol. IV. Modern History. 9s. each.

Verses, Wise or Otherwise. By ELLEN THORNEYCROFT FOWLER. 3s. 6d.

War and Peace, Memories and Studies of. By ARCHIBALD FORBES, LL.D. *Original Edition*, 16s. *Cheap Edition*, 6s.

Water-Colour Painting, A Course of. With Twenty-four Coloured Plates by R. P. LEITCH, and full Instructions to the Pupil. 5s.

Westminster Abbey, Annals of. By E. T. BRADLEY (Mrs. A. MURRAY SMITH). Illustrated. With a Preface by the DEAN OF WESTMINSTER. 63s.

Wild Birds, Familiar. By W. SWAYSLAND. Four Series. With 40 Coloured Plates in each. (In sets only, price on application.)

Wild Flowers, Familiar. By F. E. HULME, F.L.S., F.S.A. With 200 Coloured Plates and Descriptive Text. *Cheap Edition.* In Five Vols., 3s. 6d. each.

Wild Flowers Collecting Book. In Six Parts, 4d. each.

Wild Flowers Drawing and Painting Book. In Six Parts. 4d. each.

Windsor Castle, The Governor's Guide to. By the Most Noble the MARQUIS OF LORNE, K.T. Profusely Illustrated. Limp cloth, 1s. Cloth boards, gilt edges. 2s.

World of Wit and Humour, Cassell's New. With New Pictures and New Text. Complete in Two Vols., 6s. each.

With Claymore and Bayonet. By Col. PERCY GROVES. With 8 Plates. 3s. 6d.

Work. The Illustrated Journal for Mechanics. Half-Yearly Vols. 4s. each.

"Work" Handbooks. A Series of Practical Manuals prepared under the Direction of PAUL N. HASLUCK, Editor of *Work.* Illustrated. Cloth, 1s. each.

World of Wonders, The. With 400 Illustrations. *Cheap Edition.* Two Vols., 4s. 6d. each.

ILLUSTRATED MAGAZINES.

The Quiver. Monthly, 6d.

Cassell's Magazine. Monthly, 6d.

"Little Folks" Magazine. Monthly, 6d.

The Magazine of Art. Monthly, 1s. 4d.

Cassell's Saturday Journal. Weekly, 1d.; Monthly, 6d.

Chums. The Illustrated Paper for Boys. Weekly, 1d.; Monthly, 6d.

Work. The Journal for Mechanics. Weekly, 1d.; Monthly, 6d.

Building World. Weekly, 1d.; Monthly, 6d.

Cottage Gardening. Illustrated. Weekly, ½d.; Monthly, 3d.

*** *Full particulars of* CASSELL & COMPANY'S Monthly Serial Publications *will be found in* CASSELL & COMPANY'S COMPLETE CATALOGUE.

Bibles and Religious Works.

Bible Biographies. Illustrated. 1s. 6d. each.
   The Story of Joseph. Its Lessons for To-Day. By the Rev. GEORGE BAINTON.
   The Story of Moses and Joshua. By the Rev. J. TELFORD.
   The Story of Judges. By the Rev. J. WYCLIFFE GEDGE.
   The Story of Samuel and Saul. By the Rev. D. C. TOVEY.
   The Story of David. By the Rev. J. WILD.

   The Story of Jesus. In Verse. By J. R. MACDUFF, D.D. 1s. 6d.

Bible, Cassell's Illustrated Family. With 900 Illustrations. Leather, gilt
   edges, £2 10s. ; best full morocco, £3 15s.

Bible, Cassell's Guinea. With 900 Illustrations and Coloured Maps. Royal 4to.
   Leather, 21s. net. Persian antique, with corners and clasps, 25s. net.

Bible Educator, The. Edited by E. H. PLUMPTRE, D.D. With Illustrations,
   Maps, &c. Four Vols., cloth, 6s. each.

Bible Dictionary, Cassell's Concise. By the Rev. ROBERT HUNTER, LL.D.,
   Illustrated. 7s. 6d.

Bible Student in the British Museum, The. By the Rev. J. G. KITCHIN,
   M.A. *Entirely New and Revised Edition.* 1s. 4d.

Bunyan, Cassell's Illustrated. With 200 Original Illustrations. *Cheap Edition*,
   3s. 6d.

Bunyan's Pilgrim's Progress. Illustrated. *Cheap Edition*, cloth, 3s. 6d ; cloth
   gilt, gilt edges, 5s.

Child's Bible, The. With 200 Illustrations. Demy 4to, 830 pp. 150*th Thousand*.
   Cheap Edition, 7s. 6d. *Superior Edition*, with 6 Coloured Plates, gilt edges, 10s. 6d.

Child's Life of Christ, The. Complete in One Handsome Volume, with about
   200 Original Illustrations. *Cheap Edition*, cloth, 7s. 6d. ; or with 6 Coloured Plates,
   cloth, gilt edges, 10s. 6d.

Church of England, The. A History for the People. By the Very Rev. H. D. M.
   SPENCE, D.D., Dean of Gloucester. Illustrated. Vols. I., II., and III., 6s. each.

Church Reform in Spain and Portugal. By the Rev. H. E. NOYES, D.D.
   Illustrated. 2s. 6d.

Commentary for English Readers. Edited by Bishop ELLICOTT. With Contributions by eminent Scholars and Divines:—
      New Testament. *Original Edition.* Three Vols., 21s. each ; or in half morocco, £4 14s. 6d.
         the set. *Popular Edition.* Unabridged. Three Vols., 4s. each.
      Old Testament. *Original Edition.* Five Vols., 21s. each ; or in half-morocco,
         £7 17s. 6d. the set. *Popular Edition.* Unabridged. Five Vols., 4s. each.
   ⁎⁎ *The Complete Set of Eight Volumes in the Popular Edition is supplied at 30s.*

Commentary, The New Testament. Edited by Bishop ELLICOTT. Handy
   Volume Edition. Suitable for School and General Use.

St. Matthew. 3s. 6d.	Romans. 2s. 6d.	Titus, Philemon, Hebrews,
St. Mark. 3s.	Corinthians I. and II. 3s.	and James. 3s.
St. Luke. 3s. 6d.	Galatians, Ephesians, and	Peter, Jude, and John. 3s.
St. John. 3s. 6d.	Philippians. 3s.	The Revelation. 3s.
The Acts of the Apostles.	Colossians, Thessalonians,	An Introduction to the New
3s. 6d.	and Timothy. 3s.	Testament. 2s. 6d.

Commentary, The Old Testament. Edited by Bishop ELLICOTT. Handy Volume
   Edition. Suitable for School and General Use.

Genesis. 3s. 6d.	Leviticus. 3s.	Deuteronomy. 2s. 6d.
Exodus. 3s.	Numbers. 2s. 6d.	

Dictionary of Religion, The. An Encyclopædia of Christian and other
   Religious Doctrines, Denominations, Sects, Heresies, Ecclesiastical Terms, History,
   Biography, &c. &c. By the Rev. WILLIAM BENHAM, B.D. *Cheap Edition*, 10s. 6d.

Doré Bible. With 200 Full-page Illustrations by GUSTAVE DORÉ. *Popular
   Edition.* In One Vol. 15s. Also in leather binding. (*Price on application.*)

Early Days of Christianity, The. By the Very Rev. Dean FARRAR, D.D., F.R.S.
   LIBRARY EDITION. Two Vols., 24s. ; morocco, £2 2s.
   POPULAR EDITION. In One Vol. ; cloth, gilt edges, 7s. 6d. ; tree-calf, 15s.
   CHEAP EDITION. Cloth gilt, 3s. 6d.

Family Prayer-Book, The. Edited by the Rev. Canon GARBETT, M.A., and
   the Rev. S. MARTIN. With Full-page Illustrations. *New Edition.* Cloth, 7s. 6d.

Gleanings after Harvest. Studies and Sketches. By the Rev. JOHN R. VERNON, M.A. Illustrated. *Cheap Edition.* 3s. 6d.

"Graven in the Rock;" or, the Historical Accuracy of the Bible confirmed by reference to the Assyrian and Egyptian Sculptures in the British Museum and elsewhere. By the Rev. Dr. SAMUEL KINNS, F.R.A.S., &c. &c. Illustrated. *Library Edition*, in Two Volumes, cloth, with top edges gilded, 15s.

"Heart Chords." A Series of Works by Eminent Divines. In cloth, 1s. each.

My Father. By the Right Rev. Ashton Oxenden, late Bishop of Montreal.

My Bible. By the Rt. Rev. W. Boyd Carpenter, Bishop of Ripon.

My Work for God. By the Right Rev. Bishop Cotterill.

My Object in Life. By the Very Rev. Dean Farrar, D.D.

My Aspirations. By the Rev. G. Matheson, D.D.

My Emotional Life. By Preb. Chadwick, D.D.

My Body. By the Rev. Prof. W. G. Blaikie, D.D.

My Soul. By the Rev. P. B. Power, M.A.

My Growth in Divine Life. By the Rev. Prebendary Reynolds, M.A.

My Hereafter. By the Very Rev. Dean Bickersteth.

My Walk with God. By the Very Rev. Dean Montgomery.

My Aids to the Divine Life. By the Very Rev. Dean Boyle.

My Sources of Strength. By the Rev. E. E. Jenkins, M.A.

My Comfort in Sorrow. By Hugh Macmillan, D.D.

Helps to Belief. A Series of Helpful Manuals on the Religious Difficulties of the Day. Edited by the Rev. TEIGNMOUTH SHORE, M.A., Canon of Worcester, 1s. each.

CREATION. By Harvey Goodwin, D.D., late Lord Bishop of Carlisle.

MIRACLES. By the Rev. Brownlow Maitland, M.A.

PRAYER. By the Rev. Canon Shore, M.A.

THE DIVINITY OF OUR LORD. By the Lord Bishop of Derry.

THE ATONEMENT. By William Connor Magee, D.D., Late Archbishop of York.

Holy Land and the Bible, The. A Book of Scripture Illustrations gathered in Palestine. By the Rev. CUNNINGHAM GEIKIE, D.D., LL.D. (Edin.). *Cheap Edition*, with 24 Collotype Plates, 12s. 6d.

Life of Christ, The. By the Very Rev. Dean FARRAR, D.D., F.R.S.

CHEAP EDITION. With 16 Full-page Plates. Cloth gilt, 3s. 6d.

POPULAR EDITION. With 16 Full-page Plates. Cloth gilt, gilt edges, 7s. 6d.

LARGE TYPE ILLUSTD. EDITION. Cloth, 7s. 6d. Cloth, full gilt, gilt edges, 10s. 6d.

LIBRARY EDITION. Two Vols. Cloth, 24s.; morocco, 42s.

Moses and Geology; or, the Harmony of the Bible with Science. By the Rev. SAMUEL KINNS, Ph.D., F.R.A.S. Illustrated. *Library Edition*, revised to date, 10s. 6d.

New Light on the Bible and the Holy Land. By BASIL T. A. EVETTS, M.A. Illustrated. Cloth, 7s. 6d.

Old and New Testaments, Plain Introductions to the Books of the. Containing Contributions by many Eminent Divines. In Two Vols., 3s. 6d. each.

Plain Introductions to the Books of the Old Testament. 336 pages. Edited by Bishop ELLICOTT. 3s. 6d.

Plain Introductions to the Books of the New Testament. 304 pages. Edited by Bishop ELLICOTT. 3s. 6d.

Protestantism, The History of. By the Rev. J. A. WYLIE, LL.D. Containing upwards of 600 Original Illustrations. Three Vols., 27s.

"Quiver" Yearly Volume, The. With about 600 Original Illustrations and Coloured Frontispiece. 7s. 6d. Also Monthly, 6d.

St. George for England; and other Sermons preached to Children. *Fifth Edition.* By the Rev. T. TEIGNMOUTH SHORE, M.A., Canon of Worcester. 5s.

St. Paul, The Life and Work of. By the Very Rev. Dean FARRAR, D.D., F.R.S.

CHEAP ILLUSTRATED EDITION. 7s. 6d.

CHEAP EDITION. With 16 Full-page Plates, cloth gilt, 3s. 6d.

LIBRARY EDITION. Two Vols., cloth, 24s.; calf, 42s.

ILLUSTRATED EDITION, One Vol., £1 1s.; morocco, £2 2s.

POPULAR EDITION. Cloth, gilt edges, 7s. 6d.

Searchings in the Silence. By the Rev. GEORGE MATHESON, D.D. 3s. 6d.

Shall We Know One Another in Heaven? By the Rt. Rev. J. C. RYLE, D.D., Bishop of Liverpool. *New and Enlarged Edition.* Paper covers, 6d.

Shortened Church Services and Hymns, suitable for use at Children's Services. Compiled by the Rev. T. TEIGNMOUTH SHORE, M.A., Canon of Worcester. *Enlarged Edition.* 1s.

"Six Hundred Years"; or, Historical Sketches of Eminent Men and Women who have more or less come into contact with the Abbey and Church of Holy Trinity, Minories, from 1293 to 1893, and some account of the Incumbents, the Fabric, the Plate, &c. &c. By the Vicar, the Rev. Dr. SAMUEL KINNS, F.R.A.S., &c. &c. With 65 Illustrations. 15s.

"Sunday:" Its Origin, History, and Present Obligation. By the Ven. Archdeacon HESSEY, D.C.L. *Fifth Edition*, 7s. 6d.

Educational Works and Students' Manuals.

Agricultural Text-Books, Cassell's. (The "Downton" Series.) Fully Illustrated. Edited by JOHN WRIGHTSON, Professor of Agriculture. **Soils and Manures.** By J. M. H. MUNRO, D.Sc. (London), F.I.C., F.C.S. 2s. 6d. **Farm Crops.** By Professor WRIGHTSON. 2s. 6d. **Live Stock.** By Professor WRIGHTSON. 2s. 6d.

Alphabet, Cassell's Pictorial. Mounted on Linen, with Rollers. 2s. Mounted with Rollers, and Varnished. 2s. 6d.

Arithmetic:—Howard's Art of Reckoning. By C. F. HOWARD. Paper, 1s.; cloth, 2s. *Enlarged Edition*, 5s.

Arithmetics, The "Belle Sauvage." By GEORGE RICKS, B.Sc. Lond. With Test Cards. (*List on application.*)

Atlas, Cassell's Popular. Containing 24 Coloured Maps. 1s. 6d.

Blackboard Drawing. By W. E. SPARKES. With 52 Full-page Illustrations by the Author. 5s.

Book-Keeping. By THEODORE JONES. FOR SCHOOLS, 2s.; or cloth, 3s. FOR THE MILLION, 2s.; or cloth, 3s. Books for Jones's System, Ruled Sets of, 2s.

British Empire Map of the World. New Map for Schools and Institutes. By G. R. PARKIN and J. G. BARTHOLOMEW, F.R.G.S. Mounted on cloth, varnished, and with Rollers or Folded. 25s.

Chemistry, The Public School. By J. H. ANDERSON, M.A. 2s. 6d.

Cookery for Schools. By LIZZIE HERITAGE. 6d.

Dulce Domum. Rhymes and Songs for Children. Edited by JOHN FARMER, Editor of "Gaudeamus," &c. Old Notation and Words, 5s. N.B.—The Words of the Songs in "Dulce Domum" (with the Airs both in Tonic Sol-Fa and Old Notation) can be had in Two Parts, 6d. each.

England, A History of. From the Landing of Julius Cæsar to the Present Day. By H. O. ARNOLD-FORSTER, M.P. Fully Illustrated. 5s.

English Literature, A First Sketch of, from the Earliest Period to the Present Time. By Prof. HENRY MORLEY. 7s. 6d.

Euclid, Cassell's. Edited by Prof. WALLACE, M.A. 1s.

Euclid, The First Four Books of. *New Edition.* In paper, 6d.; cloth, 9d.

French, Cassell's Lessons in. *New and Revised Edition.* Parts I. and II., each 1s. 6d.; complete, 2s. 6d. Key, 1s. 6d.

French-English and English-French Dictionary. 3s. 6d. or 5s.

French Reader, Cassell's Public School. By GUILLAUME S. CONRAD. 2s. 6d.

Galbraith and Haughton's Scientific Manuals.
Euclid. Books I., II., III. 2s. 6d. Books IV., V., VI. 2s. 6d. Mathematical Tables. 3s. 6d. Mechanics. 3s. 6d. Hydrostatics. 3s. 6d. Algebra. Part I., cloth, 2s. 6d. Complete, 7s. 6d. Tides and Tidal Currents, with Tidal Cards, 3s.

Gaudeamus. Songs for Colleges and Schools. Edited by JOHN FARMER. 5s. Words only, paper, 6d.; cloth, 9d.

Geometry, First Elements of Experimental. By PAUL BERT. Illustrated. 1s. 6d.

German Dictionary, Cassell's. German-English, English-German. *Cheap Edition*, cloth, 3s. 6d.; half-morocco, 5s.

German Reading, First Lessons in. By A. JÄGST. Illustrated. 1s.

Hand and Eye Training. By GEORGE RICKS, B.Sc., and JOSEPH VAUGHAN. Illustrated. Vol. I. Designing with Coloured Papers. Vol. II. Cardboard Work. 2s. each. Vol. III. Colour Work and Design. 3s.

Hand and Eye Training. By G. RICKS, B.Sc. Two Vols., with 16 Coloured Plates in each. 6s. each. **Cards for Class Use.** Five Sets. 1s. each.

Historical Cartoons, Cassell's Coloured. Size 45 in. × 35 in., 2s. each. Mounted on canvas and varnished, with rollers, 5s. each. (Descriptive pamphlet, 16 pp., 1d.)

Italian Lessons, with Exercises, Cassell's. In One Vol. 2s.

Latin Dictionary, Cassell's. (Latin-English and English-Latin.) 3s. 6d.; half-morocco, 5s.

Latin Primer, The New. By Prof. J. P. POSTGATE. 2s. 6d.

Latin Primer, The First. By Prof. POSTGATE. 1s.

Latin Prose for Lower Forms. By M. A. BAYFIELD, M.A. 2s. 6d.

Laws of Every-Day Life. For the Use of Schools. By H. O. ARNOLD-FORSTER, M.P. 1s. 6d.

Lessons in Our Laws ; or, Talks at Broadacre Farm. By H. F. LESTER, B.A. In Two Parts. 1s. 6d. each.

Little Folks' History of England. By ISA CRAIG-KNOX. Illustrated. 1s. 6d.

Making of the Home, The. By Mrs. SAMUEL A. BARNETT. 1s. 6d.

Map Building for Schools. A Practical Method of Teaching Geography (England and Wales) By J. H. OVERTON, F.G.S. 6d.

Marlborough Books:—Arithmetic Examples. 3s. French Exercises. 3s. 6d. French Grammar. 2s. 6d. German Grammar. 3s. 6d.

Mechanics, Applied. By JOHN PERRY, M.E., D.SC., &c. Illustrated. 7s. 6d.

Mechanics for Young Beginners. By the Rev. J. G. EASTON, M.A. *Cheap Edition*, 2s. 6d.

Mechanics and Machine Design, Numerical Examples in Practical. By R. G. BLAINE, M.E. *New Edition, Revised and Enlarged.* With 79 Illustrations. Cloth, 2s. 6d.

Models and Common Objects, How to Draw from. By W. E. SPARKES. Illustrated. 3s.

Models, Common Objects, and Casts of Ornament, How to Shade from. By W. E. SPARKES. With 25 Plates by the Author. 3s.

Natural History Coloured Wall Sheets, Cassell's New. Consisting of 16 subjects. Size, 39 by 31 in. Mounted on rollers and varnished. 3s. each.

Object Lessons from Nature. By Prof. L. C. MIALL, F.L.S., F.G.S. Fully Illustrated. *New and Enlarged Edition.* Two Vols. 1s. 6d. each.

Physiology for Schools. By ALFRED T. SCHOFIELD, M.D., M.R.C.S., &c. Illustrated. 1s. 9d. Three Parts, paper covers, 5d. each ; or cloth limp, 6d. each.

Poetry Readers, Cassell's New. Illustrated. 12 Books. 1d. each. Cloth, 1s. 6d.

Popular Educator, Cassell's. With Revised Text, New Maps, New Coloured Plates, New Type, &c. Complete in Eight Vols., 5s. each ; or Eight Vols. in Four, half-morocco, 50s.

Readers, Cassell's "Belle Sauvage." An Entirely New Series. Fully Illustrated. Strongly bound in cloth. (*List on application.*)

Reader, The Citizen. By H. O. ARNOLD-FORSTER, M.P. Cloth, 1s. 6d. ; also a Scottish Edition, cloth, 1s. 6d.

Readers, Cassell's Classical. Vol. I., 1s. 8d. ; Vol. II., 2s. 6d.

Reader, The Temperance. By J. DENNIS HIRD. 1s. or 1s. 6d.

Readers, Cassell's "Higher Class." (*List on application.*)

Readers, Cassell's Readable. Illustrated. (*List on application.*)

Readers for Infant Schools, Coloured. Three Books. 4d. each.

Readers, Geographical, Cassell's New. With Numerous Illustrations in each Book. (*List on application.*)

Readers, The Modern Geographical. Illustrated throughout. (*List on application.*)

Readers, The Modern School. Illustrated. (*List on application.*)

Rolit. An entirely novel system of learning French. By J. J. TYLOR. 3s.

Round the Empire. By G. R. PARKIN. With a Preface by the Rt. Hon. the Earl of Rosebery, K.G. Fully Illustrated. 1s. 6d.

Science Applied to Work. By J. A. BOWER. Illustrated. 1s.

Science of Every-Day Life. By J. A. BOWER. Illustrated. 1s.

Sculpture, A Primer of. By E. ROSCOE MULLINS. Illustrated. 2s. 6d.

Shakspere's Plays for School Use. Illustrated. 9 Books. 6d. each.

Spelling, A Complete Manual of. By J. D. MORELL, LL.D. 1s.

Technical Educator, Cassell's. A New Cyclopædia of Technical Education, with Coloured Plates and Engravings. Complete in Six Vols., 3s. 6d. each.

Technical Manuals, Cassell's. Illustrated throughout. 16 Vols., from 2s. to 4s. 6d. (*List free on application.*)

Technology, Manuals of. Edited by Prof. AYRTON, F.R.S., and RICHARD WORMELL, D.SC., M.A. Illustrated throughout. (*List on application.*)

Things New and Old ; or, Stories from English History. By H. O. ARNOLD-FORSTER, M.P. Fully Illustrated. Strongly bound in cloth. Seven Books from 9d. to 1s. 8d.

World of Ours, This. By H. O. ARNOLD-FORSTER, M.P. Fully Illustrated. *Cheap Edition.* 2s. 6d.

Young Citizen, The ; or, Lessons in our Laws. By H. F. LESTER. Fully Illustrated. 2s. 6d.

Books for Young People.

Two Old Ladies, Two Foolish Fairies, and a Tom Cat. The Surprising Adventures of Tuppy and Tue. A New Fairy Story. By MAGGIE BROWNE. With Four Coloured Plates and Illustrations in text. Cloth, 3s. 6d.

Micky Magee's Menagerie; or, Strange Animals and their Doings. By S. H. HAMER. With 8 Coloured Plates and other Illustrations by HARRY NEILSON. Coloured Boards, 1s. 6d.

The Victoria Painting Book for Little Folks. Containing about 300 Illustrations suitable for Colouring, 1s.

"Little Folks" Half-Yearly Volume. Containing 480 pages of Letterpress, with Six Full-page Coloured Plates, and numerous other Pictures printed in Colour. Picture boards, 3s. 6d. ; or cloth gilt, gilt edges, 5s.

Bo-Peep. A Treasury for the Little Ones. Yearly Vol. With Original Stories and Verses. Illustrated with Eight Full-page Coloured Plates, and numerous other Pictures printed in Colour. Elegant picture boards, 2s. 6d. ; cloth, 3s. 6d.

Beneath the Banner. Being Narratives of Noble Lives and Brave Deeds. By F. J. CROSS. Illustrated. Limp cloth, 1s. ; cloth boards, gilt edges, 2s.

Good Morning ! Good Night ! Morning and Evening Readings for Children, by the Author of "Beneath the Banner." Fully Illustrated. Limp cloth, 1s., or cloth boards, gilt edges, 2s.

Five Stars in a Little Pool. By EDITH CARRINGTON. Illustrated. 3s. 6d.

Merry Girls of England. By L. T. MEADE. 3s. 6d.

Beyond the Blue Mountains. By L. T. MEADE. Illustrated. 5s.

The Cost of a Mistake. By SARAH PITT. Illustrated. *New Edition.* 2s. 6d.

The Peep of Day. Cassell's Illustrated Edition. 2s. 6d.

A Book of Merry Tales. By MAGGIE BROWNE, SHEILA, ISABEL WILSON, and C. L. MATÉAUX. Illustrated. 3s. 6d.

A Sunday Story-Book. By MAGGIE BROWNE, SAM BROWNE, and AUNT ETHEL. Illustrated. 3s. 6d.

Story Poems for Young and Old. By E. DAVENPORT. 3s. 6d.

Pleasant Work for Busy Fingers. By MAGGIE BROWNE. Illustrated. 2s. 6d.

Magic at Home. By Prof. HOFFMAN. Fully Illustrated. A Series of easy and startling Conjuring Tricks for Beginners. Cloth gilt, 3s. 6d.

Little Mother Bunch. By Mrs. MOLESWORTH. Illustrated. *New Edition.* 2s. 6d.

Heroes of Every-Day Life. By LAURA LANE. With about 20 Full-page Illustrations. 256 pages, crown 8vo, cloth, 2s. 6d.

Ships, Sailors, and the Sea. By R. J. CORNEWALL-JONES. Illd. 2s. 6d.

Gift Books for Young People. By Popular Authors. With Four Original Illustrations in each. Cloth gilt, 1s. 6d. each.

The Boy Hunters of Kentucky. By Edward S. Ellis.	Jack Marston's Anchor.
	Frank's Life-Battle.
Red Feather: a Tale of the American Frontier. By Edward S. Ellis.	Major Monk's Motto ; or, "Look Before you Leap."
Fritters; or, "It's a Long Lane that has no Turning."	Tim Thomson's Trial; or, "All is not Gold that Glitters."
Trixy; or, "Those who Live in Glass Houses shouldn't throw Stones."	Ursula's Stumbling-Block.
	Ruth's Life-Work; or, "No Pains, no Gains."
Rhoda's Reward.	Uncle William's Charge.

"Golden Mottoes" Series, The. Each Book containing 208 pages, with Four Full-page Original Illustrations. Crown 8vo, cloth gilt, 2s. each.

"Nil Desperandum." By the Rev. F. Langbridge, M.A.	"Honour is my Guide." By Jeanie Hering (Mrs. Adams-Acton).
"Bear and Forbear." By Sarah Pitt.	"Aim at a Sure End." By Emily Searchfield.
"Foremost if I Can." By Helen Atteridge.	"He Conquers who Endures." By the Author of "May Cunningham's Trial," &c.

"Cross and Crown" Series, The. With Four Illustrations in each Book. Crown 8vo, 256 pages, 2s. 6d. each.

Heroes of the Indian Empire; or, Stories of Valour and Victory. By Ernest Foster.	Adam Hepburn's Vow: A Tale of Kirk and Covenant. By Annie S. Swan.
Through Trial to Triumph; or, "The Royal Way." By Madeline Bonavia Hunt.	No. XIII.; or, The Story of the Lost Vestal. A Tale of Early Christian Days. By Emma Marshall.
Strong to Suffer: A Story of the Jews. By E. Wynne.	
By Fire and Sword: A Story of the Huguenots. By Thomas Archer.	Freedom's Sword: A Story of the Days of Wallace and Bruce. By Annie S. Swan.

Albums for Children. Price 3s. 6d. each.

The Album for Home, School, and Play. Set in bold type, and illustrated throughout.

Picture Album of All Sorts. Illustrated.

The Chit-Chat Album. Illustrated.

"Wanted—a King" Series. *Cheap Edition.* Illustrated. 2s. 6d. each.

Fairy Tales in Other Lands. By Julia Goddard.

Robin's Ride. By Ellinor Davenport Adams.

Wanted—a King; or, How Merle set the Nursery Rhymes to Rights. By Maggie Browne.

"Peeps Abroad" Library. *Cheap Editions.* Cloth gilt, 2s. 6d. each.

Rambles Round London. By C. L. Matéaux. Illustrated.

Around and About Old England. By C. L. Matéaux. Illustrated.

Paws and Claws. By one of the Authors of "Poems Written for a Child." Illustrated.

Decisive Events in History. By Thomas Archer. With Original Illustrations.

The True Robinson Crusoes.

Peeps Abroad for Folks at Home. Illustrated throughout.

Wild Adventures in Wild Places. By Dr. Gordon Stables, R.N. Illustrated.

Modern Explorers. By Thomas Frost. Illustrated. *New and Cheaper Edition.*

Early Explorers. By Thomas Frost.

Home Chat with our Young Folks. Illustrated throughout.

Jungle, Peak, and Plain. Illustrated throughout.

Three-and-Sixpenny Books for Young People. With Original Illustrations. Cloth gilt, 3s. 6d. each.

Told Out of School. By A. J. Daniels.

† Red Rose and Tiger Lily. By L. T. Meade.

The Romance of Invention. By James Burnley.

† Bashful Fifteen. By L. T. Meade.

The King's Command. A Story for Girls. By Maggie Symington.

A Sweet Girl Graduate. By L. T. Meade.

† The White House at Inch Gow. By Sarah Pitt.

† Polly. By L. T. Meade.

† The Palace Beautiful. By L. T. Meade.

"Follow my Leader."

For Fortune and Glory.

Lost among White Africans.

† A World of Girls. By L. T. Meade.

Books marked thus † can also be had in extra cloth gilt, gilt edges, 5s. each.

Books by Edward S. Ellis. Illustrated. Cloth, 2s. 6d. each.

A Strange Craft and its Wonderful Voyage.

Pontiac, Chief of the Ottawas. A Tale of the Siege of Detroit.

In the Days of the Pioneers.

The Phantom of the River.

Shod with Silence.

The Great Cattle Trail.

The Path in the Ravine.

The Hunters of the Ozark.

The Camp in the Mountains

Ned in the Woods. A Tale of Early Days in the West.

Down the Mississippi.

The Last War Trail.

Ned on the River. A Tale of Indian River Warfare.

Footprints in the Forest.

Up the Tapajos.

Ned in the Block House. A Story of Pioneer Life in Kentucky.

The Young Ranchers.

The Lost Trail.

Camp-Fire and Wigwam.

Lost in the Wilds.

Lost in Samoa. A Tale of Adventure in the Navigator Islands.

Tad; or, "Getting Even" with Him.

Cassell's Picture Story Books. Each containing 60 pages. 6d. each.

Little Talks.

Bright Stars.

Nursery Joys.

Pet's Posy.

Tiny Tales.

Daisy's Story Book.

Dot's Story Book.

A Nest of Stories.

Good Night Stories.

Chats for Small Chatterers.

Auntie's Stories.

Birdie's Story Book.

Little Chimes.

A Sheaf of Tales.

Dewdrop Stories.

Illustrated Books for the Little Ones. Containing interesting Stories. All Illustrated. 9d. each.

Bright Tales and Funny Pictures.

Merry Little Tales.

Little Tales for Little People.

Little People and Their Pets.

Tales Told for Sunday.

Sunday Stories for Small People.

Stories and Pictures for Sunday.

Bible Pictures for Boys and Girls.

Firelight Stories.

Sunlight and Shade.

Rub-a-dub Tales.

Fine Feathers and Fluffy Fur.

Scrambles and Scrapes.

Tittle Tattle Tales.

Dumb Friends.

Indoors and Out.

Some Farm Friends.

Those Golden Sands.

Little Mothers and their Children.

Our Pretty Pets.

Our Schoolday Hours.

Creatures Tame.

Creatures Wild.

Up and Down the Garden.

All Sorts of Adventures.

Our Sunday Stories.

Our Holiday Hours.

Wandering Ways.

Shilling Story Books. All Illustrated, and containing Interesting Stories.

Seventeen Cats.

Bunty and the Boys.

The Heir of Elmdale.

Claimed at Last, and Roy's Reward.

Thorns and Tangles.

The Cuckoo in the Robin's Nest.

John's Mistake.

Diamonds in the Sand.

Surly Bob.

The History of Five Little Pitchers.

The Giant's Cradle.

Shag and Doll.

The Cost of Revenge.

Clever Frank.

Among the Redskins.

The Ferryman of Brill.

Harry Maxwell.

Eighteenpenny Story Books. All Illustrated throughout.

Wee Willie Winkie.
Ups and Downs of a Donkey's Life.
Three Wee Ulster Lassies.
Up the Ladder.
Dick's Hero; & other Stories.

The Chip Boy.
Roses from Thorns.
Faith's Father.
By Land and Sea.
The Young Berringtons.
Jeff and Leff.

Tom Morris's Error.
"Through Flood—Through Fire."
The Girl with the Golden Locks.
Stories of the Olden Time.

Library of Wonders. Illustrated Gift-books for Boys. Cloth, 1s. 6d.

Wonders of Animal Instinct.
Wonderful Balloon Ascents.

Wonders of Bodily Strength and Skill.

The "World in Pictures" Series. Illustrated throughout. *Cheap Edition.* 1s. 6d. each.

All the Russias.
Chats about Germany.
Peeps into China.
The Land of Pyramids (Egypt).

The Eastern Wonderland (Japan).
Glimpses of South America.
Round Africa.
The Land of Temples (India).
The Isles of the Pacific.

Two-Shilling Story Books. All Illustrated.

Margaret's Enemy.
Stories of the Tower.
Mr. Burke's Nieces.
The Top of the Ladder: How to Reach It.

Little Flotsam.
The Children of the Court.
The Four Cats of the Tippertons.
Little Folks' Sunday Book.
Two Fourpenny Bits.

Poor Nelly.
Tom Heriot.
Aunt Tabitha's Waifs.
In Mischief Again.
Peggy, and other Tales.

Half-Crown Story Books.

On Board the *Esmeralda*; or, Martin Leigh's Log.
Esther West.
For Queen and King.

Perils Afloat and Brigands Ashore.
Working to Win.
At the South Pole.

Pictures of School Life and Boyhood.

Cassell's Pictorial Scrap Book. In Six Books, each containing 32 pages, 6d. each.

Books for the Little Ones. Fully Illustrated.

Rhymes for the Young Folk. By William Allingham. Beautifully Illustrated. 1s. 6d.

The Sunday Scrap Book. With Several Hundred Illustrations. Boards, 3s. 6d.; cloth, gilt edges, 5s.

The New "Little Folks" Painting Book. Containing nearly 350 Outline Illustrations suitable for Colouring. 1s.

Cassell's Robinson Crusoe. With 100 Illustrations. Cloth, 3s. 6d.; gilt edges, 5s.

The Old Fairy Tales. With Original Illustrations. Cloth, 1s.

Cassell's Swiss Family Robinson. Illustrated. Cloth, 3s. 6d.; gilt edges, 5s.

The World's Workers. A Series of New and Original Volumes by Popular Authors. With Portraits printed on a tint as Frontispiece. 1s. each.

John Cassell. By G. Holden Pike.
Charles Haddon Spurgeon. By G. Holden Pike.
Dr. Arnold of Rugby. By Rose E. Selfe.
The Earl of Shaftesbury.
Sarah Robinson, Agnes Weston, and Mrs. Meredith.
Thomas A. Edison and Samuel F. B. Morse.
Mrs. Somerville and Mary Carpenter.
General Gordon.
Charles Dickens.
Florence Nightingale, Catherine Marsh, Frances Ridley Havergal, Mrs. Ranyard ("L. N. R.").

Dr. Guthrie, Father Mathew, Elihu Burritt, Joseph Livesey.
Sir Henry Havelock and Colin Campbell, Lord Clyde.
Abraham Lincoln.
David Livingstone.
George Müller and Andrew Reed.
Richard Cobden.
Benjamin Franklin.
Handel.
Turner the Artist.
George and Robert Stephenson.
Sir Titus Salt and George Moore.

⁎⁎⁎ The above Works can also be had Three in One Vol., cloth, gilt edges, 3s.
